"Why have you dragged me in here, Jordan?"

"I thought it might be a good idea if we got married tomorrow." Jordan made the suggestion with a casualness that would have been entirely appropriate if he'd been suggesting that she might like to try out a new restaurant for brunch on Sunday.

Emily clutched the back of the nearest chair. *Jordan had asked her to marry him.* She was quite sure she'd heard him do that. Unless she was hallucinating. Was she? She felt her mouth start to drop open again, and she hurriedly closed it.

"I don't think marriage would work out too well for us," she said, trying to keep her voice soft and nonthreatening. She even managed a small, reassuring smile. When dealing with lunatics, it was best to be gentle. "Thanks for asking, Jordan, but if you remember, we don't like each other. I have this quaint, old-fashioned dislike of men who sleep with other men's wives."

D0974341

Dear Reader,

Long before I became a romance writer, I was an avid reader of all types of romances. I love Cinderella stories, and stories in which the heroine transforms herself from quiet, mousy wimp into a strong, sexy, achieving woman. Best of all, I confess to enjoying the marriage-of-convenience plot, even though it could be considered among the most artificial and contrived of romantic story lines.

In days gone by, women often found themselves in situations from which the only possible escape was to make a marriage of convenience. Consequently, authors of historical fiction can have a lot of fun playing with this theme. But nowadays, with endless opportunities open to most women, it's much harder for an author of contemporary romances to dream up circumstances in which a woman might consider making a marriage of convenience.

Emily Sutton, the heroine of *His Brother's Finacée,* is an educated, professional woman from a loving family background, and yet, she finds herself agreeing to marry Jordan Chambers, the outcast younger son of the upper-crust Chambers family. Of course, the temporary marriage of convenience soon begins to turn into a passionate affair of the heart, although there are a few obstacles to be overcome along the way before Emily and Jordan can have their happy ending.

I hope you find their story fun, and that you will enjoy this new installment of the TRUEBLOOD, TEXAS series.

Sincerely,

Jasmine Cresswell

TRUEBLOOD, TEXAS

Jasmine Cresswell

His Brother's Fiancée

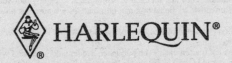

HARLEQUIN®

TORONTO • NEW YORK • LONDON
AMSTERDAM • PARIS • SYDNEY • HAMBURG
STOCKHOLM • ATHENS • TOKYO • MILAN • MADRID
PRAGUE • WARSAW • BUDAPEST • AUCKLAND

Jasmine Cresswell is acknowledged as the author
of this work.

For Angela Naylor Candlish,
who likes to read all the same books I do!

HARLEQUIN BOOKS
225 Duncan Mill Road, Don Mills,
Ontario, Canada M3B 3K9

ISBN-13: 978-0-373-65079-8
ISBN-10:   0-373-65079-5

HIS BROTHER'S FIANCÉE

Visit us at www.eHarlequin.com

Printed in U.S.A.

TRUEBLOOD, TEXAS

THE TRUEBLOOD LEGACY

THE YEAR WAS 1918, and the Great War in Europe still raged, but Esau Porter was heading home to Texas.

The young sergeant arrived at his parents' ranch northwest of San Antonio on a Sunday night, only the celebration didn't go off as planned. Most of the townsfolk of Carmelita had come out to welcome Esau home, but when they saw the sorry condition of the boy, they gave their respects quickly and left.

The fever got so bad so fast that Mrs. Porter hardly knew what to do. By Monday night, before the doctor from San Antonio made it into town, Esau was dead.

The Porter family grieved. How could their son have survived the German peril, only to burn up and die in his own bed? It wasn't much of a surprise when Mrs. Porter took to her bed on Wednesday. But it was a hell of a shock when half the residents of Carmelita came down with the horrible illness. House after house was hit by death, and all the townspeople could do was pray for salvation.

None came. By the end of the year, over one hundred souls had perished. The influenza virus took those in the prime of life, leaving behind an unprecedented number of orphans. And the virus knew no boundaries. By the time the threat had passed, more than thirty-seven million people had succumbed worldwide.

But in one house, there was still hope.

Isabella Trueblood had come to Carmelita in the late 1800s with her father, blacksmith Saul Trueblood, and her mother, Teresa Collier Trueblood. The family had traveled from Indiana, leaving their Quaker roots behind.

Young Isabella grew up to be an intelligent woman who had a gift for healing and storytelling. Her dreams centered on the boy next door, Foster Carter, the son of Chester and Grace.

Just before the bad times came in 1918, Foster asked Isabella to be his wife, and the future of the Carter spread was secured. It was a happy union, and the future looked bright for the young couple.

Two years later, not one of their relatives was alive. How the young couple had survived was a miracle. And during the epidemic, Isabella and Foster had taken in more than twenty-two orphaned children from all over the county. They fed them, clothed them, taught them as if they were blood kin.

Then Isabella became pregnant, but there were complications. Love for her handsome son, Josiah, born in 1920, wasn't enough to stop her from growing weaker by the day. Knowing she couldn't leave her husband to tend to all the children if she died, she set out to find families for each one of her orphaned charges.

And so the Trueblood Foundation was born. Named in memory of Isabella's parents, it would become famous all over Texas. Some of the orphaned children went to strangers, but many were reunited with their families. After reading notices in newspapers and church bulletins, aunts, uncles, cousins and grandparents rushed to Carmelita to find the young ones they'd given up for dead.

Toward the end of Isabella's life, she'd brought together more than thirty families, and not just her orphans. Many others, old and young, made their way to her doorstep, and Isabella turned no one away.

At her death, the town's name was changed to Trueblood, in her honor. For years to come, her simple grave was adorned with flowers on the anniversary of her death, grateful tokens of appreciation from the families she had brought together.

Isabella's son, Josiah, grew into a fine rancher and married Rebecca Montgomery in 1938. They had a daughter, Elizabeth Trueblood Carter, in 1940. Elizabeth married her neighbor William Garrett in 1965, and gave birth to twins Lily and Dylan in 1971, and daughter Ashley a few years later. Home was the Double G ranch, about ten miles from Trueblood proper, and the Garrett children grew up listening to stories of their famous great-grandmother, Isabella. Because they were Truebloods, they knew that they, too, had a sacred duty to carry on the tradition passed down to them: finding lost souls and reuniting loved ones.

CHAPTER ONE

EMILY SUTTON'S fiancé caught up with her in the library of the elegant San Antonio mansion where he lived with his parents. Michael Chambers was normally blessed with a ready smile, but Emily noticed that today he looked somber, even a little nervous. How odd, she thought. Michael's self-confidence was usually as vast as the state of Texas; it was one of the characteristics that had first attracted her to him.

"Hi, Michael, what's up? You're looking worried." She was already running late for her appointment at Finders Keepers, but she paused in the doorway, her arms clutched around the massive three-ring binder that contained the complex details of their wedding arrangements.

Emily shifted the heavy weight of the binder from one arm to the other. There were moments when she felt sure the inauguration of the president of the United States couldn't necessitate more paperwork than the elaborate wedding ceremony her mother and Mrs. Chambers had planned over the past three months. Her mother had loved every minute of the planning, of course, even though she and Mrs. Chambers both complained repeatedly that the engagement was much too short for them to put on a truly stylish affair.

Thank goodness Michael needed to have the wedding ceremony behind him before he embarked on his election campaign for governor of Texas, Emily reflected wryly. Otherwise she couldn't begin to visualize what their respective mothers might have attempted. Importing the royal guards from Buckingham Palace, maybe?

Emily grinned, glad that she'd been able to make her mother so happy just by saying yes to all her fancy wedding plans. She leaned against the door, once again shifting the weight of the binder to her other arm. Michael still remained silent and she felt her first twinge of true concern.

"You look really worried, honey. Tell me what's wrong."

He didn't respond and her stomach lurched with a premonition of disaster. "Michael, talk to me. Has there been an accident? Oh my gosh, is it one of my parents?"

"No, not that..."

"Is your dad's heart playing up again? Please don't try to cushion the blow—you're just making me more scared."

He shifted from one foot to the other, so ill at ease that his discomfort seemed almost feigned. "I can't marry you," he said, avoiding her gaze. "We have to call off the wedding."

Shock momentarily paralyzed Emily. Then relief surged through her, leaving her knees feeling shaky. She suppressed a slightly impatient sigh. She'd noticed before that she didn't share Michael's rather cruel sense of humor, and she was too busy today to be tactful.

Glancing at her watch, she gave a weak smile. "Michael, I'm sorry, but I don't have time to play games. I'll see you this evening at five o'clock. Remember we have the cocktail reception for the bridal party and family members at your father's club, and then we have the dinner for out-of-town guests right afterward."

Compulsively organized as always, she opened the file and read out the column of arrangements that affected Michael. "It's black tie tonight, of course. My parents are bringing me, so there's no need for you to pick me up. By now, your brother should already have left for the airport to pick up your groomsmen who are flying in from Dallas. Harrison Turner and Carter Blayne. Those are the two groomsmen I've never met, if you remember. They'll need transportation tonight, because they're not renting cars for some reason. I have written in on my schedule that your brother will drive them to the dinner, but he hasn't been pinned down on this, and you know Jordan is always a law unto himself. He may choose to cooperate, or then again he's just as likely to blow off the entire night's events."

She snapped the ring binder shut, taking a calming breath. The mere thought of Jordan was enough to provoke a frisson of irritation so, with the ease of long practice, she switched her train of thought. "Oh, and if you have a spare second, you might go and say a couple of soothing words to your mother. She's fussing about the dinner menu again, and Sidney is beginning to lose his cool."

Emily managed a tired smile, although her prospective mother-in-law had been really hard to manage this morning. "Try to convince her that serving smoked pheasant appetizers simply isn't an option at this point. She'll have to be content with the ten varieties of hors d'oeuvres she's already selected."

Michael rubbed his forehead. "Who is Sidney?"

"Oh, sorry. I've spoken to him so often, I forgot you wouldn't know. He's the chef at your dad's club."

She turned to go, but Michael hurried across the room and grabbed her arm, interposing himself between her and the door. "Damn it, Emily, will you stand still for a minute and stop rattling off lists? I shouldn't have allowed you to go on about all those arrangements." He crossed his arms and stared at her with a touch of defiance. "I wasn't joking just now. I can't marry you. We have to call off the wedding.''

''Call off the wedding?'' Once again, it seemed to Emily that the world stopped. Only this time it didn't immediately start moving forward again. She blinked and swallowed hard, trying to bring her vision back into focus. ''Not…marry me?''

Michael drew in another deep breath and shook his head. ''That's right. I'm sorry, but we have to call off the wedding. I just can't go through with it.''

Panic froze her in midbreath. Michael was a decent man, her good friend. There was only one rational explanation for what he was saying. She gasped, frantically trying to suck in enough air to speak. ''Oh, my God! You've discovered you're suffering from some incurable disease!''

''No.'' His manner was so brusque she knew he had to be hiding something terrible.

''Don't try to protect my feelings—''

''I'm not protecting you!'' Michael yelled. He lowered his voice with visible effort. ''I'm fine, Emily, never healthier. But I can't marry you.''

He was serious, Emily realized. Dead serious. Michael was just fine, except that he wanted out of their marriage. Her brain, overloaded with details ranging from the color of the table linen for the prenuptial bridal dinner—cream with centerpieces of yellow rosebuds—to the gifts for her six bridesmaids—specially designed gold pins from Tiffany's—refused to find space for the unpalatable fact that the reason for all these elaborate preparations had just vanished. On a whim of Michael's, with no reference to her wishes, the wedding was off.

It was now ten-thirty on Friday morning. On Saturday evening, in less than thirty-six hours, fifty important out-of-town guests and three hundred movers and shakers from the state of Texas expected to see Emily Sutton, heiress to the Sutton land development fortune, married to Michael Chambers, candidate for governor of Texas. Unfortunately, it seemed that half the bridal couple wouldn't be available.

Moving with great care, Emily walked across to the antique burled-wood desk and set down the ring binder. The 150-page tome of meticulous planning had suddenly been rendered as useless as a dead battery.

"Is there some special reason why you no longer want to marry me?" she asked. Amazingly, shock had so stifled her emotions that her voice emerged sounding coolly interested rather than heartbroken.

"There are a lot of reasons," Michael said vaguely. He shoved his hands into his pockets and paced the library, seeming to regain his natural confidence. "For one thing, there's obviously no sexual spark between the two of us. I know we agreed on this marriage for practical reasons, but in this day and age, doesn't it bother you that we've been engaged for three months and we haven't found the time to take a weekend away and actually make love to each other?"

Now he noticed that they'd never made love? She'd been wondering for weeks why not. Emily flushed, touching her engagement ring. The four-carat diamond solitaire—big enough to make a statement, not big enough to be vulgar—suddenly felt heavy and out of place on her finger. Twisting the ring, she decided this wasn't the very best moment to confess that she hadn't made any sexual overtures to Michael because their celibate relationship had been a source of considerable relief to her.

She gave an explanation she hoped he would accept. "We have frantically busy schedules, both of us. I'm sure our sexual relationship will be just fine once we get around to it."

"Once we get around to it?" Michael shot her an incredulous glance. "You're attractive, but you seem to have almost no sex drive. When we kiss, it's as if we're friends, not potential lovers. That's strange, really, considering—'' He pulled himself up short. ''Anyway, I know this marriage of ours was never supposed to be a love match...''

Wasn't it? Emily wondered, no longer listening to Michael's attempt to explain the inexplicable. No, she supposed she had to grant him that much. She'd been determined to make her marriage last a lifetime, and she'd promised as much when Michael asked her to marry him. But neither of them had exchanged vows of everlasting love. Neither of them had mentioned passion. They'd simply committed themselves to a relationship based on friendship, mutual trust and loyalty. The qualities her adoptive parents shared in their marriage. The very qualities Emily had always wanted in her own marriage.

Michael was amazingly good-looking, Emily thought, watching his lips move without hearing a word of what he was saying. She wondered why she'd never felt even a twinge of physical attraction toward him. She pondered this for a second or two, then dismissed the question as one that no longer held any interest for her.

Despite the fact that she had never lusted for Michael's body during their engagement, she'd intended to be the best possible wife for him, and she'd recognized that included being an active sexual partner. Just last week she'd bought a sexy black negligee for their honeymoon. Surely that proved she was willing to do whatever it took to keep her husband happy.

Sex had always struck her as a significantly overrated activity, but she wasn't neurotic about it. Damn it, she was *not* neurotic about sex. Just because she was more aware than some of her contemporaries that getting carried away by passion could have serious consequences, it didn't mean she was a prude. She wanted children, she knew men liked to have sex on a regular basis, and she was quite sure she could learn to enjoy a modest program of sexual activity. That's why she'd carefully selected a prospective husband who looked as if he'd know how to go about the whole thing tastefully, without the excessive panting and pawing she found such a turnoff.

Besides, she'd assumed that what she and Michael shared was something much more important than messy emotions like lust and desire. She liked Michael's company, admired his achievements, and envied his deep family roots. Surely those were better—stronger—grounds for marriage than a physical attraction that was likely to burn itself out within weeks of the honeymoon.

Emily felt a spurt of betrayal when she thought back over the past three months. Michael had assured her numerous times that she was going to be the perfect wife for him, the ideal partner for a man burning up miles on the trail to the governor's mansion. Only last week, after their dinner with Senator Drysdale and his wife, he'd told her that she was the sort of woman most political candidates could only dream of finding. Socially gracious, well educated, but never pushy, she burnished his image whenever they appeared together, Michael had said proudly. What had happened between last Wednesday and today to change his mind?

Emily realized she'd been so wrapped up in her own thoughts that she'd given less than half her attention to Michael's rambling explanation as to why he was calling off the wedding. In the end, though, perhaps it didn't matter that she wasn't much wiser about his motives now than she had been ten minutes ago. What could he possibly say that would justify such a crazy decision, anyway?

"I'm counting on you to help me come up with a reasonable explanation for this last-minute cancellation," Michael was saying, in a jolting echo of her own thoughts. "Neither of us wants to provide any more fodder for the scandal sheets than we need. Our breakup is bound to be reported by the local San Antonio media, especially coming right before the wedding like this. If we're unlucky, this is a story that could get picked up by the national tabloids. We can't forget how easily my campaign for governor could hit a roadblock. I know I don't need to remind you, honey, how important it is that we don't do anything to derail my fund-raising prospects at this stage of the game. These days, if you can't please the moneymen, you can't hope to run a campaign.''

She winced at the endearment, but she could see he hadn't even noticed the casual intimacy of the way he'd called her *honey*. Hurt made her angry. ''Yes, I can see that your fund-raising prospects are your first priority right now.''

Michael gave no indication that he noticed the sarcasm dripping from her reply. ''I knew you'd understand, Emily. I value your opinion, you know, even though I can't marry you, and I sure would appreciate anything you can think of that would keep my campaign moving along on an upward swing.''

How about a swift kick in the pants, Emily thought wildly. That ought to give him some satisfactory upward propulsion.

''It's vital for us to have some sort of plausible story to tell before tonight's dinner,'' Michael said. He sent her a smile that Emily found infuriatingly patronizing. ''I'm perfectly agreeable to pretending that it's you who called it off.'' His smile deepened, then changed into a warm chuckle. ''Who knows? If you're seen ditching me, maybe that'll increase my sympathy ratings with the women voters.''

''Or maybe they'll all start wondering what I found wrong with you,'' she said.

His worried frown instantly reappeared. ''Damn! I was

joking, but you have a point. Hmm…we'll have to think about that some more. There must be some way for us to pull this one out of the hat.''

"Consult with your campaign manager," she said, her jaw clenched. "I'm sure Jeff Greiff will have an opinion. He always does. After all, this is a political issue, isn't it? There don't seem to be many emotions involved."

"You're wrong," he said, suddenly solemn. "At least on my side, there's quite a lot of feeling, even though we both recognized this was pretty much a marriage of convenience. I really do care about you, Emily. It's just that I need to be so careful—" He pulled himself up short. "Anyway, thanks for suggesting I should get in touch with Jeff. That was a great idea, I'll give him a call."

"Sure. Don't let me keep you."

Her sarcasm finally penetrated Michael's cloud of self-absorption. He had reached for his cell phone, but he put it down on the desk without dialing, his expression contrite and faintly ashamed. "I'm real sorry, Emily. But this will turn out for the best, you'll see."

He leaned forward and, to her horror, she realized he was planning to hug her, or maybe even give her a comforting kiss. She hastily stepped backward, out of his reach.

"Don't touch me!" She was humiliated by the hurt and panic that she could no longer screen out of her voice.

Michael's expression softened into a sympathy that she didn't want and couldn't bear to see. "I have a high regard for you and your adopted family, Emily, a very high regard. Even though things haven't worked out between the two of us, I'm glad that my father and yours have already entered into a business partnership for that new land development in Laurel Acres. And I want you to know that if I can count on your father for the promised campaign contributions, then he can count on me to get him all the introductions he can possibly use for his other business projects. Any doors that might have been closed to him in the past...well, I'll personally guarantee to make sure that they spring open. The Chambers family name carries a lot of power in this state, and you've earned the right to have me use some of that power on behalf of your adoptive family.''

Earned the right? The shock was well and truly wearing off, Emily realized. She was so hurt by Michael's suggestion that their engagement had been nothing more than a subsidiary clause in a business deal, and so disgusted by his casual shattering of their promises to each other, that she was about to say all sorts of things she would undoubtedly regret. Thinking first and speaking much later had prevented her from making a lot of bad mistakes in her life. No point in changing the habits of a lifetime at this traumatic moment. What she needed to do right now was to get out of here so that she could draw the tattered remnants of her pride and dignity back around her.

Averting her eyes, she picked up the wedding arrangements binder and clutched it to her chest, deriving irrational comfort from its familiar weight, even though all the documents tucked carefully inside were now so much waste paper.

''I can't stay talking to you any longer, Michael. I have an appointment all the way across town.'' She was fiercely glad now that she'd never told him about her decision to consult with Dylan Garrett of Finders Keepers. Especially glad that she'd never even breathed a hint as to why she might want to hire the services of a private investigator. Her desire to find her birth mother seemed an intimate yearning that she was glad she'd never shared with Michael.

She glanced at her watch, surprised that some part of her brain was still functioning clearly enough to enable her to note that it was 10:38. "Unless the traffic is miraculously light, I'm going to be late."

"Of course, don't let me keep you. We're just about finished here, aren't we?"

"You could certainly say that."

"Then I'll let you go." Michael was obviously as anxious to get away from her as she was to get away from him. She could see his fingers quivering over the buttons of his cell phone. "I really appreciate how understanding you've been about this, Emily. I knew you would be, though. You're one class act, but you know that, don't you?" He looked at her almost wistfully. "In so many ways, you'd have made the perfect governor's wife."

She was a class act in grave danger of tossing her cookies if she didn't get out of this room in the next thirty seconds. Without saying another word, Emily swung out of the library, proud that she was sufficiently in control to close the door quietly behind her.

Emily had never made a scene in her life, and she wasn't about to give Michael Chambers the satisfaction of seeing her create one now. When you had no idea where you came from, it wasn't a good idea to give people cause to ask questions about your stability, or even your manners.

Ever the lady—even if she hadn't been born one—Emily walked quietly from the room.

CHAPTER TWO

THE NEXT TIME Emily was consciously aware of her surroundings, she found herself facing a set of imposing barred wrought-iron gates. Unable to proceed, she was forced to stop driving. She drew her Ford Explorer to a halt, her hands starting to shake on the steering wheel when she realized that she had arrived at the Double G Ranch on the far northwestern outskirts of San Antonio.

Good grief, if she was at the Double G, she must have driven clear across town at the height of midday traffic! Try as she might, she couldn't summon a single memory of seeing another vehicle, or stopping for a traffic light. She could only be thankful that she hadn't killed anyone in the process of getting here.

Although a traffic accident might be one solution to her dilemma, she thought with a touch of hysteria. Maybe she could stage a fake accident, smash up the car a bit, and feign head injuries. How about pretending to have amnesia? Then Michael could sorrowfully announce to the 350 assembled guests that since his fiancée had lost her mind, they were postponing the wedding.

Three hundred and fifty guests. Emily's hands started to shake again. She'd tried so hard to be a source of pride to her parents. The Suttons had showered her with love and attention from the day they picked her up at the adoption agency, when she was only two weeks old. Achieving her maximum potential had seemed the least she could do to demonstrate her gratitude. Now she appeared doomed to shatter their pride in a big way, in the most public of settings. How in the world was she going to face them?

Her hands simply wouldn't stop shaking. She gripped the wheel, forcing herself back to an approximation of calm. Take things one step at a time. By chance, she'd made it here to the ranch without mishap. On time, no less, so she might as well keep her appointment. When she'd finished her consultation with Dylan Garrett, there would be more than enough hours left in the day to track down her parents and pass on the shocking news that their weekend schedule suddenly had plenty of free time in it.

First she had to get through the closed gates. Small tasks seemed very difficult when half your brain was nonfunctioning. Emily rubbed her pounding forehead. How was she supposed to get inside? There were video monitors mounted on the decorative stone gate posts, but she couldn't see any handles or locks on the gates themselves. Belatedly, she remembered that Carolyn had warned her about the secured entrance to the ranch. She'd been instructed to press the buzzer right below the videocam and request admittance.

Okay, Emily decided. She could manage that.

Hot, humid air assailed her as she rolled down the window. The temperature had been in the nineties for the past several days, and there was no rain in the five-day forecast, no expectation of a return to the eighties anytime soon. She'd been happy about the dry spell when she heard the forecast this morning. Now she wished rain would pour down in torrents. If there could only be a flood, just a little one, with nobody drowning, would that be sufficient excuse to call off the wedding?

Despite a fervent prayer for lightning bolts and thunder claps, the sky remained stubbornly cloudless, without the tiniest hint of an impending shower, let alone a flood of torrential rain. Thunderstorms, she could only conclude, were not delivered on demand to save people from social embarrassment.

Sighing, she pressed the intercom button. "This is Emily Sutton. I have an appointment with Dylan Garrett of Finders Keepers."

"Hi, Emily. This is Carolyn. I'll let you in."

The gates swung open, but Emily didn't drive through them. Instead, she stared at the electronic speaker as if it had sprouted fangs and poison pincers. Carolyn St. Clair! *Her maid of honor.* Good grief, she was truly losing her mind. How could she possibly have forgotten that Carolyn would be here, at the Double G Ranch? How could she have forgotten that the main reason she'd chosen Dylan Garrett to be her investigator was because her best friend Carolyn worked for Finders Keepers?

"Hey, Em, are you there? Or have we lost you to a daydream about your honeymoon?" Even over the intercom system, Emily could hear that Carolyn's voice was tinged with friendly laughter. What in the world was she going to tell her? Carolyn was probably the kindest, most sympathetic woman in San Antonio, but that didn't make it any easier for Emily to confess that she'd been dumped by her fiancé, hours before the wedding.

Whatever story she settled on, Emily decided, she couldn't break the news over an intercom. She cleared her throat. "I'm here, Carolyn, and the gates are open. I'll be with you in a couple of minutes."

"Okay. I'll meet you at the head of the stairs. When you've parked the car, you'll see the signposts to our office."

The gates swung closed behind her, and Emily followed the winding, tree-shaded drive to the ranch. The driveway was almost long enough and wide enough to be considered a road, and on another day, in different circumstances, she might have been intrigued by this chance to observe one of the San Antonio region's oldest and most successful cattle ranches. As it was, her brain was so stuffed full of worry that she could just as easily have been driving to the local mall for all the attention she paid to the view.

Parking on a flagstone apron shaded by a pair of giant live oaks, she followed rustic wooden signs that pointed her to a side entrance and a stairway that led up to the second-floor offices of Finders Keepers.

As promised, Carolyn greeted her at the head of the stairs. "I'm glad you could make it, Em. With the wedding tomorrow, I half expected to get a phone call saying that some last-minute glitch in the arrangements was keeping you in town."

"No." Emily drew in a shaky breath. "I decided to get the hell out of Dodge for an hour or two and leave everyone else to cope with the disasters."

Carolyn laughed. "I should have known you would be much too well organized to be panicked just because several hundred of the most important people in Texas are coming to watch you get married. Now me, I'm already chugging antacids just because I'm going to be your maid of honor. I know people aren't going to pay the least bit of attention to anyone except you, and maybe a glance or two at Michael, but I'm not used to moving in the sort of high-society circles that you inhabit, and I don't want to mess up." She rolled her eyes. "The Chambers family is so nose-in-the-air Old Money that I'm never quite sure whether to curtsey or tell them to lighten up and get a life."

This was simply awful. Emily wondered if she should faint, have hysterics, or cut short her torture by jumping out of the nearest window. "Look, Carolyn, you probably need to know that you don't have to worry anymore about being—"

A man came out of a door to her left. "Ms. Sutton? I'm

Dylan Garrett, one of the partners in Finders Keepers. I've been looking forward to meeting you.''

Years of social training took over and Emily extended her hand, smiling politely. "Yes, I'm Emily Sutton. It's good to meet you, Dylan.''

"I'll get back to straightening out the petty cash accounts," Carolyn said with a quick wave. "See you tonight, Em. I'm looking forward to it.''

Oh, God! Should she keep Dylan waiting while she told Carolyn what had happened? Panic started to whirl in Emily's stomach and she leaned against the banister, afraid she might pass out if she didn't grab on to some solid support.

"Come into my office and we'll get started," Dylan said, taking the decision of what to do next out of her hands. "I know how busy you must be, and I'll try to do this as fast as we can.'' He held the door, standing back so that she could pass him.

He would never know what an effort of will it required to straighten her shoulders, move away from the support of the stair rail, and follow him into his office, Emily thought.

"What a pleasant room," she said as Dylan closed the door behind them. Her reaction was mechanical, but as she spoke, she realized she had instinctively responded to the simple, masculine comfort of the room. As a trained interior designer, it was second nature for her to notice the settings people chose to live and work in, and she heartily approved Dylan's taste.

The office had walls of natural stone and rough-hewn timber, contrasted with sections of whitewashed plaster that gave the whole room an airy feel that was simultaneously timeless and fashionably rustic. The furniture was obviously custom-designed to fit the niches and contours of the room, and the natural clutter of a working office was cleverly contained within several purpose-designed cabinets and open tray systems.

"You have wonderful natural light, and you've made the most of the available space," she said, looking around. "You must enjoy working here."

"I sure do. It's turned out well, hasn't it?" Dylan sat down behind an oversize desk and gestured for her to take the comfortable armchair that faced him. "It's hard to imagine that this second floor has been part of the ranch for a hundred years, but it wasn't much more than wasted space until my sister and I decided to convert the area into our offices."

"With Carolyn to keep the administration running smoothly, and this great setting to impress your clients, I'm sure Finders Keepers will soon be the most successful investigative firm in the state."

Dylan grinned. "We can only hope. But let's get down to business. I know this is a very busy day for you and I'm sorry we couldn't arrange to get together any earlier. You're the only person I know whose schedule is more full than mine right now."

Emily managed a sickly smile. If only he realized just how empty her schedule was about to become.

Dylan gave her an intent look, then leaned back in his chair, deliberately casual. "Tell me what you would like Finders Keepers to investigate for you, Ms. Sutton. Carolyn said that it was a family matter, but that's all she told me."

"Call me Emily, please." She had agonized over her decision for weeks before coming to consult with Dylan Garrett. Ironically, now that she was here, her emotions were so numb that it didn't seem such a big deal after all. "I'm here because I need you to find my birth mother," she said.

"Need?" Dylan asked mildly. "Do you really need to

find your birth mother for something like medical reasons, or was that just a figure of speech?''

''A figure of speech. At least I think it was.'' Emily smiled wryly. ''I don't have any hereditary diseases as far as I know, and psychologically I'm sure I'll survive if I never find out who my birth mother was, but I guess I've grown more and more curious about my origins as I've gotten older. Don't get me wrong. My parents, Sam and Raelene Sutton, are wonderful people. They've given me a great education, a secure home, and lots of material possessions. Most of all, they've loved me more than any child could possibly hope for. In fact, they were such terrific parents I made it all through the teenage years without ever once being tempted to run away to search for my 'real' mom. So I guess it kind of took me by surprise a couple of months ago when I found myself wondering about my birth mother.''

''You never thought about her before? That's unusual for an adopted child.''

''I thought about her occasionally, but not with any real intensity. On my birthdays, I would wonder if she remembered the day I was born, and if she missed me. But suddenly, after twenty-seven years, I have this nagging sense of urgency, and I've even started to dream about her at night. It's as if time's running out for me to find her. When I'm awake, the feeling of urgency isn't so strong, but I keep asking myself how she'd feel if she knew her daughter was about to get married—'' Emily stopped abruptly.

Fortunately, Dylan misinterpreted the reason for her sudden silence. ''It's not surprising that you should start questioning the circumstances of your birth now you've reached the point in your life when you might have children of your own. Even so, before I agree to proceed with the investigation, I'd like to reassure myself that you're aware of the risks involved.''

"Risks?"

"Emotional risks, chiefly. Although sometimes there are practical risks, too."

"I've considered the risks," Emily said. "I realize this search will impact my adoptive parents as well as me. Obviously, I don't want to hurt them—"

"Have you told them what you're planning to do?"

Emily shook her head. "No, not yet."

Dylan sent her a quizzical look and she acknowledged his tacit question with a rueful smile. "I'm not chickening out. Honest. I don't think they'll be hurt by the idea that I've chosen to look for my birth mother, but they'll be...anxious. Why worry them needlessly? Carolyn says your success rate in finding missing family members is very high, but even you must have the occasional failure. I didn't want to get everyone worked up over something that might fizzle out into nothing."

"You have a point. But we're proud of our record, even though we've only been in business a short time, so I'm optimistic that we can find your mother. However, there are still a couple of warnings I need to run by you before we start the investigation. Until quite recently adoptions were governed more by custom than by law. Nowadays, most states insist on full disclosure, and open adoptions are the norm, with all the important facts on the table. But thirty years ago, case workers figured birth records were closed forever, and nobody was going to be hurt if they polished the truth to make it more palatable to adoptive parents."

"I just want to know who my mother is and why she chose to give me up for adoption," Emily said. "I'm prepared to face whatever you find."

"Are you certain? Even if it turns out that you were born while your mother was in prison? Or maybe she had so many sexual partners nobody has any idea who your father is? Or how about if she's a married woman, living in the suburbs with a second family and children she chose not to give up for adoption? How badly is that going to hurt you? Then there are the practical risks I talked about. You're a successful professional woman, with wealthy parents. What if your adoptive mother hits you up for money?''

''Actually, I've thought about all those possibilities, and I've decided I want to know the truth, whatever it is,'' Emily answered without hesitation. Surprisingly, a fierce desire to find her birth mother was one of the few emotions she could still feel through the numbness induced by Michael's rejection.

She realized she was gripping the edge of the desk, and she uncurled her tense fingers. ''I appreciate the warnings, Dylan, and I'm prepared to face the worst, but I don't think I'll have to. The adoption agency provided some pretty specific details about my background. They said my birth mother was a nineteen-year-old student at the University of Texas. My father was also a college student, although he was a couple of years older. They had a brief affair, but by the time my birth mother found out she was pregnant, my father had already graduated—''

Dylan shook his head, interrupting her. ''Emily, every client who walks through these doors seems to have been told a version of the same story. Middle-class couples were more willing to adopt babies from middle-class backgrounds, so that's what the agencies provided—babies supposedly born to innocent young girls who had made a mistake. The truth might really have been that the birth mother was an illegal immigrant toiling in a factory sweatshop and boosting her income by working as a prostitute, but somehow she always got transformed into a college student who made a mistake.''

"Sometimes it must have happened that way, though. College students do have unplanned babies."

"Yeah. Sometimes. Not as often as you might expect." Dylan leaned forward, his gaze intent. "I had a case where an older woman found out the truth about her past and wished she hadn't. The illusions of a lifetime were badly shattered and she's coping with information she'd have preferred not to have. Let me give you one last warning, Emily. Don't open the box unless you're one hundred percent sure you want to see the contents."

Emily knew adoption agencies often lied about the circumstances of the birth parents…knew that her mother might be someone society would deem unworthy. Her dubious genetic heritage was one of the reasons she had always been so anxious not to disgrace Raelene and Sam. She didn't want to give people cause to whisper that bad blood always tells in the end. But the time had come in her life when she needed to replace comforting myths with the truth.

"I'm prepared for whatever you find out," she said quietly. "I want to open the box."

"Okay, I believe you." Dylan relaxed and gave her a warm smile. "Now I'm finally going to quit with the dire warnings and tell you one of my favorite adoption stories. Almost the first client this agency had was a man in his forties. His adoptive mother had just died, and he'd decided to start a search for his birth mother. We found her without too much difficulty, and they had a great reunion. It turned out his birth mother had been widowed a year earlier and had been looking for her son ever since. But it gets even better. Yesterday, I had a phone call from my client. His birth mother and his adoptive dad have just gotten engaged and he called to invite me to the wedding. Isn't that a great story?"

"It sure is. It's the sort of fairy-tale ending every

adopted child dreams of." Emily concentrated on feeling happy for the bride and groom, and not wallowing in self-pity for herself and her broken engagement.

"I have a bunch more great adoption stories, but with your tight schedule, I guess we need to get down to business." Dylan's manner became brisk. "I'll need your birth certificate and the name of the agency that arranged the adoption. I assume you can give me that much?"

Emily nodded. "I sure can. The adoption was arranged through the Lutheran Family Services. Unfortunately, their records were all destroyed in a fire, and the agency itself is no longer in business, which is why I couldn't take this investigation any further myself. I didn't know where to start."

She laid a brown envelope on the desk. It contained the meager records of her adoption. "Other than the story I told you about both my parents being students at the University of Texas, I don't have any leads to give you, I'm afraid."

"Don't worry. It's my business to generate leads. That's why we charge the big bucks."

Emily acknowledged his smile. "Yes, Carolyn already provided me with your fee schedule. It took me a couple of days to recover, but I'm no longer in a state of total shock."

"Good." Smiling, Dylan pushed back his chair and rose to his feet. "Don't worry, Emily, we earn our high prices. We've traced birth parents with less information than you've given me, and quite quickly, too. So my advice is that you should enjoy your wedding, have fun on the honeymoon, and by the time you're back in town again, I hope to have news for you."

He glanced down at some notes on his desk. "I have your address and phone number here—365 Market Street. Is that going to change after you're married?"

Emily felt her smile freeze. Good grief, here was another problem she hadn't thought of. She was about to become a homeless person! She'd sold her small but beautiful condo with views over the River Walk because she'd expected to move into Michael's self-contained apartment within the Chambers mansion. Her furniture was in storage, and she'd been camping out for the past ten days at her parents' house. The new owners had already moved into her condo, and she had no place to go. Because much as she loved her parents, she simply wasn't going to continue living with them. She never again wanted to put herself at the mercy of their well meant but smothering protection.

It took significant effort, but she managed not to let her worry show. "I'm not living at the Market Street address anymore, but I'll make sure Carolyn has my new address and phone number," she said. "I'll be in touch in a couple of days."

Dylan wasn't a detective for nothing. She'd thought she managed to convey that information rather calmly, but he sensed the anxiety lurking only a hairbreadth beneath the cool surface.

"Emily, what's bothering you?" he asked quietly. "I assumed it was the search for your birth mother that had you on the edge, which is why I pressed you hard about the risks involved. But I've been watching you closely, and I'm fairly sure it's not this investigation that has you half a step away from full-blown panic. It's something else. Can I help?"

"No, but I really appreciate the offer. It sounded genuine."

"It was. I have broad shoulders if you feel the need to unload a problem."

It occurred to her that Dylan would be an easy man to confide in. It also occurred to her that he must encounter people all the time who were struggling with heartbreaking, life-or-death dilemmas. She suddenly realized that 350 disgruntled guests didn't amount to a life-or-death problem. As for heartbreaking... Her heart, now that she stopped to think about it, seemed remarkably unscathed by Michael's casual termination of their engagement. Her pride was rubbed raw and she was panicked by the sudden upheaval in her plans for her future, but there was no gaping wound in her emotions. In fact, for a bride jilted almost at the altar, she was embarrassingly free of grief.

Emily flashed Dylan her first genuine smile in several hours. "I've just this minute come to the conclusion that I don't have much of a problem at all. Other than the fact that I've been indulging in an exaggerated case of self-pity, which I plan to snap out of right now. Thank you again for your excellent advice."

"You're welcome." Dylan grinned. "Sometime you must let me know what I said that was so insightful." He walked her to the door. "You'd probably like to see Carolyn before you leave. Her office is two doors down. You can't miss it."

"Thanks. I'll look forward to hearing from you as soon as you have any news about my birth mother." Emily said a final goodbye and marched purposefully down the hallway to Carolyn's office. The door was open and she stepped inside without knocking.

"I'm not going to marry Michael," she announced. "You're the first person to hear the news."

The sky didn't fall and the walls of the building remained standing. In fact, her announcement seemed considerably less amazing once she'd actually spoken it out loud.

Carolyn, who'd been working at a computer, swiveled around on her chair and looked at Emily without saying anything. Her expression revealed nothing at all about what she was thinking, not even that she was surprised.

"You want to sit down and tell me about it?" Carolyn asked finally.

"No, I don't want to talk about it. Not yet." Whatever story she invented for the benefit of the world at large, Carolyn was her best friend and would have the plain, unvarnished truth. But not right now. Not today.

"I've been really stupid, and it still feels too frightening to talk about," Emily said by way of explanation. Her heart might not be shattered, but it could still ache for dreams and hopes that weren't going to be fulfilled. "Give me a few hours to get my head fixed on straight and then I'll share all the gory details."

"Okay. Subject closed. So what shall we do tonight?" Carolyn rallied like the trooper she was. "Want to come to my place and eat popcorn and watch bad movies? Hop on a plane to Dallas? Drive into the country and spend the night at a motel, drinking champagne and dissing men? You name it, I'm game."

"Thank you," Emily said, feeling tears spring into her eyes. "You're a wonderful friend, Caro. But I think what you should do tonight is attend the Sutton-Chambers bridal dinner at the San Antonio Federal Club. Trust me, the food's going to be spectacular. The champagne is all from France, and there are a bunch of cute guys coming, and most of them dance really well."

"But I thought you said you weren't going to marry Michael?"

"I'm not. But it's too late to cancel the bridal dinner. Everything will have to be paid for anyway, so somebody might as well eat all the fancy food Mrs. Chambers has spent three months selecting." Emily was quite proud of her smile. "The bride and groom will be missing, but that should at least make for some interesting table gossip."

"Well, I don't know, Em..."

"Go, Carolyn. Please. I want you to. You bought a super new dress, you told me so. You might as well wear it and leave all the men of San Antonio eating their hearts out because you're so unattainable."

Carolyn laughed. "You've got me mixed up with you," she said. "You're the one who left a trail of broken hearts when you accepted Michael's proposal."

Emily sent her friend a grateful smile. It was so typical of Carolyn to say something to boost her morale. "Thanks, Caro. I wish we could have lunch together so you could pay me lots more slick compliments, but I ought to get back, I suppose. I can't put off talking to my parents any longer."

"Do you want me to call any of the guests? Warn the other bridesmaids? Anything along those lines?"

Emily felt herself break out in a cold sweat at this reminder of what she would shortly be facing. "I don't know what to say...." She drew in a steadying breath. "No. Don't tell anyone that the wedding's off. I think it's best if we just let everyone turn up for the bridal dinner tonight and then my parents will have to make some kind of an announcement."

Carolyn sent her a look of real sympathy. "You went a bit white around the gills when you said that. Are you okay to drive yourself home, Em?"

"Yes, I'll manage. I'm fine, really." She looked at her watch and realized that she'd left the Chambers' home well over two hours ago. "Wow! I *really* have to get back and face the music. I'll be in touch soon, I promise. Take care, Carolyn."

"You, too, Em. Drive carefully. Love ya."

"Love you, too, babe."

Carolyn watched her friend leave. "But you didn't love Michael," she muttered under her breath. "Thank goodness you realized that in time to get out of marrying him."

CHAPTER THREE

EMILY DIDN'T NEED to ask where everyone was when she finally managed to fight her way through the crush of city traffic and return to the Chambers's house. The sound of loud, angry voices informed her she would find a large gathering of furious people in the family room at the rear of the house.

Feet dragging, she walked slowly down the hallway, fighting a cowardly urge to hide in one of the formal reception rooms, where the heavy antique furnishings provided cover, and Victorian oil portraits of Chambers ancestors looked down at the goings-on of their descendants with bland indifference.

The irate voices grew progressively louder, with Mr. Chambers's upper-crust baritone booming over a cacophony of other speakers. Her mother sounded as if she might be crying, and Emily winced in anticipation. The prospect of opening the door to the family room and facing the hurt and disappointment of her parents was almost enough to have Emily turn tail and run as fast as her legs could carry her in the opposite direction. But the thought of Mr. Chambers berating her mother put some steel into her flabby backbone. Reminding herself that a canceled wedding barely rated as an earthshaking problem in the grand scheme of things, Emily opened the door.

The family room was little used and quite small, converted from a combination of the old butler's pantry and housekeeper's sitting room. Right now it appeared crammed to overflowing with irate people. Her parents. Mr. and Mrs. Chambers. Michael. Jeff Greiff, his campaign manager. Michael's brother, Jordan, was also there, standing a little apart from the others and staring out of the window. He was the only person who wasn't yelling, shouting or crying.

Emily swallowed hard. The tension swirling around the room was powerful enough to squeeze the air out of her lungs. Her vocal chords stubbornly refused to function and she pressed her hands to her rib cage, trying to speak, but no words came. Surprisingly, it was Jordan who noticed her arrival first, even though his back was toward the door.

"Emily's here," he said, half turning. He spoke quietly, but his cool tones penetrated the hullabaloo, and the babble of exasperated voices stopped for a few seconds while everyone swiveled around to stare at her. She'd noticed before that Jordan rarely needed to raise his voice in order to make his presence felt, and she wondered why his family seemed unaware of the fact that on the rare occasions when he wanted to, Jordan could dominate any situation he found himself in.

Amelia Chambers spoke first, her voice acid with sarcasm. "Well, it's the vanishing bride! How good of you to put in an appearance. Finally. I suppose we should be grateful for small mercies."

Emily flushed. "I had an appointment on the far side of town, Mrs. Chambers. I'm sorry to have kept everyone waiting."

Amelia was standing by the fireplace, her hand resting on the mantelpiece. At Emily's reply, she drew herself up to her full, imposing five feet nine inches and squinted down her narrow, patrician nose, her nostrils flaring with temper.

"You had an appointment across town?" She sounded

incredulous, as if Emily had admitted to taking off for a brief trip to the planet Mars.

"It was a long-standing commitment. A business appointment."

"Oh, well, that explains everything. I appreciate your finding time to squeeze us into your busy schedule." Amelia rarely lost her temper, but when she did, her sarcasm could corrode steel. "Perhaps, now that you're here, you'd be kind enough to give us some clue as to why you've chosen to ruin my son's life?"

"You've no call to talk to my daughter in that nasty tone of voice!" Raelene Sutton, plump and petite, sprang to her daughter's defense like a sparring bantam hen, giving Emily no chance to speak for herself. "If she's called off her engagement to your son, you can be sure she has a good reason for it."

"Yes, and I'd like to know what that reason is," Sam Sutton said fiercely. "What did your son do to my little girl that she doesn't want to marry him anymore?"

Sam was a good six inches shorter than Michael, but that didn't deter him from confronting his daughter's former fiancé. Hands on hips, lower lip thrust out, he looked as if he'd as soon punch Michael's nose as listen to an explanation.

Michael stepped back, alarmed. "I didn't do anything to your daughter!" he protested, sounding aggrieved. "Emily, tell everyone the truth! Explain to your parents that *you* called off our engagement because we were incompatible. You have to convince them you're okay with this! Nobody seems to believe me."

Emily sent him an astonished glance, although she didn't really look at him. Couldn't look at him and maintain any pretense of being in control. Was this how Michael had resolved the dilemma of explaining that he'd called off their wedding? By blaming it all on her? If she hadn't felt so numb—so *bludgeoned*—she thought she might have been angry.

How little Michael understood her, she reflected wearily. After three months as her fiancé, he still didn't recognize that she was a conformist to the core of her being. But unlike Michael, her parents knew her well enough to realize she would never have suggested canceling the wedding at this late date except in the most dire of circumstances. No wonder they were worried sick, imagining what those dire circumstances could be.

When she didn't immediately speak up, Michael came and stood at her side, his confident manner suggesting that he harbored no real doubt that she'd go along with his version of events. He obviously assumed she was still such a captive of his charm that she would meekly accept whatever story he cooked up, Emily thought, seething at his attitude. Had she really been such a wimp in their relationship? Was it only a few hours earlier that she had found his arrogance appealing?

"Tell everyone that you want to call off the wedding, Emily. Help me out here." Michael flashed one of his cajoling smiles, reminiscent of Bruce Willis at his most endearing. Smiles she had previously considered irresistible and now found repellant. "Please tell them that you don't want to go through with this charade, honey. Tell them it's a mutual decision."

Emily had new insights into Michael's character now that she hadn't enjoyed this morning, and she felt sure he hadn't lied about their breakup in order to save her injured pride. He was laying the blame for their broken engagement on her doorstep simply because his jaunty confidence was a sham. Deep inside where it really counted, he was too gutless to stand up and take responsibility for a mess that was entirely his own creation.

Despite her anger, if he wanted to pile all the blame on

her, she didn't really care. Nothing could avoid the humiliation that was building inexorably toward tomorrow's climax, when 350 guests would gather for a wedding that wouldn't happen. In the circumstances, did it matter how the guilt was apportioned? In fact, she could only agree with Michael about their incompatibility. Whatever the true reasons for his last-minute decision to call off the wedding, she probably ought to be grateful that he wanted out. After today's events, there was no avoiding the conclusion that they were wildly unsuited to each other. It seemed inevitable that their marriage would have ended in crushing failure. Better that it never take place.

Right now, though, it was difficult to feel gratitude, with Holt and Amelia Chambers looking so disgruntled and her parents looking so devastated. Still, she couldn't give her parents false hope. The wedding was off and, since there was no way to change that, she needed to confirm that the break between her and Michael was beyond mending. There were business considerations at stake here, in addition to everything else. Holt Chambers and her father had signed a preliminary agreement to develop Laurel Acres, a major construction project in the hill country region north of San Antonio. If her marriage to Michael didn't take place, that deal might be at risk. Her father had old-fashioned values and tried to do business only with people whom he respected. He might not want to continue in partnership with the Chamberses if he decided that Michael had treated her badly.

Michael's father wasn't a warmhearted man, but he'd been as kind to her as his uptight nature permitted, and she knew he needed the projected partnership a great deal more than her father, whose canny judgment and hard work had made him a millionaire many times over. By contrast, since her engagement, she'd come to realize that the Chambers family was long on ancient lineage and seriously short of ready cash.

Emily knew she had it within her power to wreak revenge on Michael simply by telling the truth. For a moment she was tempted, then her better nature won out. No point in punishing Holt Chambers because Michael had turned out to be a jerk.

Her silence had already gone on way too long, and she spoke quickly, before her good intentions melted in the heat of disgust for Michael's behavior. "A marriage between the two of us would never have worked," she said woodenly. "We don't love each other enough to make a go of our relationship. Under the circumstances, we decided to cancel the wedding ceremony tomorrow. I'm sorry for the inconvenience. Very sorry."

She spoke to a spot angled somewhere between her parents' concerned faces. Which, by an unfortunate fluke, brought her slap bang into visual contact with Jordan Chambers. He looked at her quizzically and she felt heat flare in the pit of her stomach. From the time of their disastrous encounter in Mary Christine Bernauer's bedroom, Michael's brother always produced that effect on her, and Emily intensely disliked the sensation.

Cheeks burning, she dropped her gaze and stared fixedly at her shoes. Even though she could no longer see him, she knew instinctively that Jordan continued to look at her. She felt the touch of his gaze as a physical entity, unsettling, but compelling. His silent inspection continued and the heat in her cheeks spread through her body, blazing all the way to her toes.

With a liberating sense of release, Emily realized there was no longer any reason for her to conceal her dislike of Michael's brother. She jerked her head upward and sent him a gaze of fulminating fury. Here was a genuine blessing about her broken engagement, she thought grimly. At least she would never have to be polite to Jordan again.

He held her gaze for several tense seconds, then turned back to his original position at the window, staring outside as if fascinated by the view of the barren, sun-drenched courtyard. Emily drew in a shaky breath, determined to get a grip on herself. She could only hyperventilate about one disaster at a time, and right now, her antagonistic relationship with Jordan Chambers shouldn't even be registering on her personal disaster scale. She had bigger problems to worry about.

She was concentrating so hard on ignoring Jordan that she jumped when Jeff Greiff spoke. "You and Michael need to come up with a better explanation for the breakup than being incompatible," the campaign manager said. "When a celebrity couple splits and tries to claim incompatibility, the media just invent a more interesting story. Gone are the days when keeping a discreet silence ensures that gossip dies down faster. Nowadays, silence is an open invitation to scandal. Mega scandal."

Jeff puffed out his cheeks, looking self-important and vaguely ridiculous to Emily's jaundiced eyes. "You can't afford scandal right now, Michael," he went on. "Quite apart from the disastrous effect on our fund-raising potential, you're just starting to get some name recognition with the voters. Negative publicity could sink your positive ratings to a point where they can't be salvaged. We can't afford any negative press right now." He scowled at Emily. "The timing for this breakup really sucks, you know."

Emily almost apologized, then stopped herself just in time. Michael's campaign problems were not of her making and she had zero sympathy for his plight. In fact, given the weakness of character he'd revealed today, a dose of negative publicity might not be a bad thing. The people of

Texas deserved better than a man who broke promises and then tried to weasel out of the consequences.

She finally brought herself to look squarely at her former fiancé, letting him see her scorn. He stared back at her somewhat helplessly, then ran his hand through his thick, glossy hair, looking a great deal more worried now than he had when he announced the ending of their engagement. "This is a hell of a mess," he said, handsome jaw clenched.

"You could certainly say that," Emily agreed. "Personally, I suggest we stop tossing around blame and make up our minds what we're going to say to the 350 people who are expecting to watch us get married tomorrow."

Michael sucked in a nervous gulp of air, then scowled. "My God, this is a public relations nightmare."

"You should have thought of that earlier, I guess."

"I did think about it. But I didn't have much choice—" He scowled. "Damn! Why couldn't all this have come to light weeks ago? There would be no story for any reporters to run with if it weren't for the fact that the wedding's only hours away."

"You're right. It's the wedding ceremony itself that's the real problem." Jeff Greiff paced nervously. "The guest list includes three U.S. senators and the secretary of defense—"

"Dear lord," Amelia whispered, fanning herself. The poor woman looked truly ill. "What in the world are we going to do? What shall we say?"

"The out-of-town guests are all due at the dinner tonight, so there's no way to head them off," Jeff said with gloomy relish. "They'll have left Washington already. What kind of spin can we put on this? My God, Michael, if you'd set out to piss off the movers and shakers who've supported your candidacy for governor, you couldn't have done a better job."

Amelia stopped glaring at Emily long enough to direct an icy glance at her son's campaign manager. "This horrible situation isn't improved by using coarse language, Jeff."

"Sorry, ma'am." Jeff turned away, rolling his eyes once he was out of Amelia's line of vision.

Raelene broke into a fresh burst of tears. "I don't care about the senators or any of your other fancy guests," she wailed. "All I care about is my daughter. I don't understand, Emmie. You looked so beautiful when we went for the final fitting on your wedding dress yesterday. You seemed so calm, so sure of yourself...."

"I'm sorry, Mom," Emily interrupted, unable to bear any more reminders of how naively content she'd been a mere twenty-four hours earlier. "I guess Michael and I discovered we weren't in love—"

"Now, now, muffin, you know we aren't going to believe that load of garbage." Her father took her hand, patting it as much to comfort himself as to reassure her. "We're not angry with you, Emmie, we just want to understand. At breakfast you gave us no hint—none!—that you were having second thoughts. What happened between breakfast and lunch to make you change your mind?"

Emily opened her mouth, then shut it again, unable to think of a single intelligent thing to say. She wanted to help Mr. Chambers salvage his business partnership with her dad, but she realized that might be impossible. Her parents simply knew her too well to believe the story Michael was trying to pass off on them.

"I know it's out of character for me to do something like this," she said in a final attempt to make the incredible sound reasonable. "The truth is—"

"The truth is that you and I need to talk," Jordan interrupted. "Now, Emily, before you say anything more."

"Excuse me?" Emily stared at him, sufficiently astonished to forget that looking at Jordan invariably produced an absurd and troublesome rush of heat. Their eyes met and, on cue, her cheeks flamed, but for once she ignored the sensation. "I can't think of a single thing that you and I might need to discuss, Jordan."

"You're not handling this the right way," he responded coolly. "Trust me, Emily, we need to talk."

She glared at him. "Have you ever noticed that it's only people who are completely untrustworthy who tell you to trust them?"

Jordan flashed her a brief, hard smile. "Darling, this isn't going to get us anywhere, you know. We need to discuss the situation privately. Just the two of us."

He'd called her *darling.* Emily's stomach performed a back flip. She was sufficiently stupefied by Jordan's endearment that she forgot to reply, just stared at him with her mouth hanging open. What in the world was going on? This was the man she despised, the man who had never yet spent ten minutes in her company without saying something that provoked an argument. Was the entire Chambers family going mad?

If *they* weren't collectively nuts, perhaps *she* was. Maybe this crazy cancellation of the wedding was a nightmare, and she would wake up any second. Surreptitiously, Emily gave her arm a hard pinch and waited in hope.

Unfortunately, it seemed that she wasn't dreaming. Jordan walked across the room and touched his finger to her chin, gently closing her mouth. She opened it again to speak, but Jordan closed it once more, this time with considerable firmness.

"Not here, dearest."

First *darling,* and now *dearest.* She'd definitely slipped down a rabbit hole into Wonderland, Emily decided.

Jordan turned to the assembled company. From their silence, Emily deduced they were all as bewildered as she was. "Excuse us," he said. "Give us fifteen minutes, will you?"

He didn't wait for a response, just put his hand under Emily's elbow and propelled her from the crowded family room, shutting the door on the explosion of questions that followed their exit.

"They'll be hot on our tail within minutes," he said as soon as they were in the hall. "We'll have to use the library. That's the only room with a lock on the door."

"I have no intention of going anywhere with you, least of all into a room where we're locked in—"

Jordan swung her up into his arms, carried her into the library, and set her down on her feet, turning the key in the door behind them. "Sorry about that," he said, strolling over to the fireplace and standing with one foot resting on the old-fashioned fender, his hands shoved into the pockets of his pants. "I'm not trying to lock you in, Em, I'm trying to keep everyone else out while we talk."

Emily tugged at the linen jacket of her suit, her breathing shallow and her heart thudding. She refused to let him see the turmoil she felt, and she addressed him coolly. "Tell me, Jordan, is the insanity you and your brother suffer from hereditary? If so, I guess I should be grateful that your brother decided to dump me. Much as I want to have children, I'd prefer them not to be crazy."

Instead of appearing insulted, Jordan grinned. "You might have had girls," he said. "I've heard rumors that the Chambers women usually escape the family afflic-tion."

"You mean insanity really does run in your—" Emily broke off, pressing her hands to her forehead. "No, of course it doesn't. You're not going to do this to me today, Jordan."

"Do what?"

"Distract me. Confuse me." She hadn't intended to admit that he had the power to discompose her, and she hurried on. "We're going to have a brief, rational conversation and then I'm going back to talk with my parents. Why have you dragged me in here, Jordan?"

"I thought it might be a good idea if we got married tomorrow." Jordan made the suggestion with a casualness that would have been entirely appropriate if he'd been suggesting that she might like to try out a new restaurant for brunch on Sunday.

Emily clutched the back of the nearest chair. *Jordan had asked her to marry him.* She was quite sure she'd heard him do that. Unless she was hallucinating. Was she? She felt her mouth start to drop open again, and she hurriedly closed it.

This library was not a good place to be alone with a Chambers male, she decided. First Michael had called off their wedding for no reason at all. Now Jordan was suggesting something even more totally crazy. So crazy, in fact, that Emily felt a spurt of genuine alarm. She hadn't been serious in suggesting Jordan and Michael were suffering from the onset of insanity. Maybe she should have been.

"I don't think marriage would work out too well for us," she said, trying to keep her voice soft and nonthreatening. She even managed a small, reassuring smile. When dealing with lunatics, it was best to be gentle. "Thanks for asking, Jordan, but if you remember, we don't like each other. I have this quaint, old-fashioned dislike of men who sleep with other men's wives."

Damn! If he was mentally unstable, maybe she shouldn't have mentioned the fact that they disliked each other. Much less reminded him of their disastrous second meeting, a couple of days after their formal introduction, when she had discovered Jordan romping under satin sheets with

Mary Christine, the twenty-three-year-old wife of Emily's sixty-year-old client, Ted Bernauer.

All things considered, escape from the study seemed like a truly excellent plan. Either Jordan was nuts or she was. Why hang around to find out who? She was closer to the door than Jordan, so keeping her smile fixed in place, she tried to back up toward it without drawing attention to her movements.

Jordan might have lost his mind, but his vision remained acute, and his physical coordination excellent. In three quick strides, he crossed the room and pulled her away from the door, spread-eagling his body between her and her escape route.

"Sorry," he said, sounding sincerely apologetic as he pocketed the key. "But I really need you to listen to my proposal."

"I already had one of those from Michael," she replied tightly. "I believe I'm a little burned out on proposals from the Chambers men."

His gaze narrowed. "*Proposition* might be a better word in my case. I'm offering you a face-saving deal, Emily. You owe it to yourself to listen. Marry me tomorrow, and the joint business venture between my father and yours can go on as planned. Marry me tomorrow, and the ceremony will probably be over before half the guests even notice that you're exchanging rings with the wrong brother."

"Thanks again for the generous offer, Jordan, but before we get carried away, let's remember there's one teensy-tiny problem with your scheme."

"What's that?"

"Half the guests might not notice that I'd married the wrong brother, but I would." Emily spoke more harshly than she'd intended, mostly because for a few insane seconds, she'd actually found herself considering his proposition. Surely she was hitting a new low to even contemplate accepting Jordan's proposal just because it would provide a groom for tomorrow's ceremony.

Jordan shrugged. "It wouldn't be a lifetime sentence," he said. "We can have the big, splashy wedding our parents planned, and then, in a few months, we can get a quiet, civilized divorce."

"Divorce is never civilized," Emily said. "It's a heartbreaking betrayal of promises."

"There would be no heartbreak in our case. You can't betray promises that were never made. We're not promising each other anything except to go through a ceremony and live in the same house just long enough for the media to lose interest in the Chambers family. These days, I'd figure that's about a week."

"You're forgetting Michael's campaign for governor."

"Hmm...true. In view of my brother's prominent position, the media interest might have a lingering half life. I guess we'd better agree up front that we'll stick it out until the start of the new year. Michael's campaign should be firmly established by then."

"That's more than four months from now!"

Jordan shrugged. "Four months is hardly a life sentence. We don't have to live in each other's pockets the whole time. In fact, we should probably give the marriage a year. That would allow the Chambers-Sutton land development deal ample time to get off the ground."

"Oh," she said, suddenly understanding Jordan's motives in making the offer to marry her. She quashed an entirely irrational twinge of disappointment. "So that's what this proposal is really about—money. You're worried that my father's money is going to vanish from the Chambers bank accounts if I don't marry your brother."

Jordan didn't contradict her. "Your father and mine have put together a complicated business deal that requires a lot of trust on both sides. My family is giving up land that we've owned for generations. Your father is supplying development capital and design ideas. A feud between the two parties isn't going to make for a successful development. If this project isn't a success, both parties could end up losing their shirts.''

She was surprised that Jordan had been paying sufficient attention to know some of the details of the proposed Laurel Acres partnership deal. He was notorious for his lack of involvement in his family's investment and banking business. To his parents' dismay, he had dropped out of college in his junior year and struck out on his own, claiming that he wanted to become a carpenter. The Chamberses considered any profession that involved sweat and hammers beneath them, so they were seriously unhappy about his choice of career. Their complaints got louder and more frequent as Jordan's circle of blue-collar friends expanded and his visits to the family mansion became less and less frequent. Even Michael was annoyed by his brother's refusal to participate in the complicated network of social events that bound together the rarefied world of Texas high society.

Jordan remained unmoved by his family's reproaches. He never argued with them—he simply refused to change his career or drop his friends in order to suit their sense of what was socially acceptable. Ignoring bribes and threats from his parents, he designed a line of inexpensive kitchen cabinets, found financial backing, set up a manufacturing plant out in the boonies, and seemed to make enough money to live comfortably. He often disappeared for weeks at a stretch, leaving no clue as to where he had gone or what he was doing. His parents and brother, whose business, social and political ambitions were tightly interwoven, found his elusiveness absolutely infuriating.

Unlike the Chamberses, Emily had no problem with Jordan's choice of career, and she admired his ability to make a success, however modest, without turning to his father for startup capital. She even understood his need for independence, since she'd struggled with similar issues with her own parents. It was his moral code she couldn't tolerate, especially the fact that his romp with Mary Christine was rumored to be only one in a long series of affairs with married women.

"Why the sudden interest in the Laurel Acres project?" she asked him. "I thought you made a big deal out of the fact that you weren't involved in any of the Chambers business ventures."

If she'd hoped to penetrate Jordan's self-possession, she should have known better. "I made an exception in this case. I got involved."

"Running short of money, Jordan?"

He sent her a glance that was somewhere between cynical and indifferent. "I don't need my father's money. I have access to plenty of my own."

"Got a new rich girlfriend?" she asked spitefully, then wondered why Jordan invariably managed to provoke her into bad behavior.

His smile betrayed not a twinge of shame. "Of course."

She turned abruptly, more hurt than she understood or wanted to acknowledge. "Jordan, this conversation is crazy. I would like to go back to the family room so that we can start a serious discussion of exactly what we're going to say to the guests tonight."

"Before you worry about what you're going to tell the guests, don't you think you should at least tell your parents the truth?" he asked.

"What do you mean?"

"Your engagement didn't end by mutual agreement," Jordan said. "Michael called it off. He left you absolutely no choice in the matter, and yet you're still protecting him. Why? I don't believe you love him that much.''

"How do you know Michael called off the engagement?'' she demanded.

"You don't lie very well, Emily. Besides, I'm a hundred percent sure you'd never have pulled a stunt like this hours before the ceremony was due to take place.''

"You don't know me as well as you think—''

"Maybe not. But you already told me yourself that Michael was responsible.''

"I told you? Of course I didn't—''

"'Is the insanity you and your brother suffer from hereditary?'' he quoted. '''If so, I guess I should be grateful that Michael decided to dump me.'''

She *had* said that, Emily realized. It was yet another of the disconcerting things about being with Jordan. Her normal barriers seemed to crumble and she let drop information she would never have revealed to another person.

"I'm not protecting your brother,'' she said tiredly.

"No? Seems to me he dumped you, knowing darn well you'd cover his ass. And he was right.''

She flushed. "There just doesn't seem to be any point in getting everyone angry with everyone else. The engagement is over, there isn't going to be a wedding, and we need to move on.''

"Good thinking,'' he said. "Is that what you plan to say at the bridal dinner tonight?''

Jordan asked the question without expression, yet Emily reacted with a sickening lurch of her stomach. She knew she spent too much of her life worrying about making a good impression, but however much she wished she could throw the inhibitions of a lifetime out the window, she couldn't. She cared that she was going to humiliate herself and her parents in front of a very large crowd of very important people.

To her dismay, her throat tightened and she felt tears well in her eyes. It had been an exhausting, emotion-charged day, and she was afraid that if she started crying, she would be sobbing hysterically within seconds. She fumbled in the pocket of her tailored pants for a tissue and remembered they were all in her purse, which was still in the family room.

The first tears started to roll down her cheeks. She ordered herself to stop crying, but before she could get herself back under control, Jordan was at her side.

"Don't cry," he said softly, taking her into his arms, stanching the flow of tears with his thumbs. "Come on, Em, cheer up. It's only a bunch of stuck-up old geezers who aren't worth worrying about."

She would have expected mockery from Jordan, or at least indifference. His sympathy was so unexpected that it had the disastrous effect of shattering what small remnant of self-control she still possessed. Aware at some deep level that she was allowing herself to do something incredibly dangerous, she laid her head against Jordan's chest and gave way to the luxury of a noisy, uninhibited bout of weeping.

She heard the tattoo of multiple footsteps coming down the hallway but paid no attention until the pounding began on the study door.

"What's going on in there?" Michael demanded.

"Let us in!" her father said. "Emily, Jordan—it's been fifteen minutes already."

"Are you all right?" Raelene asked anxiously. "Emily, honey, I can hear you crying!"

Jordan's arms tightened fractionally around her. "I have to let them in," he said.

"Yes, I know you do." She tried to drag herself back together again.

He held her at arm's length, wiping away a final tear. "You okay?"

She nodded. "Yes." She looked at him, unsure of herself, but surprisingly unembarrassed. "Thanks, Jordan."

"You're welcome." He unlocked the door and everyone spilled into the library.

"Why are you crying?" Michael demanded.

"What did you need to discuss so urgently with Emily, Jordan?" Amelia sounded barely more friendly to her son than she had been earlier when speaking to Emily.

Jordan was still standing close enough to her that she could see the almost imperceptible flicker of a muscle in his jaw. "We were deciding that Emily really needed to tell you the truth about her broken engagement," he said.

Her father sent Jordan an approving look. "That's about the only sensible remark I've heard so far today. Since you seem to know what's going on here, and Emily won't tell us, why don't you explain why the wedding's been called off at the last minute?"

Jordan clamped his arm around Emily's waist. "She wants to marry me," he said. "We've been trying to fight our feelings for each other, but we couldn't. Since you have a wedding planned for tomorrow anyway, we were hoping you'd all agree to go ahead on schedule. Except with me as the substitute groom."

CHAPTER FOUR

ON THE VERY DAY that Michael and Emily became engaged, Amelia Chambers announced her decision to host the prewedding bridal dinner at the San Antonio Federal Club. Founded the year after the Republic of Texas joined the United States, the club was originally intended as a meeting place for the city's leaders, and its role hadn't changed much during the 155 years of its existence. Its decor remained stuffy Victorian, with nineteenth-century English hunting prints on the walls, plaid carpet in the bar, and enough walnut paneling to rival a French château. The most powerful people in San Antonio still belonged to the club, and mere money wasn't enough to get a person elected. For that, you needed the sort of connections the Chambers family had enjoyed for generations. Connections that Holt, Amelia and Michael Chambers continued to cultivate with painstaking care.

Sam Sutton, by contrast, had been too busy establishing a profitable business to waste time acquiring the type of friends who could get him drafted into the inner circle of San Antonio's social elite. It was only in the past couple of years that he'd started to think how nice it would be to give Raelene the pleasure of belonging to the same snooty club where her granny had washed dishes during the Depression—and been grateful for any leftover food she was allowed to take home.

He had to admit he'd originally thrown Michael and his daughter together in hopes that they might hit it off, and he wouldn't deny that it had been mighty useful when Emily decided to marry the guy. Holt Chambers's offer to propose Sam for membership in the prestigious club would never have happened if Emily hadn't been marrying his son, and the Laurel Acres deal would have been a lot more difficult to negotiate.

By the same token, it was darned inconvenient that his daughter had decided not to marry Michael—and at the very last minute, too. Lord knew, if Emily had been trying to screw things up, she couldn't have picked a more sure-fire method. Not to mention how her behavior was going to set tongues wagging.

But Sam was a father first and a businessman second. He would never want Emily to hook up with a man she didn't love. Not for the sake of the Laurel Acres project, that was for sure, and much less for the sake of membership in a club where you paid too much money to eat dubious food with fancy French names. Names that left you wondering just what the heck you were actually swallowing. Raelene lived in mortal dread that one of these days she'd order rattlesnake or snails or alligator, all wrapped up in puff pastry and stuffed with truffles.

But for all that he wanted his little girl to be happy, Sam believed in calling a spade a spade, and he never swept problems under the rug, so there was no getting around the fact that Emily's broken engagement left him *real* worried about the future of his dealings with the Chambers family. His gut told him that a personal link between the two families was necessary if Holt Chambers was going to honor the complex verbal agreements that underpinned the official Laurel Acres contracts. Sam had worked damned hard and made a tidy profit over the years—enough to make him mighty proud of what he'd achieved. But the Laurel Acres project was among the biggest developments he'd ever tackled, and if it didn't work out, he could lose enough money to hurt. To hurt pretty bad, in fact. The knowledge that Michael had his finger firmly on the pulse of his family's business interests had been reassuring, keeping Sam's stomach from feeling too queasy as he poured truckloads of money into the initial stages of the development.

Sam tried to comfort himself with the thought that Emily wasn't completely severing her link to the Chambers family. After all, Jordan was a Chambers, too, and marriage to him ought to forge just as tight a connection as marriage to Michael. Ought to, but probably wouldn't, since Jordan seemed to be ignored by his father and brother as far as business dealings were concerned. Jordan had never put in an appearance at a negotiating session and never signed a single legal document connected to the Laurel Acres project. As far as Sam could tell, he hadn't even been consulted about the decision to sell land that had been in the Chambers family for over a hundred years.

Under the circumstances, Sam had to wonder if Emily's marriage to Jordan would prove a strong enough bond to keep the deal on track. If Michael Chambers was pissed off with his brother—not to mention angry with Emily—he could make things difficult for everyone. Mighty difficult, in fact.

Despite these very real concerns, Sam had been surprised to discover that he felt more relief than anything else when Michael had dropped his bombshell and announced that Emily no longer wanted to marry him. Sam didn't entirely cotton to Michael Chambers, even though the guy was considered San Antonio's most eligible bachelor. His campaign for governor added the perfect finishing touch to his already desirable image, but it didn't reassure Sam any. Not now that he knew the guy a little better.

Sam had been impressed by Michael when they first met, and Raelene had been thrilled to think that their daughter—their own sweet Emily—might one day become the First Lady of Texas. But the better he got to know Michael, the less Sam liked him. The guy was too much of a slick politician, with smiles that came a tad too easily, and a way of conversing that had him managing to agree with two or three different viewpoints all at once. Sam's exuberance over the match had cooled dramatically in recent weeks, and even the prospect of having Emily living in the governor's mansion hadn't been enough to rekindle his enthusiasm.

There had always been something wrong with the relationship between Michael and his daughter, Sam reflected, handing his car keys to the parking valet and offering his arm to escort his wife up the steps into the club. From day one of Emily's engagement, he'd sensed an off note. Now that he'd seen his daughter with Jordan, he realized what the problem had been. Sam smiled to himself. It had been a real simple problem when you got right down to it: Emily had agreed to become engaged to Michael for the wrong reasons. She'd never been in love with him, at least not top-over-tail crazy, the way she ought to have been. Instead, his prim-and-proper darling had fallen for Jordan, the bad boy of the Chambers family. No wonder Sam had noticed increasing tension on Emily's part as the wedding day approached. Now he understood why: she'd been trying to work up the courage to follow her heart and break off her engagement to the oh-so-eligible Michael.

Sam chuckled inwardly, then turned to look at his daughter, thinking how pretty her golden brown eyes were, and how elegant her long chestnut hair looked, all swept up on top of her head, with just a few curls clustering at her neck. She'd brought him and Raelene so much joy over the years. He wished there had been more time for the three of them to talk before they had to rush out again to this stuffy party. He wanted to hear how she and Jordan had met, and when they'd fallen in love, but they hadn't had a moment to chat. Emily and Jordan had hurried off to get a marriage license, something that had proved difficult to achieve, even pulling strings and calling in favors from everyone that Holt Chambers knew at the county clerk's office. Once Emily got back to the house, there had barely been time to take showers and get changed for tonight's shindig. There'd been no time at all for finding out how his daughter's thoroughly conventional relationship with Michael had given way to a passionate, not at all conventional relationship with Jordan.

However it had happened, Sam sure was glad that his daughter had found real love at last. He wasn't a man who felt at ease expressing mushy sentiments, but he knew that without Raelene at his side, he'd never have made it through the lean years while he struggled to get his business established. Even more important, without Raelene and Emily, there would have been nobody to share the success with when it finally came.

Feeling a sudden lump in his throat, Sam patted his wife's arm, then turned and gave Emily a beaming smile, pleased to see how lovely she looked, despite the stresses of the past few hours.

Emily returned his smile, but her eyes didn't light up the way they usually did. "You okay, muffin?" Sam asked. He didn't understand why Emily set such great store by always doing the right thing, but he knew her well enough to guess that tonight was going to be torture for her.

"I'm fine, Dad, thanks." Despite the confident words, she drew in an audible breath, and her voice shook when she continued speaking. "I guess I'll be relieved when this evening's over, that's all."

"Don't you give another thought to what people are going to say about this, muffin." Sam tried his best to reassure her. "Just remember what's important. You and Jordan are in love and you want to get married. In the long run, that's all that matters. Five years from now, nobody will remember you and Michael were ever an item."

"I'm sure you're right, Dad." At least outwardly, Emily had already managed to recover her poise, which was no surprise to Sam. His daughter was a grand master at concealing her true feelings.

"Thanks for being so supportive," she said quietly. "You've been really understanding about all this. I honestly don't know how I...we...ended up in such an impossible situation. I'm sorry to be causing you and Mom so much embarrassment...."

Her voice trailed off again, and Sam waited for Raelene to jump in with some words of encouragement. When none were forthcoming, he gave his daughter a quick hug. "Emmie, you've never caused either of us a moment's embarrassment in your entire life. I reckon you've earned the right to one night when you give the gossips something to talk about. Right, Raelene?"

"Right," his wife said faintly. "You can't marry Michael if you don't love him. Of course you can't, Emmie. But are you absolutely sure you love Jordan? I mean, how did you manage to get to know him? Maybe it's just a passing infatuation—"

"Our Emmie is too sensible to confuse love and infatuation," Sam said.

"Is she? Then why did she get engaged to Michael in the first place? Apparently she didn't really love him. If she made one mistake, how can she be so darn sure that she loves Jordan?"

"Emmie wouldn't be doing this unless she was sure, honey." Sam smothered a sigh. Raelene was worried sick about the turn of events, but he'd bring her around. Truth be told, he didn't care if Emmie's behavior seemed a bit illogical. What did love have to do with logic, anyway? Frankly, he was relieved to discover that his daughter had enough fire in her belly to spurn Michael and follow her heart.

He appreciated somebody with a solid sense of duty, but Emily paid way too much attention to what the world considered right, regardless of the cost in terms of her own emotional needs. It was good to see his little girl swept off her feet by love. When you got right down to it, without a bit of passion to grease the gears of everyday life, no marriage could hope to survive. He sometimes worried that his daughter concentrated too much on the pragmatic side of things and forgot about the sparkle of magic that made all the practical struggles worthwhile.

"Good evening, sir. Mrs. Sutton. Ms. Sutton." The club's general manager greeted them with an obsequious nod. "Mr. and Mrs. Chambers are expecting you. They're waiting upstairs in the ballroom, if you would care to follow me."

"Thanks," Sam said. "Much obliged." He'd eaten at the famous club several times in the past few months, and he had to admit that he rather liked the opulent marble columns, the statues of ancient Greek heroes, and the plush crimson carpet on the stairs. Not the sort of style he'd ever want in his own home, but it was satisfying to know that Sam Sutton, son of a handyman, grandson of an itinerant peddler, had earned the right to enter a fancy place like this. And tonight, the food was preordered, so he and Raelene didn't have to worry about snails, snakes or alligators turning up on the menu. So what did it matter if they were going to give grist to San Antonio's notorious gossip mills? What could the stuffy dragon ladies of the upper crust say, after all, except that his daughter had followed her heart? And thank God for it.

Sam gave Emily another encouraging hug. "Come on,

muffin, chin up. Where's that radiant smile of yours? I can't wait for Jordan to see how beautiful you look in that dress.''

AMELIA CHAMBERS heard the sounds of approaching footsteps and glanced around the ballroom, reassuring herself once again that everything was in order. The grandiose setting struck her as imposing rather than ugly or outdated, and from her point of view, imposing was good. The club's atmosphere of pompous formality was ideally suited to impressing her friends and intimidating her inferiors—the latter a large group that comprised every last one of the guests invited to this evening's dinner by Raelene and Sam Sutton.

Impressing her friends was even more important to Amelia than intimidating her social inferiors, and in recent years it had become more and more difficult to keep up the expensive facade that the Chambers name merited and her own position as doyenne of San Antonio society demanded. She tried not to concern herself with finances—it was so *blue collar* to worry about money—but she was enough of a realist to recognize that the Chambers Investment Bank teetered on the brink of failure, and her husband's coffers were in desperate need of an infusion of ready cash. Sam Sutton's development project undoubtedly offered the best chance of making a couple of quick million before disaster struck.

Even so, despite what was at stake, Amelia had never quite reconciled herself to the idea of having Emily Sutton as the wife of her beloved Michael. Bad enough if the girl had actually been a flesh-and-blood daughter to the Suttons, but she wasn't. She was adopted, and who knew what horrible defects she might be introducing into the Chambers gene pool? Look at all those babies who'd been imported from Eastern Europe. They'd seemed so cute until their adoptive parents found out that half of them were sociopaths, or suffering from deadly inherited diseases. Of course, Emily had been born in the States, but that was no guarantee her pedigree was acceptable. On the contrary. If she was so perfect, why had she been given up for adoption?

During one of their planning sessions for the wedding, Raelene had confided that Emily's birth mother was a college student who'd made one terrible mistake, and then had lacked sufficient funds to keep her baby. Amelia gave a mental snort, just as she had when she first heard the unlikely story. If Raelene wanted to believe the fairy tales spun by the adoption agency, then good luck to her. Amelia wasn't so gullible.

When you adopted a child, you never knew what potential problems you were letting yourself in for, as she'd pointed out to Michael weeks ago. She'd recommended that he take a look into Emily's true antecedents. Quite apart from the risk of choosing a woman who was an unknown quantity to be the mother of his children, he needed to be quite sure that some enterprising reporter wasn't going to turn up any facts about Emily's birth parents that might embarrass him now that his campaign for governor was poised to go into high gear. They absolutely didn't want some drunken street person turning up on the campaign trail, announcing to the world that she was Emily's real mother.

Amelia didn't know if Michael had actually ordered a background search, but her reservations about Emily had been proven amply justified today, with the shocking announcement that the wretched girl was breaking off her engagement to Michael at the very last minute. And all because she had fallen in love with Jordan! A lack of taste that was just what Amelia would have expected from a child raised by Raelene and Sam Sutton. *Of course* a lower class nobody like Emily would feel more at home with a man like Jordan, who actually enjoyed working with his hands. *Of course* she would feel awkward with a man like Michael, who was such a credit to his ancient and distinguished lineage.

She glanced across at her younger son, who was drinking a beer with apparent pleasure. A beer, for heaven's sake. Amelia shuddered involuntarily. She couldn't imagine where her younger son's peasantlike tastes sprang from. Certainly not from her side of the family—the Beaumonts were even more refined than the Chamberses. Sadly, these days they also had even less money.

As she watched Jordan take a final swig before setting his glass on the table, Amelia frowned. Thank goodness he wasn't drinking from the bottle the way he often did. For a man who made his living banging nails into kitchen cabinets, he certainly had more than his fair share of self-confidence. Here he was in the most exclusive establishment in San Antonio, managing to make it look as if beer were the beverage of choice for the world's social elite.

Instead of being impressed by her son's aura of power, Amelia was offended, as if Jordan's ability to look at ease without her blessing were some sort of subtle insult. But she didn't let her irritation show. She couldn't afford to. She needed to get through the next thirty-six hours without giving her social rivals any chance to pounce. And God knew, that was going to take every ounce of skill she could muster. She needed this wedding to go off smoothly, despite Emily Sutton's best efforts to turn the event into a comic spectacle. Amelia reminded herself to keep focused on what was truly important: Michael's campaign for governor, and her husband's need for money.

She sighed, then told herself that she could do this. She'd spent her life sacrificing for the sake of the family heritage—she could certainly do it one more time.

EMILY HAD EATEN at the club with Michael on several occasions, and she normally spent a good part of each meal mentally refurbishing the hideous decor. Tonight, though, she had far too much on her mind to take refuge in her usual mental games. Oppressed by the weight of her parents' justifiable concern, she hardly dared look at either of them, although her father was being kindness itself, and her mother was doing her best to hide the fact that she hovered on the verge of tears.

The atmosphere of the club seemed stifling as she walked up the curving staircase toward the second-floor ballroom, and by the time they arrived at the arched entrance, the single strand of her tasteful pearl necklace felt as if it might choke her.

Struggling to get a grip on her chaotic emotions, Emily followed her parents into the ballroom, absorbing the fact of Jordan's presence before letting her gaze settle on Michael, Holt and Amelia Chambers. The three of them stood together beside a buffet table laden with hors d'oeuvres, although no one was actually eating. If their stomachs felt anything like hers, she understood why. Even the sight of food was enough to bring on a wave of nausea.

She risked another glance toward Jordan, who stood to one side of the carved granite fireplace, noticeably removed from the rest of his family. Apart from their encounter in the Bernauers' bedroom, when he'd been naked, Emily had never seen him wearing anything except worn jeans and casual shirts. It was a shock to see him in a dinner jacket, even more of a shock to see how at ease he appeared wearing formal clothes. She wondered what he was feeling now that they were poised on the brink of announcing their supposed passion to the world, but his expression was remote and self-contained, making it impossible for her to guess.

With a sudden unwelcome flash of insight, she wondered if Jordan's aloof expression might be as much of a defense mechanism as her own. She had always thought of Jordan as indifferent to the opinion of the other members of his family. Tonight, for the first time, it occurred to her that perhaps he stood apart not because he wanted to, but because he wasn't welcome within the tight-knit circle of the Chambers family.

Emily was astonished to feel a spurt of anger on his behalf. Why was Jordan getting the cold shoulder when Michael was the real cause of the problem? Then she remembered that Jordan wouldn't need to be here tonight, facing his family's hostility, if he hadn't made his outrageous claim that the two of them were madly, passionately in love.

She directed an explosive glance at her soon-to-be-husband, castigating him silently. *Too bad if you don't like the mess you've gotten us both into,* she muttered beneath her breath. She hardened her heart against any more flashes of sympathy. *You interfered when you didn't need to, and now you can face the consequences.*

She refused to listen to the annoying voice inside her head that kept pointing out she was far from blameless in the current situation. She could have told everyone the simple truth. She could have explained that Michael was the one who'd broken off the engagement, and that she was devastated by his rejection. She could certainly have denied Jordan's ridiculous statement that they'd fallen in love weeks ago, the first time they met.

But she hadn't said a word. When Jordan made his outrageous claims, she'd just stood there—a silent coconspirator in his mad scheme. Because of her excessive pride, she hadn't contradicted him when he told her parents that the two of them had been fighting against their deepest feelings almost the entire time she was engaged to his brother. She hadn't so much as blinked when Jordan stated that with the wedding to Michael looming within days, the two of them had no longer been able to contain their passion.

She'd had the grace to blush when Jordan invented a tale about how they'd ended up in each other's arms yesterday and been forced to admit the truth of their feelings for each other. But everyone had misinterpreted her blushes and nobody had asked her any direct questions—perhaps because they feared her answers would make for embarrassing listening. Even Michael appeared to have been taken in by his brother's lies. He'd erupted in fury as Jordan's tale of suppressed passion unfolded.

Just thinking about the scene in the library was enough to make Emily break out in a cold sweat. What had possessed her? Why hadn't she spoken up? More to the point, once she was alone with her parents, why hadn't she quietly and calmly explained the truth to them? In retrospect, she couldn't believe that she had tamely accompanied Jordan to get a marriage license. And what in the world was she doing here at San Antonio's most famous club, about to announce a change in groom with rather less forethought than she had given last week to changing the color of the orchids planned for her wedding bouquet?

Emily couldn't answer her own questions, but that didn't bother her as much as it should have. She was in no mood to listen to the reproaches of her conscience. Damn it, she was the victim here. She had been spurned by Michael and exploited by Jordan for reasons that were still a mystery. She'd been badly used by both the Chambers brothers, and she intended to wallow in her justifiable sense of injustice. Squaring her shoulders, she tilted her chin defiantly upward and prepared to greet her future in-laws. At least that hadn't changed since yesterday, she thought with a touch of hysteria. The groom might have changed, but the Chamberses were still going to become her parents-in-law.

Holt and Amelia Chambers acknowledged the Suttons' arrival with icy formality, but they maintained a facade of courtesy. Michael, on the other hand, turned his back on them without speaking, as if he had washed his hands of the debacle that was about to unravel.

Emily's bravado disappeared, wiped out by Michael's rejection. She wondered why earthquakes never happened when you needed them. The tension swirled around the room, thick enough to choke anyone unwary enough to get trapped inside. Her parents must have shared her discomfort, since neither one of them said anything beyond a mumbled greeting. Emily tried to think of some topic of conversation that would cut through the oppressive atmosphere, but came up with nothing.

She was approaching the point of desperation when Jordan stepped forward and took her hands, cradling them against his cheek in a gesture that managed to seem more intimate than a kiss. Her skin prickled and her stomach performed its standard back flip. One of the few things she had carried from her old life into this new, uncharted territory seemed to be the annoying physical reaction she had to Jordan's presence. Now that he was her fiancé, though, she couldn't just stare through him and pretend the feeling didn't exist.

She swallowed over the lump lodged in her throat. "Hi, Jordan."

"Hi, Emily."

His voice was very soft, and his expression seemed almost tender. She gazed at him, hypnotized by the realization that although his eyes appeared dark brown when viewed from a distance, up close they had a fascinating silvery halo around the pupils. His hair was long enough to touch his collar at the back, and although she normally preferred men with short, neat haircuts like Michael's, she felt a surprising urge to reach out and run her fingers through the thick, dark-brown strands. Of course, she didn't. Emily didn't approve of people who allowed trivial sexual urges to overcome their better judgment.

"You look lovely," Jordan said quietly. "Blue always suits you, but that deep shade is just perfect on you."

"Th-thank you."

"She didn't choose it for you," Michael said, his scowl ferocious. "She chose it for me."

"I hope she chose it for herself," Jordan said mildly, his gaze fixed on Emily.

She decided that she was about one second away from screaming. Why did Michael care about her dress and who she'd chosen it for? Wasn't he the man who'd spurned her only a few hours earlier? Good grief, was it really less than twelve hours ago that her world had seemed entirely normal, with nothing to worry about but the schedule for picking up guests at the airport?

Emily's hands were ice-cold and, to her embarrassment, she could feel them shaking. Jordan must have felt the tremble because he stroked his thumb over her knuckles in a gesture that was curiously comforting. His thumb eventually traced a loop around her engagement ring, coming to rest on the four-carat diamond solitaire that Michael had placed there three months earlier.

"I guess you forgot to take this off," he said.

She looked down at the ring, symbol of so many dashed hopes, and for a painful moment thought she was going to cry. But once again, pride came to her rescue. Damned if she would give Michael the satisfaction of seeing her weep over his rejection. She lifted her head and stared straight at him, challenging him even at this late stage to come clean and reveal what had really happened between the two of them this morning.

When he said nothing, she turned back to Jordan, her pain transforming into anger at Michael's cowardice. How dare he be angry with her and Jordan because they were trying to salvage something from the wreckage he had created?

"You're right," she said to Jordan. "I did forget to take off Michael's ring. Everything was such a rush. Going for the license, and then getting ready for this dinner tonight."

"No problem. Let's take care of it now, shall we?" Jordan's gaze was steady, almost reassuring, as he slid the ring off her finger with slow deliberation. "What would you like to do with this?" he asked, holding it out to her on the palm of his hand.

Throw it away. Stamp on it. Crush it under the heel of my shoe. Of course she didn't say that. Clinging to the outward forms of politeness was the only way Emily knew to get through the next twenty-four hours. She looked up at Jordan because—amazingly—of all the people in the room, he seemed to pose the least threat. "I should probably give it back to Michael," she said.

"Yes, you damn well should give it back to me," Michael said, finding his voice at last. "That's eight thousand bucks of my money you're holding, *little brother.*"

"Then take it back, by all means," Jordan offered.

"I sure will." Michael snatched the ring from his brother's outstretched hands. "This circus is more than I can stand," he announced, shoving the ring into the pocket of his dinner jacket. "I'm leaving. I'm not going to be a player in this farce any longer. I damn well refuse to act as best man at what was supposed to be my own wedding!"

"Oh, no, Michael, please don't go!" Amelia pleaded. "I know how difficult this must be for you, but we have to think of appearances—"

"To hell with appearances—"

"Michael, calm down," Holt said sharply. "You can't afford to have a temper tantrum. You have your campaign to think of. Governor Kincaid is vulnerable if you manage to garner enough support from people in key positions across the state. Have you forgotten that a lot of potential donors are coming tonight, expecting to talk with you? We can't afford to offend them, or give them cause to think you're not suited to be governor. I appreciate what you must be feeling, but you have no choice but to put the best possible face on this. Unfortunately, none of us has any choice." He accompanied his final words with a glare in Emily's direction.

Michael kept his back to Emily and spoke through gritted teeth. "I guess you're right, Dad, although I hate to admit it. Okay, for the sake of my campaign, I'll put in an appearance when the guests start to arrive."

His voice boiled with suppressed fury, and Emily winced. In the surreal world she had been living in for the past several hours, it no longer seemed absurd that Michael, who had terminated their engagement, should be furious with her, rather than the other way around.

Jordan spoke quietly, his words only for her. "Don't look so stricken, Em. You have no reason to feel guilty because my brother chooses to behave badly. I know it's difficult, but try to keep a sense of perspective about all this."

She blinked, and dragged her gaze back to Jordan. "My name is Emily," she said stiffly, because it was easier to be snippy with him than to sort out what she was really feeling.

"Em suits you better," Jordan said, oblivious to her snub. "Come on, Em, let down your hair a bit. Relax and enjoy the party. You're not nearly as stuffy as you try to pretend, you know."

Stuffy? He was accusing her of being *stuffy,* just because

she felt a little uptight about switching fiancés hours before the wedding? Emily was speechless. Before she could gather her wits enough to deliver a suitably scathing reply, he had changed the subject. With a casual gesture, he reached into the pocket of his dinner jacket and pulled out a small, blue velvet box. He flipped the lid open with his thumb.

"I have a friend who designs jewelry," he said. "I stopped by her workshop this evening and picked this out for you. It isn't a traditional engagement ring, but I thought it was just the right style for you. For us."

Emily glanced down at the box, silenced by the sheer beauty of the ring Jordan was holding out to her. A gold band supported a slender spray of tiny diamonds, reminiscent of the tail of a shooting star. A slightly larger diamond, perfect in clarity and color, represented the star itself. She guessed the ring was much less valuable than the one she'd just given back to Michael, but it was at least twice as pretty, and ten times more original.

Jordan slipped the ring onto her finger, then lifted her hand and turned it palm upward, pressing a kiss against her finger and the band of the ring. "You have to make a wish on a shooting star," he said.

The touch of Jordan's lips against her palm sent a tremor racing down Emily's spine and she had to wait a moment before she could speak. "Did you make a wish?" she asked.

Jordan's eyes met hers, clear and silvery cool. "Yes."

Emily looked down at the ring and, with an intensity that shocked her, wished that it symbolized something more important than her own false pride, and the desire of Jordan Chambers to keep the Laurel Acres deal on track.

"You made a wish," Jordan said.

It was a statement on his part, not a question, but she answered anyway. "Yes."

Michael came back into the ballroom. "Senator and Mrs. Drysdale have just arrived," he said. "Jeff Greiff is escorting them upstairs right now. Carolyn St. Clair and another couple of bridesmaids are on their way, too." He punctuated his words with a glare in his brother's direction, followed by a scornful glance at Emily.

Her fingers clenched Jordan's hand tightly, the weight and shape of her new engagement ring feeling totally alien as he returned the pressure. "We can do it, Em. Let's put on a good show for the mob."

Emily drew in a breath deep enough to kill the butterflies dancing in her stomach. This was it, then. The masquerade was about to begin.

She had only a few seconds to wonder when the unmasking would occur, and what price she would eventually pay for tonight's deception. Then she was smiling and greeting Senator and Mrs. Drysdale just as if she were a completely normal person, instead of a woman who had taken leave of her senses several hours earlier and showed no sign of regaining them anytime soon.

CHAPTER FIVE

BY THE TIME the guests arrived at the church for the Sutton-Chambers wedding ceremony, most of them had already heard the incredible news that there had been a change of groom. As a TV newscaster commented sarcastically on *Sunrise San Antonio,* the city's wedding of the year was going ahead exactly as planned, except for the minor fact that Michael Chambers was now going to be best man, and Jordan Chambers would be the groom.

The minister, persuaded to conduct the ceremony by means of an extremely generous donation to the church building fund, delivered a pointed lecture on the solemnity of the marriage vows, and the distressing tendency of modern couples to make their sacred promises with too much haste and far too little prayer. Marriage, he reminded the congregation, was a sacred commitment, not to be entered into frivolously, even if most people in twenty-first century America seemed to behave as though getting married was more about throwing an elaborate party than dedicating your life to a loving partnership with another human being.

Emily would probably have agreed with the minister's disapproving sermon if she had been able to hear a word that he said. Fortunately—or unfortunately, depending on your point of view—she was in such a state of mental paralysis that she was basically blind and deaf to the world.

She had woken after a restless, dream-filled night, shaking with panic. Her panic had intensified throughout the long hours of waiting for the ceremony to begin, but by the time she actually got to walk down the aisle, her emotions had congealed into a state of frozen apathy. The numbness was so complete that it created a thick veil between her and reality. All her senses failed to operate. Not only was her vision blurred and her hearing blocked, but her bouquet had no scent, and her skin registered no sensation as Jordan slid a slim gold wedding band onto her finger. The ring fit quite well, and she noted with a distant flicker of relief that it wasn't the one she and Michael had chosen together six weeks earlier. That tiny flicker of relief was as close as she came to experiencing any emotion.

If she'd been capable of feeling surprise, she would have been impressed that Jordan had been efficient enough to buy a set of wedding rings in the few hours available to him this morning. His parents always complained that their younger son was hopelessly impractical and disorganized. Jordan's offer to volunteer as Michael's substitute groom might be highly impractical, Emily thought, but nothing about his behavior over the past twenty-four hours suggested that he was disorganized. Quite the opposite, in fact.

Her own fingers were nerveless, and she would have dropped the ring Carolyn St. Clair handed to her if the minister hadn't helped her to push it onto Jordan's finger. Once it was there, she stared at it with the same abstract interest she had viewed her own. Jordan had heavy calluses on his fingers, she noted, but his hand was perfectly steady, whereas hers shook like a leaf in a high wind. Her fingertips appeared bloodless with cold, although she wasn't conscious of feeling chilled. How amazing to be cold in San Antonio in August.

After that brief flirtation with awareness, Emily sank back into apathy, and even when Jordan bent his head and kissed her lightly on the mouth, the only thing she felt was mild relief that the wedding must now be over. Apparently they had made it through the ceremony without totally disgracing themselves. That had to be a cause for celebration, provided she didn't focus too hard on the fact that if the ceremony had ended, she must now be Mrs. Jordan Chambers.

"Smile," Jordan murmured in her ear. "You're supposed to be deliriously happy."

Emily responded automatically to the note of command in his voice and turned to face the assembled congregation with a dazzling smile that was all show and no substance. Applause greeted them as she walked back down the aisle, clinging to Jordan's arm, followed by their retinue of bridesmaids and groomsmen. In another example of his unexpected efficiency, Jordan had found time to call two of his friends and invite them to be part of the wedding. Amazingly, given the short time frame, they even wore tuxedos that fit. As for the rest of the groomsmen, Emily doubted if Jordan had actually met any of them prior to last night's dinner. At least she'd known all five of her bridesmaids for several years. Was that a consolation?

Having produced a facial expression that everyone seemed to find appropriate to the occasion, Emily couldn't seem to change it. She smiled through the receiving line, smiled through the various toasts and speeches, smiled through the dinner—which she didn't eat—and then continued smiling brightly as Jordan led her out for their first dance as a married couple.

"You can stop smiling now," Jordan said, drawing her into a traditional ballroom dancing hold. "Try looking dreamy eyed instead."

"I can't." Emily couldn't imagine what might happen to her precarious self-control if she relaxed the muscles that held her lips fixed into a grin. That smile was her best defense, even if it was beginning to feel more like a rictus of rigor mortis than a happy sign of newlywed bliss. If she didn't smile, she was afraid her whole body might crumble into a limp, pathetic heap like the Wicked Witch of the West when sprayed with water.

Jordan swung her in a graceful loop around the small dance floor, looking down at her with the same expression she'd noticed yesterday. The one that seemed almost tender. "Poor old Em. It's been a rotten couple of days for you, hasn't it?"

His way of saying "poor old Em" sounded more like an endearment than all Michael's "sweethearts" and "darlings." But Emily couldn't risk responding to the tenderness, which she'd probably imagined anyway. So she ratcheted up her smile a notch until it reached a new level of gleaming teeth and brittle insincerity.

"It sure has been rotten," she agreed. "And just think, the worst is still to come."

He gave her a quizzical glance. "What does that mean, precisely?"

She was puzzled that he needed clarification. "It means we have at least four months of fake marriage still to get through. More than a year if we wait until after the election to get a divorce."

"Oh," he said. "I thought you were talking about the honeymoon."

Emily tripped over her own feet, and Jordan tightened his hold, guiding her expertly into a twirl dramatic enough to provoke friendly applause from the watching guests. When they were back in each other's arms, spinning more sedately, Emily stared up at him with such intensity that she forgot to blink.

The honeymoon. *The honeymoon.* Good grief, she seemed to have lost the use of those few brain cells that might have been expected to remain functional. How else to explain that until this moment she'd been so focused on the problems of the prenuptial dinner and the wedding reception that she hadn't given a single moment's thought to the fact that when the reception ended, the honeymoon would begin?

"You've lost your smile," Jordan murmured. "I have to say your new look of haunted dread isn't much of an improvement."

"I was thinking about the honeymoon," Emily croaked.

"Mmm…I guessed as much." He flashed her a charming smile. "I've confirmed all new plane reservations and so on, so don't worry, Em. It was one thing to borrow Michael's wedding ceremony wholesale, but I wanted to do my own honeymoon."

"I just bet you did," she muttered.

He grinned. "Yeah, well, honeymoons are my kind of thing. Anyway, relax. We're not going to Tahiti. That struck me as being the sort of place Michael would choose, not you. I decided we'd both enjoy a few days in Colorado. I've arranged for us to stay at a house in Elk Meadow. That's near Blue Lake, in the Rocky Mountains."

"In Colorado?"

"Yes. Have you ever been there?"

"No. Never." He was right that Tahiti had been Michael's choice, not hers. Equally correct to guess that she would enjoy spending time in Colorado. But choice of destination hadn't figured anywhere on Emily's mental list of concerns about their honeymoon.

She had no chance to explain this to Jordan, however, since he stopped dancing without warning and bent her back over his arm, kissing her with amazing thoroughness while the drummer obliged by delivering a long tattoo on the drums, climaxing in a noisy clash of cymbals. Jordan caught Emily at the waist, lifted her high in the air, and then slowly and suggestively let her glide down his body until her toes touched the floor.

While the guests laughed and their applause intensified,

Emily contemplated killing either Jordan or herself, or—better yet—both of them.

Arm still around her waist, Jordan escorted Emily back to their table, and the dance floor was filled by guests, leaving her free to regain her smile and then concentrate once again on not succumbing to hysterics. The smiling part was pretty easy, but she only managed to avoid hysterics by jerking her thoughts away from the topic of honeymoons whenever they started to slither in that ominous direction.

By the time Carolyn St. Clair came to help her get changed into her going-away outfit, Emily had reached the end of her rope. She was emotionally spent and physically exhausted.

Carolyn was normally a perceptive person, but the events of the past couple of days were bizarre enough to throw even her off the scent. She seemed to be convinced that the match between Jordan and Emily was based on passionate, romantic love and she was ecstatic on her friend's behalf. She'd already dropped a couple of hints to the effect that she considered the switch from Michael to Jordan a giant step in the right direction. Hints that surprised Emily, because she would have expected all her friends to prefer Michael. He was, after all, handsome, well connected, ambitious, and conservative in his lifestyle—everything women seemed to want in a marriage partner.

Emily planned to tell Carolyn the truth about her marriage to Jordan eventually, but so far there had never been either time or privacy for such a complicated explanation. They now had a modicum of privacy, although one of the other bridesmaids might put in an appearance at any minute. Besides, Emily was in no mood for a general confession. Especially to Shannon and Erin Sutton, her cousins, who would immediately blab the whole story to her father, their favorite uncle. She couldn't do it, Emily realized. She lacked the energy to start an explanation of something as complicated as her true reasons for marrying Jordan Chambers. Even if she could fathom what those reasons really were.

Carolyn unzipped her dress and Emily stepped out of the multiple layers of frothy organza. Taking off her taffeta petticoat, she tried to remember the exact process that had led from Michael's announcement that he wanted to break off their engagement to this moment when she was preparing to set off on a honeymoon with Jordan.

There was no way to get from there to here, Emily decided. Try as she might, she could no longer remember how she'd slipped from the devastating scene in the library with Michael to this bridal changing room at the famous Hyatt Hill Country Resort, just outside San Antonio.

Carolyn helped Emily fasten the row of tiny buttons on the lightweight eau-de-nile silk dress she'd spent three weeks choosing as her going-away outfit. That meant she'd spent approximately two weeks, six days, twenty-three hours and forty-five minutes longer selecting her going-away outfit than she had choosing the groom who would be accompanying her.

Emily and the Fifteen Minute Bridegroom. It sounded like the title for a really bad TV movie.

The situation suddenly struck Emily as so ridiculous that she gave a tiny gasp of laughter. Laughter that hovered dangerously close to hysteria. Carolyn heard the edge of nervousness, but apparently interpreted it as excitement. She hugged Emily, her eyes bright with a sheen of tears.

"When you look back, Emily, you'll realize this has been a super day, with lots of great memories for you and Jordan. I've heard guests saying what a lovely ceremony it was, and what a terrific party your parents have put on. Everyone seems to agree the food was delicious and the band is just great. Not to mention the fact that you were a stunningly beautiful bride.''

''You're too kindhearted, Caro. What was everyone saying about the fact that the groom and his brother just happened to switch roles?''

''Not much. At least not to me. I guess they were smart enough to figure out they hadn't better make any snide comments when I was in hearing distance.'' Carolyn grinned. ''Besides, one look at you and Jordan dancing together, and nobody could have any doubts about whether you ended up married to the right brother. And that's the only important thing, isn't it?''

Emily had no idea how her best friend—normally a woman of perception—could be so mistaken. ''I'm glad you think the guests had fun,'' she said, trying to hang on to her self-control for just a few more minutes. ''I'm truly grateful for all your help, Caro. I'd never have made it through the ceremony without you there to poke and prod me into making all the right moves.''

''My pleasure. I know you were stressed to the max, but it's over now. You've got nothing more to do except relax and enjoy the honeymoon.'' Carolyn chuckled. ''Somehow, I'm guessing you and Jordan are going to have a real good time, wherever you go.''

Emily glossed over the word *honeymoon*, and was surprised to hear herself laugh almost naturally. ''Caro, you may be the world's biggest optimist, but even you can't seriously believe that there's nothing left for me to stress about. The media aren't going to let this story die anytime soon. Not to mention what San Antonio's infamous circle of gossips will make of it. In some ways, this is a very small town.''

''There'll be a lot of talk for a few days,'' Carolyn acknowledged. ''And you're right, the local media will give the story plenty of coverage, especially when Michael intensifies his schedule of campaign appearances. But most people have real short attention spans, and I'm willing to bet that a month from now the story will be deader than the dinosaurs."

Emily winced. "Bad example, Caro. In case you haven't noticed, dinosaurs are the most newsworthy dead animals in the history of the universe."

"Okay, bad analogy, but so what? Anyway, does it matter all that much if people gossip? Your friends and family know the truth, and that's what's important." Carolyn leaned forward, speaking with sudden forcefulness. "You had a choice, Em, and you made the right decision. Thank goodness you didn't marry a man you don't love, just because you were afraid to face a little gossip. That wouldn't have been any more fair to Michael than it would have been to you and Jordan. You can't marry a man you don't love. Not unless you're looking for a huge amount of heartache."

Emily recognized that Carolyn was at least half right: a marriage between her and Michael would have been disastrous. Even more disastrous than marriage to Jordan, because she would have married Michael full of hope and naive expectations that he clearly wouldn't have been able to fulfill. At least with Jordan there was no hope of a happily-ever-after. Still, she worried about Caro's reaction when she found out that Emily and Jordan had married not because they were deeply, desperately in love, but because she was a wimp who wanted to avoid social disgrace, and Jordan wanted to keep Sutton money flowing into the depleted Chambers family coffers. Carolyn—or any other ethical person—was bound to be disgusted by two such rotten reasons for marriage.

What a miserable couple Jordan and I make, Emily thought wearily. *We almost deserve each other.*

A knock at the door heralded the arrival of her remaining bridesmaids and put a stop to any further private conversation with Carolyn. Emily forced herself to join in the chatter of her cousins and friends, and felt weak-kneed with relief when she realized that she only had to get through one more round of farewells and good wishes before she would be free.

If you could describe leaving with Jordan for their honeymoon as *freedom*. She could handle it, Emily decided. She'd survived Michael's rejection and today's wedding ceremony without making a total idiot out of herself, which was more than she'd expected. With luck, she'd manage to hold everything together long enough to make it quite clear to Jordan that her agreement to marry him had definitely not included having sex. It was only rational to keep their relationship platonic, and Jordan would be smart enough to realize that. The situation they'd created was complicated enough without adding sex to the mixture. She was absolutely clear and firm on that in her own mind.

There would be no sex.

CHAPTER SIX

FROM THE INGLORIOUS moment of their meeting in Ted Bernauer's bedroom, Jordan had never had any difficulty deciphering exactly what Emily was thinking. When she was around him, of course, her feelings tended to be monochromatic, shifting in a gray spectrum between disapproval and total condemnation. But even when he watched her with other people, he found her moods transparent, her courteous facade an inadequate shield that constantly leaked information about her true thoughts.

He'd heard Michael complain that her face never revealed any emotion, which made Jordan wonder if his brother had ever taken the time to actually look at his former fiancée. Emily tried to convey the impression that she was a woman with an even temperament, not much given to deep feelings or intense emotional reactions. Jordan wasn't sure why she was so anxious to conceal her true nature, but he'd never been deceived by her touch-me-not exterior. Passion and extravagant emotion simmered beneath the surface of Emily's genteel facade, all the more enticing because it wasn't instantly accessible to every casual observer.

Right now, as they rode the elevator up from the ballroom to the hotel suite he'd reserved for the first night of their honeymoon, Jordan could see Emily was in turmoil, despite the carefully blank expression she was maintaining. Unfortunately for him, he could read her thoughts almost as clearly as if she'd spoken them out loud.

She was trying to work out how to tell him that there wasn't going to be any sex tonight.

Jordan appreciated the ironies of life as well as the next man, and he'd spent a fair part of the past twenty-four hours trying to feel wryly amused at the absurdity of the situation in which he found himself. His control had been wearing increasingly thin as the night progressed, and he was no longer in the mood for irony and cynical detachment. What he and his testosterone-flooded body wanted to do right now was to grab Emily's hand, drag her into their hotel room, and fling her onto the bed. There they would make wild, tempestuous love until he finally got rid of the sexual tension that had been building, day by excruciating day, for three long, hard months.

Regrettably, he knew better than to indulge his fantasy. Instead of enjoying hours of wild sex, if he wanted to have any chance of making this farcical marriage work out, he needed to steel himself to resist temptation.

All things considered, he could safely say that it was going to be one hell of a long night.

But better than the many long nights that had preceded it, since now he could allow himself to hope. For three months he'd lived with the knowledge that Emily was destined to become his brother's wife. In comparison, sleeping in the same room with her and not having sex should be relatively easy.

Or maybe not, Jordan thought ruefully, as the elevator halted and Emily rocked momentarily against him, igniting desires he'd spent the past hour ruthlessly extinguishing.

Making no comment on the fact that she scooted away from contact with him as if he were a certified carrier of bubonic plague, Jordan indicated that she should turn right.

"We have the corner suite," he said, reaching into his pocket for the key card. "With luck, our luggage should be waiting for us in the room already."

"Thank you." Emily's voice sounded distantly courteous, but Jordan heard the trepidation rioting behind the calm facade, and almost felt sorry for her. Almost. Right now, he didn't have much sympathy to spare for anyone except himself.

The suite was spacious and attractively decorated. A minor point in the plus column, he reflected. He could lie in bed and count sheep, or curse his fate, or sneak adolescent yearning glances at Emily, secure in the knowledge that at least his surroundings were congenial, even if his mood was foul, and his libido in a major state of rebellion.

The large sitting room had French doors that opened onto a balcony, and the separate bedroom was furnished with two queen-size beds as he had requested when booking the suite. A request that had caused the well-trained registration clerk to blink several times before keying the command into his computer in discreet silence. The clerk was, after all, dealing with the groom in a wedding that had been billed as the passion-fest of the decade. Under the circumstances, Jordan figured the guy was entitled to a little astonishment. He probably thought they had some weird sexual fetish that required two beds. Jordan wasn't sure whether to laugh or groan out loud at the escalating craziness of his situation.

Emily's reaction to their honeymoon suite didn't make it any easier for him to hold on to his cool. She explored the rooms with the darting gaze of a hunted rabbit who knew the hounds were gaining fast. At the sight of the two beds, her shoulders slumped with relief.

Jordan waited for her to say something, but she seemed to decide that the less said the better. A typical Emily reaction, but one he was willing to let her get away with for now. Given that virtually everything he'd said to convince Emily to marry him had been a lie, he was in no position to complain about people who didn't have the courage to bring important issues out into the open. Jordan the rebel, the kid who'd walked away from his heritage without a backward glance, had turned into a card-carrying member of Cowards Anonymous when confronted with the possibility of confessing to Emily how he truly felt about her.

"I asked room service to send us up a light supper around eleven," he said, flinging his jacket over a chair and loosening his black tie enough to unfasten the top button of his starched and pleated shirt. "I don't know about you, but I barely ate at the reception. Every time I got a bite of food on my fork, some cousin or great-aunt would come up to congratulate me. Eventually, I gave up."

"Same with me. I never even got to eat any wedding cake, except for a mouthful while the photographer shot pictures." Emily gave him a tentative smile. "Actually, now that you mention it, I'm starving."

Her smile worked its usual devastating magic on his common sense, his hormones and his general state of rampaging sexual need. He was damn lucky his tongue wasn't hanging out. Jordan glanced at his watch, giving himself a couple of seconds to get his act back together. Emily, in the close proximity of their honeymoon suite, was not doing a thing for his state of overheated lust.

"It's almost eleven, so the food should be arriving any minute," he said, when his heart was no longer thumping in double time. Damn! This was not going to be a fun night. He hadn't felt this aroused—this unsure of himself—since his best friend in high school dared him to ask for a date with Lindsey Ibbotson, princess of the cheerleading squad and possessor of the boobs voted "best all-around" in the guys' locker room poll.

"I'll take care of the room service waiter," Jordan said. "Why don't you go ahead and unpack whatever you need for tonight? Maybe you want to take a shower and change into a robe, or something.''

Emily's hesitant smile vanished at the reminder of the obstacles that still lay ahead before she could take refuge in the safety of sleep. She linked her hands tightly in front of her, kneading them anxiously. Jordan wanted to laugh at her unmistakable embarrassment, but no laughter came. Instead, he found that he was dry-mouthed with desire.

After a few moments of tense silence, Emily cleared her throat and launched into the speech he'd been waiting for. ''Jordan, I've been trying to find some casual and sophisticated way to discuss the sleeping arrangements for tonight but I can't. So I guess I'll have to be crass and juvenile.'' Her cheeks turned pink. ''I'm sure you weren't expecting us to—to sleep together, but just in case you were, I don't think that would be a good idea.''

''I agree,'' Jordan said blandly, deliberately misunderstanding. Hell, he wasn't going to get any other satisfaction tonight, so he might as well at least have the pleasure of watching Emily squirm a little.

''You—you do?''

''Sure,'' he said. ''That's why I ordered a room with two beds. I'm a pretty restless sleeper and I've never enjoyed sleeping with my lovers, have you?''

Emily sent him an appalled glance. ''I didn't mean...I know I said *sleeping,* but I wasn't actually talking about *sleeping....*''

''No?'' Her fingers were going to snap off if she twisted them much harder, Jordan thought wryly. ''What were you talking about, then?''

She drew in a determined breath, giving up on euphemisms. ''I was talking about having sex.''

''We only need one bed for that.'' He sent her his most charming and intimate smile.

''We don't need *any* beds for that.''

He quirked an eyebrow. "You prefer the floor? The couch? A chair?" He flashed her a sexy leer. "Whatever you want, Em. I'm real flexible."

"Good heavens, no! I don't want to have sex on the floor! Or anywhere!" Her blush darkened to crimson. "This isn't coming out right," she said, pacing the room. "What I'm trying to say is that this is a marriage of convenience, based on my need not to disappoint my parents, and my even more pathetic need not to be held up as an object of pity in front of San Antonio's social elite, and your need to...well, whatever your needs were, precisely."

"I guess I thought I was pretty much saving Michael's ass," he said, provoked into a half truth.

"Well, yes, I guess you were. And he should be grateful for that, just as I am. But we still can't get sexually involved, Jordan. The situation's messy enough and sex would only make things way more complicated for both of us."

He shrugged. "Personally, I don't see a damn thing that's convenient about a marriage where there's no sex."

"Well, I can see that it's not very convenient for you to spend several months in a state of celibacy." Emily forced herself to meet his gaze. "This is obviously one of the many hundreds of things we should have discussed before today's ceremony. But we didn't, and the bottom line is that I can't fall into bed with you just because the state says it's legal. We have nothing in common except that we both want the Laurel Acres project to succeed, and that's a lousy reason to have sex with someone."

He wanted to tell her that he didn't give a damn about the success or failure of Laurel Acres, except insofar as their respective parents needed the profits the project might generate. But he wasn't ready for the discussion that admission would generate, so he kept silent.

Encouraged by his silence, Emily spoke with increasing

confidence. "I'm sure now that you've stopped to consider the situation, you'll agree that things will be a lot simpler if we keep our relationship platonic."

"No, I don't agree. We're married. Why can't we make love?"

She frowned, beginning to look irritated by his failure to comprehend. "Because we're going to get divorced in less than a year. Because we're not in love, so we wouldn't be *making love*. We'd be having meaningless sex—"

"Have you been in love with everyone you ever had sex with?" Jordan discovered that he really wanted to know the answer to that question.

She hesitated for a second or two. "I thought I was," she said finally. "I would never have sex with a man unless I cared about him. And that's not the case with us, is it?"

But she'd cared about Michael, Jordan thought bleakly, otherwise she would never have agreed to become engaged. Sometimes Emily's relationship with his brother had seemed so asexual that he'd wondered if they had actually been to bed together. A crazy hope, given Michael's predatory attitude toward women. Anyway, it was ridiculous to care. Even more ridiculous to harbor a jealous wish that his brother had never seen Emily drowsy in the aftermath of sexual climax, her defenses shattered and her barriers down. He had no possible right to resent the fact that Emily and his brother must have made love many times during the past three months.

Jordan deliberately slammed the door shut on images that led him to a place where he absolutely, positively didn't want to go. No point in dwelling on what had happened between Emily and his brother since that relationship was over, however much Emily might regret its end. He consoled himself with a reminder that the past might belong to Michael, but the future was his.

Jordan shook off a momentary desolation. Hell, he should be grateful for small mercies. Two days earlier he'd been preparing himself to watch Emily marry a man he was convinced would never make her happy. Now, with the help of a lot of fast talking, he had weeks—months— in which to convince her that she'd ended up married to the right brother.

Tonight, however, was not the appropriate time to start an in-depth exploration of the many misconceptions Emily harbored about him. She was emotionally spent, not to mention physically exhausted. In all honesty, he was pretty damned tired himself.

Crossing the room, he abandoned his slightly mocking pose. Touching her lightly on the cheek, he spoke softly, with no defensive, cynical edge to his words.

"Don't look so worried, Em. I shouldn't have teased you about this. The truth is, I never expected the two of us to make love tonight. That's why there are two beds. Although it's also true that I can be a restless sleeper."

Her spectacular golden-brown eyes looked up at him, warm with sudden gratitude. "Thank you, Jordan. I really appreciate your consideration. Given that most couples nowadays fall into bed together on their first date, and only ask each other's names afterward if they've had a real good time, I know I must seem weirdly old-fashioned."

"Mmm, you do, but pleasantly so." He smiled at her, keeping his distance because he wasn't sure he could touch her and still find the willpower to move away. "We have months of married life ahead of us. I can wait."

She started a confused explanation of why she was sure their marriage would work much better if sex was kept permanently out of the equation. A knock at the door came just in time to save her from descending into total incoherence.

Jordan grinned and walked across the room toward the door. "Saved by the bell, honey, wouldn't you say?"

She let out a shaky breath. "I'll unpack," she mumbled, escaping to the bedroom. "I think I'll take a shower, too."

Jordan agreed with the room service waiter that they would eat at the table by the window, and watched as the young man set out an attractive supper of tiny sandwiches, fresh fruit and miniature cookies.

"Compliments of the general manager," the waiter said, opening a bottle of champagne and placing it in a bucket of ice. "Enjoy your meal, sir."

"Thanks. Everything looks great." Jordan signed the bill, adding a generous tip.

The waiter left just as Emily came back into the sitting room, tying the belt on a terry-cloth robe. Her hair was wet, she was barefoot, and she'd washed off all her makeup. She looked so damn beautiful that Jordan had to hold on to the edge of his chair to prevent himself leaping up and grabbing her.

She had obviously decided to put their previous conversation behind them, as if it had never happened. *Oh yes,* Jordan thought. *Let's add a bit more evasion to our relationship. The pair of us are major league champions at not talking about topics that are important.*

She sat opposite him, smiling with determined cheerfulness. In any other woman, he would have assumed that the tantalizing glimpses of naked flesh revealed by the robe were a deliberate ploy to arouse and torment him. With Emily, he was confident she had absolutely no idea that the lapels of the robe weren't staying closed, even less idea what she was doing to him. He could have stopped the torture in an instant simply by telling her that the robe wasn't properly closed. Naturally, he was crazy enough to prefer the torment.

"Everything looks wonderful," she said as her gaze

skimmed over the champagne and a bowl of raspberries, before coming to rest on the platter of bite-size sandwiches. "I'm totally and completely starving. I think the last time I ate a proper meal was at breakfast yesterday morning."

Jordan kept his gaze focused on the food, as opposed to the enticing length of Emily's bare legs, almost touching his beneath the table. "I ordered a variety of sandwiches. That way I figured there'd be something you like."

"Where food is concerned, I'm very easy to please." She smiled, gradually relaxing as she became more confident that he wasn't going to insist on taking up their conversation where it had left off. "Tonight, you could probably even convince me to eat anchovies."

He grinned. "You don't have to sink that low. I recommend the smoked turkey breast and the cream cheese with walnuts. I tried them both, and they're good."

While she ate, Jordan poured two glasses of champagne and handed one to her. "Here's to us," he said, raising his glass.

"To us." She drank quickly, as if even that casual toast was too intimate for comfort. Then she gave a tiny laugh. "This is weird, isn't it? I mean, here we are, a regular married couple as far as the world's concerned, and yet we don't know the most basic things about each other's likes and dislikes. I don't even know where you live or where you work. I don't know who your friends are, what your dreams are for the future...."

Jordan held her gaze. "That's what a honeymoon is for," he said. "Getting to know each other. I'm looking forward to it."

Emily returned his gaze, her eyes darkening with surprise. "You know, so am I."

CHAPTER SEVEN

EMILY WAS RELIEVED that the wedding ceremony had gone off without mishap and that the first night of her honeymoon was turning out to be less of a problem than she could reasonably have expected. Despite this relief, and her state of near exhaustion, she slept very little. Perched on the bed, her body rigid with the knowledge that Jordan lay less than six feet away, she drew in steady breaths and willed herself to relax. But her muscles remained as stiff and unyielding as a Victorian corset, and sleep proved an elusive luxury.

Like anesthesia wearing off after a tooth extraction, the numbness that had kept her functional for the past twenty-four hours finally dissipated, leaving Emily to confront the painful reality that she was married to a man she barely knew. A man, moreover, whose mere presence was enough to make her skin prickle with tension.

Despite his dubious moral code, Emily had to admit Jordan had saved her from major humiliation when he stepped into the breach on behalf of his brother. Michael was supposed to be the Chambers brother who'd been blessed with most of the charm and all the social graces, but the past couple of days had revealed that Jordan possessed his own good qualities, including a sensitivity to her needs and feelings that was all the more attractive when contrasted with his brother's ruthless rejection.

Unfortunately, acknowledging that Jordan had a flair for making a woman feel appreciated brought Emily no comfort. Instead, she reflected gloomily that her husband had probably acquired his expertise during the long, sensual afternoons he'd spent seducing other men's wives. It couldn't be easy, after all, to persuade dozens of rich society matrons to commit adultery, and ferreting out his partner's emotional needs so that he could make himself agreeable would be an important part of any seducer's stock in trade.

Emily discovered that she didn't like the idea of being just one more in a long line of women her husband—that crazy word again!—chose to pamper and cosset into submission. If Jordan expected her to be an easy victim, he was going to be disappointed. Other women might fall for his sexual charisma with all the mindless enthusiasm of lemmings leaping off a cliff, but she was made of sterner stuff.

That point satisfactorily settled, Emily determined not to think about Jordan anymore. Unfortunately, her decision proved easier to make than to keep. Insomnia was a major pain in the butt, she decided, twisting onto her stomach in a vain attempt to find a comfortable position. This was the second night in a row that sleep had eluded her, and she needed to get some rest instead of chewing over facts that couldn't be changed however much she obsessed about them.

She'd counted 183 fat sheep clambering through hedges before she gave up and accepted that make-believe livestock were no competition for all-too-real visions of her husband in bed with Mary Christine. She'd tried to bury her memories of that afternoon so deeply that they couldn't resurface, but despite her best efforts, the scene in the Bernauers' master bedroom remained stubbornly vivid.

Emily flopped onto her back and scowled at the ceiling, pressing her fingertips to her eyes in an effort to induce sleep. But what she saw was a sated and tousled Mary

Christine lying in the crook of Jordan's arm, her languid smile oozing sexual satisfaction.

Even now, Emily could summon a precise image of how Jordan's hand had curved possessively around Mary Christine's shoulders, and how his hair, rumpled and slightly too long, had fallen over his eyes. Eyes that were warm, laughing and relaxed as he gazed down at the woman lying next to him. Eyes that turned blank and agate hard when he turned to look at Emily, who'd come to a dead halt in the bedroom doorway, her arms full of fabric samples and strips of wallpaper.

For an endless moment she and Jordan had simply stared at each other in a silence so encompassing it was almost tangible. Then Emily had dropped her bundle of samples, and the freeze-frame had shattered. She'd knelt to pick up the spilled fabric swatches and Jordan had reacted quickly. Muscles rippling beneath tanned, taut skin, he leaned down and grabbed a cover from the floor, throwing it over Mary Christine.

Oh yes, Jordan had moved real fast, Emily thought with uncharacteristic sarcasm. He had behaved like a perfect gentleman—provided you ignored the fact that the woman whose modesty he'd been so anxious to protect happened to be another man's wife.

Emily wished that she didn't remember how Jordan had looked on that rainy afternoon, but she did. She wished that she didn't feel a hollow ache in the pit of her stomach when the memories resurfaced, but she did. She wished that her body wouldn't grow hot with tension, but it did.

The insidious heat washed over her again, leaving her more awake than ever. The upheavals of the past few days seemed to have imbued her with an unfamiliar restlessness and she found herself questioning assumptions she had previously considered basic to her personality. Until this moment, Emily had told herself that she'd experienced nothing but disgust on finding Jordan and Mary Christine in bed together. Now she felt the need to confront the whole truth, which was something more complex than straightforward disgust.

Okay, spell it out, she told herself grimly. You were genuinely shocked by the scene that greeted you in Ted Bernauer's bedroom, but shock wasn't all you felt. You were also aroused. You were appalled by Mary Christine's betrayal of her husband, and Jordan's willingness to commit adultery, but there was a little thread of envy wound into your disapproval. You wished that you could be as uninhibited as Mary Christine. You wished that you could shed your hangups and lie naked in a man's arms in broad daylight, reveling in the knowledge that you'd brought him total sexual satisfaction.

Since she seemed to be in the mood for honesty, however unpleasant, Emily decided she might as well confess the rest, at least in the privacy of her own thoughts. The truth she'd been twisting and squirming to avoid for the past three months was this: she found Jordan Chambers sexually attractive. There, she'd said it. While she scrabbled on the floor for missing pieces of fabric, she had fantasized about what it would be like to be kissed by him, and how his hands would feel as they roamed over her body. Knowing that Jordan was her fiancé's brother, she still hadn't been able to halt her fantasies. She had wondered how it would feel to make love to him, and then lie beside him, drowsy but content.

Emily usually avoided digging into the darker layers of her subconscious, but she didn't have to dig very deep to understand that the reason she was wide-awake at two-thirty in the morning was because her overactive imagination kept presenting enticing visions of what might happen if she left her bed and climbed in next to Jordan.

With more speed than finesse, Emily slammed the door

closed on that train of thought. Oh, no, she definitely wasn't going there. The events of the past couple of days might have destroyed her lifelong struggle to always behave with impeccable correctness, but she wasn't about to throw all her values out the window. Her birth provided living proof of what could happen when two people allowed their passion to outrun their judgment, and she had no intention of falling into the trap of allowing purely physical curiosity to lead to an unwanted pregnancy. Sex for her could never be casual, so starting an affair with Jordan was out of the question. The fact that they were married was an irrelevant technicality, and one that she couldn't use as an excuse.

Hot and irritable, Emily rolled onto her side, tucking her hand under her cheek. Too late, she realized that she had turned to face Jordan, a direction she'd so far managed to avoid despite all her tossing and turning. He was lying on his stomach, spread-eagled across the mattress, his face angled toward her. His hair fell forward, just as it had on that memorable afternoon with Mary Christine, but tonight his eyes were closed and he appeared lost in peaceful slumber.

So much for his claim to be a restless sleeper, Emily thought grumpily. He had strolled out of the bathroom two hours ago, dropped onto the bed, fluffed his pillow, and instantly fallen asleep. He'd barely moved since then, which suggested that he was untroubled by bad dreams. He evidently didn't seem to be suffering from the tension that had her securely in its thrall.

She found Jordan's tranquility infuriating. Unlike her nagging subconscious, which remained in permanent lurk mode, ready to pounce the moment she relaxed, his conscience seemed easily lulled. To all appearances, the wretched man didn't have a worry in the world. The fact that he was married to a woman he scarcely knew was obviously no big deal as far as he was concerned. The fact that he was stuck with his brother's discarded fiancée for the next several months hadn't given him a case of raging insomnia. That lousy wedding gift was apparently hers alone.

As for her fear that Jordan might resent her no-sex rule and attempt to make love to her...hah! She sure needn't have worried. Judging from his state of tranquil slumber, having sex with her evoked about as much longing as having last year's tax return audited by the IRS.

Emily wondered if he found her too mousy and unattractive to be worth seducing, or if his level of desire was low because his affair with Mary Christine still continued. That prospect produced a flash of outrage so intense she jerked upright in the bed.

Good grief, was it possible that Jordan and Mary Christine were still carrying on their affair? Had she been naive to believe Mary Christine's sobbing promise that she would never again betray her husband if Emily would only keep silent about what she'd seen? Belatedly, she realized that even if Jordan was no longer involved with Mary Christine, that offered no guarantee he wasn't involved with some other woman.

Now, there was a subject that ought to have been included in one of their nonexistent prewedding chats, Emily thought with bleak irony, forcing herself to slide down the bed into a prone position before Jordan noticed she was awake. Was it too late to strike a deal that while they were married, Jordan couldn't have affairs with other women? Was it even fair to make that rule if she was refusing to have sex with him herself?

Smothering a hysterical desire to laugh, she wondered what Miss Manners might have to say about the etiquette of that knotty little problem. What were the twenty-first century rules for sexual fidelity when two people were united in a nineteenth-century-style marriage of convenience?

Except that nothing about this marriage was even remotely convenient, Emily reflected despairingly. The more she thought about the ramifications of her daily life with Jordan, the less she could understand why she had agreed to marry him. Realistically, how in the world were they going to organize their lives? She'd had a grand total of two private conversations with Jordan before the wedding, neither of them lasting longer than five minutes. During one of those conversations she'd stipulated that their bank accounts would remain separate. In another, she'd asked him for his home address, which he'd given her, but they'd been interrupted before she had time to ask if the address was for a house, condo, or rental apartment.

In retrospect, finances and the address of her new home seemed way down on the list of things she should have discussed. Instead, she should have asked him how they were going to prevent their lives from getting hopelessly intertwined. Would they have separate phone lines, with separate answering machines so that they wouldn't have to take each other's messages? Were they going to tell each other where they went each time they left the house? Or was their marriage going to be such a sham that she would never know whether Jordan's absence meant he was at his factory building kitchen cabinets, or frolicking in another woman's bedroom, making passionate love to his latest conquest?

Hell and damnation, Emily thought, punching her pillow with all the force of her pent-up frustration. How in the world had she gotten herself into this insane situation?

Jordan finally stirred, and she hastily closed her eyes, afraid that he might wake up and find her staring at him. She didn't want to create the wrong impression. She didn't want him to get the idea that she was looking at him because she was interested in him as a man, much less as a potential lover. Because, of course, nothing could be further from the truth. The fact that she found him attractive was confusing, but irrelevant. Emily didn't like messy emotions, and *messy* was the perfect word to describe her feelings toward Jordan Chambers.

She seized on that last thought because she'd finally found something that brought a measure of comfort. This whole marriage situation was messy and that was why she was such a mental and emotional wreck. She could cope with full-scale disasters that would destroy other people, but she couldn't tolerate mess, confusion and indecision. Obviously, the cure for her strange restlessness was to lay down some clear guidelines for this crazy marriage. To hell with etiquette and what was reasonable—she needed a comfort zone of agreed behavior. Some rules for their married life. Starting with the sex issue.

Tomorrow she would let Jordan know she expected him to remain celibate for the few months that their marriage would last. She would point out that they'd already caused more than enough scandal to last a lifetime, and she wasn't willing to return to face San Antonio's gossips, wondering all the time if rumors of his latest affair were already circulating.

Jordan wouldn't like the idea of celibacy one bit, but he could just suck it up, Emily decided. There was even a grim sort of satisfaction to be gained from the idea of imposing celibacy on Jordan Chambers, San Antonio's most notorious stud. He was the one who'd proposed this marriage, and he could live with the consequences.

Celibacy, Emily told herself firmly. That was definitely the way to go. She would inform Jordan of her decision before bedtime tomorrow.

CHAPTER EIGHT

VISUALIZING JORDAN condemned to a life of monklike abstinence was the only satisfaction Emily found during a long and weary night. After several more hours of staring alternately at the ceiling, the wall and Jordan's closed eyes, it was a relief when the alarm went off, warning them that they only had an hour before they needed to leave for the airport.

Jordan, fortunately, didn't seem to be any more of a morning person than she was. He wasn't grouchy, but he didn't feel any need to be chatty, and they consumed black coffee and English muffins in a silence that felt almost companionable. Their unexpected rapport at the breakfast table might be one of the weirder consequences to emerge from the past two days of almost unrelenting weirdness, Emily reflected.

Their flight left San Antonio on time and arrived a few minutes early at the Denver airport. Exhausted after two sleepless nights, Emily dozed for most of the flight, only waking up as they came in to land.

Jordan had arranged to pick up a Jeep Cherokee at the airport and they drove west out of the city for more than two hours before he turned off the interstate onto a county road that wound along the banks of the White Rocks River. Twenty minutes later he made another turn onto a single-lane gravel road that curved steeply out of the valley and up the side of Tall Chimney Mountain.

Emily felt herself unwind as the Jeep climbed steadily

upward. The worries of her sleepless night seemed far away as they drove along the deserted road, edged by banks of wildflowers. The solitude and the quiet felt heavenly after two days of unrelenting socializing.

The countryside looked so inviting that she opened the car window to its fullest extent, leaning out to get a better view. Breathing in pine-scented air that was dry enough to sting her nostrils, she watched a hawk sail across the horizon, its wings silhouetted against a sky that was brilliant, cloudless blue.

Emily watched the bird until it disappeared into a distant clump of blue spruce trees. The low rumble of the car engine made a soothing background noise, a counterpoint to the silent beauty of the hawk's flight. An unexpected sense of peace stole over her. Her jangled nerve endings, wounded by the trauma of Michael's rejection and the multiple stresses of the wedding, finally calmed down. Reveling in the view of snow-capped mountains, she rested her chin on her arms, feeling like a cat whose fur had finally been stroked back into sleekness after weathering a brutal storm.

"Almost there," Jordan said, easing into lower gear as he glanced across at her. "Are you tired? Getting to the house means a long drive on top of the flight from San Antonio, but I always think the end result is worth every minute of it."

"I'm tired," Emily acknowledged. "But this trip has been a pleasure, not a hardship. Even the stretch where we were driving along the regular highway was mostly gorgeous once we were clear of the airport."

"It's an amazing piece of interstate, isn't it? Makes a pleasant change to see herds of elk and buffalo as opposed to billboards advertising fast-food restaurants."

"Yes, it sure does."

"You mentioned that you hadn't been to Colorado before. Is it living up to your expectations? At least so far?"

There was something ridiculous about having this sort of a conversation with the man who was her husband. They sounded like two people who'd ended up as seatmates on the same vacation tour bus, Emily thought ruefully. On the other hand, politeness sure beat the tension and suppressed hostility that often hovered right below the surface of their exchanges, so she decided not to break the mood with a surly comment.

"No, I've never been to Colorado," she said. "My parents are real homebodies and we didn't travel much when I was little. We did the standard trip to Washington D.C., and a couple of vacations on the Gulf shore when I was a teenager. And we went to Acapulco with some of my cousins one year, but Mom got horrible food poisoning, so we never tried that again."

"Do you like to travel? Or are you a homebody, too?"

"I love to travel, although finding vacation time can be a problem these days. My dad's business has been growing at such a rapid pace the last few years, it's been difficult to get away."

"You do the interior design work for all his model homes?"

"Yes, and I have a few private clients, too, which makes for a really hectic schedule." Remembering that Ted and Mary Christine Bernauer had been one of those private clients, Emily hurried on. "Luckily for me, Carolyn St. Clair is a whiz at finding last-minute travel bargains, and every so often she makes reservations for two, then forces me to go with her. We've taken a couple of really fun trips together. One to New England in the fall a couple of years ago, and another last summer to Alaska."

"Did you enjoy that?"

"We loved it. The high spot of the trip was encountering

a family of polar bears on a trail walk. A mother and two cubs. It was a case of love at first sight, at least on our part. I'm not so sure about the bears.''

"They refrained from eating you, so I guess you can claim there was a certain mutual esteem."

She laughed. "I'll have to tell Caro that."

"Carolyn seems to be a really good friend. How did you meet? It wasn't at college, was it?"

"No, Caro and I have done volunteer work with the Texas Fund for Children for several years, and one day we'd both volunteered to help out with an open house. Unfortunately, there was a massive power failure just minutes after dozens of important donors had arrived. Caro and I ended up serving lukewarm tea and melted chocolate mousse by candlelight. Most of the donors were very gracious, but even so, cleaning up afterward in hundred-degree heat was a real bonding experience, let me tell you. We've been good friends ever since."

Jordan slowed down to let a pair of squirrels chase each other across the road, and Emily pointed to a waterfall that cascaded down the side of the mountain, hitting the edge of the road in a dazzling display of foaming, frothing power. "That is so beautiful. Where does all the water come from?"

"It's snowmelt," Jordan said. "This mountain is almost thirteen thousand feet high, so it takes until June for the meltdown to begin in earnest. By the beginning of October, snow will start to fall again and the waterfall will freeze. The ice crystals are sometimes two or three feet long, and clustered several yards wide. It makes for an amazing sight."

"Good grief, that's only four months without snow and ice!"

He smiled at her horrified tone. "Yeah, it's a very short summer at this elevation. There's virtually no spring, just mud season, and fall lasts about three weeks. Long enough for the aspen to change color and lose their leaves, then winter sets in. I kind of enjoy winter, though. I like to cross-country ski, and this is a perfect spot for that. And in lots of ways I think the views are even more spectacular when the mountains are covered in snow."

"I thought it was written into the state constitution that Texans are forbidden to like snow."

He grinned. "I got a special dispensation. Anyway, I'm not a complete traitor. I like the snow best when I'm admiring it from inside the house, sitting in front of a huge fire. We're not talking hardy pioneer stuff here."

Emily could barely imagine anything more magnificent than the scene that surrounded her at this moment, but she accepted Jordan's word that winter was even better. With a touch of wry amusement, she found herself thinking that marriage to Jordan Chambers was almost worth it, if it meant that she got to spend the next week in this small corner of paradise.

The contrast with what she would have been doing at this moment if her wedding to Michael had gone ahead as planned was stark. She would probably have been lying on a Tahiti beach with Michael beside her. Or maybe sipping piña coladas by the pool at the superdeluxe resort hotel he had selected for their honeymoon. Beach or poolside, she was willing to bet that Michael would have been making endless calls to political cronies from his cell phone. And then there was the ubiquitous Jeff Greiff, ever present in spirit, if not in person. Two hours without contacting his campaign manager was about as long as Michael could go during waking hours.

Michael would have expected to make love to her last night, and Emily gave an involuntary shiver at the thought. He had been right to claim that their failure to make love was indicative of a real problem in their relationship. True, she was a person who lacked interest in sex. You didn't reach the age of twenty-seven with only one lover to your credit unless you were somewhat underendowed in the sexual appetite department. Still, she should have realized there was something seriously wrong as the weeks of their engagement stretched into months, and she had never felt the slightest urgency to initiate any sexual contact.

Jordan must have noticed her shiver. "Cold?" he asked. "We've been climbing steeply for the last half hour, and it starts to get pretty chilly at this elevation. If you need a sweater, I packed a couple of extras. I could get one out for you if you like."

"Later, maybe, but right now the cool air is wonderful after the San Antonio heat. I'm fine. Great, in fact." Emily realized that she was speaking the simple truth. She felt no regret for the lost pleasures of Tahiti, and even less regret for Michael's absence. He had chosen a lousy time to break off their engagement, and his refusal to take responsibility for the break had been contemptible, but she was becoming more and more convinced that she owed him a debt of gratitude for calling off their marriage.

She'd been so happy that her engagement pleased her parents that she'd never stopped to question how much of her own pleasure derived from gratifying them, rather than herself. In organizing a grandiose wedding, she'd kept herself too busy with military-precision-style planning to dwell on the fact that the core of her relationship with Michael was hollow. Their lack of intimacy—mental as well as physical—should have been glaringly apparent, but she'd refused to see what was under her nose. Instead of probing beneath the surface, she'd deliberately disguised the emptiness with nonstop, frenetic activity.

Emily felt Jordan's gaze resting on her inquiringly, and she turned away, reluctant to answer his unspoken questions. It was one thing to admit to herself that Michael had done her a favor in breaking off their engagement, another thing entirely to confess as much to Jordan.

In a disconcerting example of his ability to pick up on her mood, Jordan didn't push for confidences, didn't even comment on her sudden silence. "As soon as we turn this corner in the road, you'll be able to see the house where we're staying," he said. "Look straight ahead. Yeah, there it is."

Emily glanced up at the note of satisfaction in his voice, then felt her heart miss a beat when she saw what he was pointing toward. She couldn't remember ever seeing a house more perfectly attuned to its setting than the one that rose ahead of them. With a cedar shake roof, rough-hewn siding, and huge windows, it had a rustic charm that soothed the eye and grabbed the heart. Jordan drew the Jeep to a halt on a concrete apron built in front of the garage. "This is Elk Meadow, one of my favorite places in the world. I hope you'll enjoy your stay here, Em."

An odd tremor rippled down her spine every time he called her Em. She supposed it must be caused by suppressed irritation at his refusal to use her proper given name. Still, the house was lovely and she chose not to pick a fight.

"It's just beautiful," she said, getting out of the car. "And that's a totally inadequate word to describe it."

"The interior has some innovative design features. I think you'll be impressed."

"I already am." She turned to him with a smile. "If there's running hot water, I'm willing to declare the place perfect."

"There's hot water. There's even a Jacuzzi tub in the master bathroom."

"Then I can't imagine anywhere I'd prefer to spend the next week." Picking up her purse and flight bag, Emily walked toward the porch that ran the entire length of the house. The sun shone with an intensity that rivaled San Antonio for fierceness, but the air was desert dry and cooled by a steady breeze. The scent of pine and wild-flowers had floated tantalizingly around her ever since she opened the car window down by the White Rocks River, but up here the scents were intense, almost heady.

"The house is built on a plateau," Jordan said, coming up behind her. "There's a meadow at the back. Take a look before we go inside." Putting his hand beneath her elbow, he guided her to the corner of the house.

Against a sky of dazzling blue, the meadow stretched for about five acres before dropping off into a ravine. The grass was lush with a feathery silver bloom, and blue columbines with yellow stamens grew tall and straight among the grasses. The breeze, its path interrupted by myriad mountain peaks, constantly changed direction, creating subtle changes in the predominant color of the meadow.

If this house were hers, Emily thought, she would take the wonderful, elusive shades of blue, gold and green and weave them into the decor of the house so there would be a seamless continuity between the magnificent natural setting and the interior design.

"I've always found this house is a pretty good place to unwind," Jordan said, standing with his hands shoved into his pockets and his gaze sweeping the horizon. "I thought we both might appreciate the chance to catch our breath for a few days, so this seemed like a good place to choose."

"We look as if we're in the middle of the wilderness, and yet we're no more than three hours from downtown Denver," Emily said. "This place is just magical, Jordan. How did you manage to discover it? Are the owners friends of yours? They must be. I can't imagine owning a house this perfect and then renting it out to anyone I didn't know well."

"Long story," he said. He paused for a moment before adding, "Actually the house is mine."

"Yours?" Emily looked at him blankly. "How in the world—" She stopped herself just in time from asking how he could possibly afford something so expensive.

"That's great," she said, recovering her polite smile. "What a terrific vacation home you've made for yourself, Jordan."

"Yeah, it is a great vacation spot." He grinned at her, his smile setting her nerve endings jangling with all their old force. "Go for it, Em," he said softly. "Forget prim and proper. For once in your life, say what's really on your mind."

"I've no idea what you mean...."

"Sure you do. My parents are always complaining that I have no money and no career, so you're dying to ask how I found the money to buy this house. Your worst suspicion is that I earned it in bed. That some grateful billionaire's wife gave it to me in return for an especially splendid orgasm."

"No orgasm is worth a house. Not even one of your best." As soon as she'd spoken, Emily wondered if the altitude was depriving her brain of oxygen. She couldn't believe what she'd just said.

Far from being offended, Jordan laughed. "Are you absolutely sure about that, Em?"

"Quite sure." Emily spoke all the more firmly because, in fact, she wasn't sure at all.

"Well, if you don't believe that I acquired it as payment for sexual services rendered, would you believe that I bought it the old-fashioned way? With money I earned as a carpenter for the down payment, and a very large mortgage from the bank for the balance?"

Emily not only believed him, she felt a surge of relief. "How unexpectedly respectable of you, Jordan."

"Isn't it just?" With a last look toward the magnificence of the ravine, he put his arm around her waist and walked her back toward the Jeep. "Don't tell anyone, Em, but I'm really a very respectable person."

"That's certainly not what the legends say."

"I know, but that's the whole point about legends, isn't it? They're much more interesting if they don't stick too closely to the facts."

She turned and looked at him intently, trying to see him without the distorting lens of his family's disapproval and the embarrassment of encountering him in bed with Mary Christine the day after they'd first been introduced. "Which parts of your legend are true, Jordan?"

He shrugged. "Not many. It's true I left home when I was still in high school, and that I dropped out of college after a single semester, but that's about where truth and legend part company. Sadly, the stories about my amazing sexual conquests far exceed the reality."

"Sadly?"

"Sure." He leaned against one of the porch posts. "I'm rumored to have had affairs with at least ninety percent of the most beautiful women in San Antonio. Hell, I wish that were true. Any man would."

"But it isn't true?"

He shook his head. "Rumor vastly exaggerates." He waited for a beat then grinned at her. "It can't possibly be more than eighty percent."

"Only eighty percent, huh?" Without thinking, she smiled back. "Well, that'll teach me to listen to gossip."

"Sorry to shatter your illusions." Jordan's expression sobered. His gaze sought hers, then held it. "And for the record, that's eighty percent of the single women in San Antonio. Contrary to what you believe, I don't make love to other men's wives."

Emily's smile vanished. "Don't lie to me," she said,

her voice tight with anger. Anger that was all the more intense because only a few seconds earlier the wretched man had actually beguiled her into joking about his sordid affairs. "I saw you in bed with Mary Christine Bernauer. That's not legend. It's not even a secondhand report. That's fact, observed by me."

"Seeing isn't necessarily a guarantee that you've understood the whole truth of the situation."

"Right. Sure. There are so many possible reasons why you might have been naked in bed with Mary Christine. Maybe you have a bible study group that meets Tuesday afternoons in her bed. Now there's a likely explanation. How crass of me to jump to the conclusion that the pair of you were committing adultery."

"Not crass. But mistaken—"

"Mistaken? Jordan, stop it! We both know damn well what I saw!"

"I meant you were mistaken about my intentions."

She shook her head impatiently. "The road to hell is paved with good intentions. And it's hard to see what there is to misunderstand about two naked bodies convulsed on a bed. And when one of them is married to someone else, I flat out disapprove." Emily drew in a deep breath, striving as always to get her emotions under control where they couldn't run wild and betray her into saying something that she would later regret.

"That's the point I'm trying to make," Jordan said quietly. "I had no idea Mary Christine was married. If I had known the truth, trust me, there wouldn't have been an affair. I promise you, Em, I may have a lot of faults, but I don't knowingly make love to other men's wives."

Emily wasn't so much angered by this obvious lie as hurt. "I have a little difficulty believing that excuse, Jordan. How could you possibly not have known Mary Christine was married?"

"Easily. We met in a bar on my side of town. Mary Christine wasn't wearing a wedding ring, and nothing about her behavior suggested she was married. She claimed to be single, and she told me straight out that there wasn't even a boyfriend in the picture. You can call me naive, or dim-witted if you like, but I believed her."

"And when you escorted her back to Ted Bernauer's seven-thousand-square-foot mansion, stuffed full of antique furniture imported from France, no red flags went up?" Emily demanded. "It didn't strike you that this was a mighty opulent home for a twenty-three-year-old single, unattached woman?"

"No, because she'd already told me she was Ted Bernauer's stepdaughter. She claimed her mother had recently married Ted. Given that Mary Christine is almost forty years younger than her husband, it was a very believable story."

What worried Emily was how much she wanted to believe Jordan was being truthful. "How come you didn't know about the huge age gap? Everybody in San Antonio had been talking about it for months."

"Everybody?" Jordan queried. "Everybody in the circles you and my brother move in maybe. But I don't spend a lot of time hanging out with San Antonio's upper crust, and I can assure you the gossip hadn't reached my part of town. When Mary Christine told me she was single, I had no reason to assume she was lying."

"It's a very convenient story, but if it's true, why didn't you tell me before? You knew what I believed about you and Mary Christine. You knew that I despised what I thought you'd done, and yet you never attempted to explain, even though I was about to marry your brother. Didn't you want to have a good relationship with your future sister-in-law?"

"Not particularly."

Emily blinked, then stared at him. "Why on earth not?"

Jordan's gaze finally veered away from her, and for the first time he hesitated before answering. "It seemed safer that way," he said finally.

"Safer?" Emily was puzzled by his choice of word.

"Yes." He turned, meeting her gaze again. "I didn't explain about Mary Christine because you were marrying my brother. The wedding date was set. On balance, it seemed safer for both of us if you had a really good reason to dislike me."

Emily felt a chill that had nothing to do with the altitude or the quickening breeze. Too much had happened in the past couple of days and she realized she was afraid of asking Jordan to expand on his cryptic answer. Okay, so she deserved her crown as Princess of Avoidance, but she wasn't ready to hear what he might reveal.

The wind was blowing her hair across her face and she used that as an excuse to swing around, pushing it out of her eyes and simultaneously turning her back on Jordan. "I'm glad you didn't know Mary Christine was married," she said, as if that ended all relevant discussion.

Jordan said nothing.

Eyes fixed rigidly ahead, Emily crossed the few feet of porch that separated her from the front door. Jordan didn't move from his position propped against one of the pillars, and even though she wasn't looking at him anymore, she could feel his tension.

Jordan wanted her to ask the question she'd so carefully avoided, Emily realized, but that didn't mean it was in her own best interests to gratify his wish. She had no reason—no need—to know why it had seemed safer to Jordan if she disliked him. Her world had already been turned upside down once in the past two days. She didn't need another threat to her mental equilibrium.

"The front door's locked," she said, trying the handle. "Do you have the key?"

"Yes, I have it."

"Could you open the door, please? I'm starting to feel a little chilled."

When he didn't respond, she slowly turned around. He hadn't moved, except to shove his hands into the pockets of his jeans, and his remote gaze still seemed fixed on some distant object on the far side of the Jeep.

Emily drew in a shaky breath. Avoidance of difficult issues had always worked well for her, but in the past couple of days, it hadn't proved a very effective coping mechanism. So what was she going to do? She could follow her standard pattern and ignore what Jordan had just said. Or she could acknowledge the tension humming between them. Tension that was all the more obtrusive because she was trying so hard to deny its existence.

What the hell. She was a married woman now, and the rules from her previous world no longer seemed to make a lick of sense. Perhaps that meant she would be wise to take a new approach?

Her decision made, Emily seized her tiny supply of courage in both hands. "You win, Jordan. I'll ask the question you're waiting to hear. Why did you want me to dislike you?"

He finally swung around, his expression so tightly controlled that it was unreadable. "Because I was afraid that if you didn't actively dislike me, I would do something we would both regret."

"Such as...what?" Emily realized her hands were balled into fists at her side, but she couldn't seem to unclench them.

"Something like this," Jordan said, closing the gap between them and bending his head to slant his mouth across hers.

The touch of his lips sent an instant jolt of sensation ripping through Emily's body. Jarred by the unexpected reaction, her lips parted. Jordan's tongue flicked against hers, and she felt a fierce quiver of unfamiliar yearning.

Since her disastrous love affair in college, she'd never much enjoyed kissing, which seemed like a frightening prelude to sex rather than an activity that could be enjoyable in itself. But Jordan's kiss felt different. Sweet. Tempting. Exciting. Recklessness churned deep inside her, bringing a liberating sensation of freedom in its wake. This man was her husband. She could kiss him if she wanted to.

Husband or not, she knew there were a thousand good reasons why kissing Jordan was a very bad mistake. Right now, though, Emily couldn't remember any of them. In defiance of the warning voice sending out urgent instructions to exercise caution, her arms went around Jordan's neck, and her body softened, molding against his. In return, he deepened the kiss, his tongue thrusting fiercely against hers and his hands roaming over her body with the sort of seductive skill she'd fantasized about during last night's sleepless vigil in the hotel. Before long, she couldn't conjure up a single reminder of why it had ever seemed important to resist.

Jordan's hands framed her face, and she could feel heavy calluses on his thumbs as he brushed them against her cheeks, tracing the contours of her face. Calluses that his mother no doubt considered shameful, since she despised men who worked with their hands.

Far from being repelled, Emily realized that she found the roughness intriguing, even stimulating. What she really wanted was for Jordan to rub those callused thumbs across her breasts. Her nipples tingled at the mere thought, and for an unguarded moment she actually contemplated taking his hand and guiding it to her breast. Then either sanity returned, or her courage failed her, she wasn't sure which.

She might lack the spunk to take any initiative to increase the intimacy of their kiss, but she could at least give herself permission to enjoy whatever Jordan initiated. Closing her eyes, she surrendered herself to sensation. Until now, she'd never known that it was possible to respond to a kiss with every part of her body. Her skin felt hot, her head light, her muscles weak, and her feet oddly heavy. And when Jordan's hands slid down her back, beneath her cotton sweater, she felt a reaction not just where he touched, but deep inside, all the way to the pit of her stomach. If they had been inside the house, in the vicinity of a bed, she wondered what might have happened next.

The realization that she was actually contemplating a sexual relationship with Jordan was enough to pour a dose of ice-cold water on Emily's overheated senses. Reality crowded in with a vengeance, and she abruptly tore herself out of his arms. Good God, even if her own birth wasn't warning enough of where careless sex could lead, how could she have forgotten the bitter lesson she had learned in college? Shawn Dooley was very like Jordan in many ways. And he, too, had been all charm and sweet promises until she really needed him.

Jordan didn't attempt to reclaim her once she'd freed herself from his arms. Emotions roiling, her body still frighteningly aroused, Emily stared at him in dazed silence, too shaken to remember any of the polite stock phrases she usually employed to dampen the enthusiasm of men who made sexual advances to her.

It was Jordan who broke the lengthening silence. "Now you know why it was better if I let you despise me. You were my brother's fiancée, after all."

And just what the hell did that remark mean, Emily wondered. The possible interpretations were limitless. Almost at once, she decided she was better off not knowing. Avoidance might not have proven an ideal coping mechanism over the past few days, but it was one that had worked mighty well for her in the past, and probably could be made to work for her again. She'd done all the probing into cryptic comments that she planned to do for the time being.

"It's really getting cold out here," she said, as if their last exchange had been an impersonal discussion of the weather instead of a passionate exchange of kisses. "Could you please let me inside the house, Jordan?"

"Yeah, sure." He took the key from the pocket of his jeans and opened the front door.

In silence, carefully not looking at him, she walked inside.

CHAPTER NINE

EXHAUSTION WAS clearly affecting his brain, Jordan decided. Or what tattered remnants of a brain he still possessed. Having spent the entire night pretending to be asleep, while actually fantasizing about jumping into Emily's bed and making love until both of them were too sated to move, he was willing to concede that he wasn't operating at peak mental efficiency. Still, he'd assumed he had a few scraps of normal brain function left. For sure it hadn't occurred to him that he was tired enough to do something as totally and completely dumb-ass as grabbing Emily and thrusting his tongue halfway down her throat.

Right now, he could probably count himself lucky that she hadn't socked him on the jaw as a warning to keep his distance. Except that Emily was way too inhibited to let rip with a punch, even when she was outraged. Which she almost certainly had been. Although—for a couple of seconds there—he'd had the impression that she was kind of getting into the kiss in her own uptight, ladylike way.

And that was sheer wishful thinking on his part, Jordan decided. If he didn't want to do irreparable damage to his long-term plans, he'd better set his mind to recovering lost ground. He needed to devote the next couple of days to convincing Emily that he wasn't going to jump her bones the minute she let down her guard. In other words, he had to keep his hands off her delectable body and his mouth off her eminently kissable lips.

Hell, that shouldn't be an impossible goal to set himself.

If he could control his adolescent urge to get laid, he might yet be able to persuade Emily that he was an okay kind of a guy, with serious potential as a husband. Someone who bore only a passing resemblance to the lazy, good-for-nothing stud portrayed by his parents and their cronies on the San Antonio gossip circuit.

There were some minor consolations to be derived from his current situation. He'd spent quite a few wakeful hours last night picturing Emily in this house he'd built, and so far, the reality of her presence was living up to his most self-indulgent fantasies. She'd clearly fallen in love with Elk Meadow as swiftly as he had the first time he saw it five years earlier. It was music to his ears to listen to her enthusiastic comments as they explored the downstairs levels of the house. He'd even been pleased that she liked the basement storage systems, and if that wasn't pathetic, he didn't know what would be.

He led her from the vaulted atrium through the living room, with its floor-to-ceiling windows, and into the kitchen, where she lingered to admire the six-burner stainless steel range, with its built-in grill.

"Do you cook?" she asked. "Or is this fancy equipment just to impress visitors?"

"I like to cook when I have time. What about you?"

She wrinkled her nose. "To my mom's despair, I'm barely adequate. I get bored at the chop, grate, peel and dice stage of most recipes, which limits what I can make."

"A set of really sharp knives helps with the grunt work."

"I guess it would help some. I like to bake cakes for special occasions, so maybe there's hope for me yet. What sort of a cook are you? Elegant European? Exotic Eastern? Down-home American?"

"Mostly down-home, with a touch of exotic thrown in for variety. I could live happily on steak and potatoes, with ice cream for dessert, seven days a week. But since I'd prefer not to drop dead on my fortieth birthday, I've learned a few recipes for fish and grilled vegetables.''

"Bet that impresses all your girlfriends," she said, smiling. Her smile was genuine, and he could see that, for a moment, she'd completely forgotten that they were officially a married couple.

"I usually take my dates out to eat. I'm too busy to cook when I'm in San Antonio. And I've never brought a girlfriend here. Until today.''

"I'm not your girlfriend," she said quickly.

"No, you're not," he agreed. "You're my wife."

She stared at him blank-eyed, having a lot of trouble wrapping her mind around the truth of what he'd just said. In all honesty, Jordan still couldn't believe they were married himself. Not wanting to make too much of his point, he walked over to the fridge and pulled open the door to check the contents.

"I called a friend of mine yesterday and asked her to buy us some groceries. It looks as if she's stocked the whole fridge. If you'd like a sandwich, there seems to be plenty of choices for fillings.''

"Thanks, but I'm not really hungry right now. I am thirsty, though.''

"The altitude will do that, especially on top of a plane journey." Jordan checked the refrigerator shelves for drinks. "Take your pick. There's fancy water in little bottles, with bubbles or without. Also Coke, milk and orange juice. And beer or wine, if you feel in the mood. Although you might be smart to lay off the alcohol for the rest of today, at least until your body adjusts to the altitude.''

She nodded. "I drank more than enough champagne yesterday to last me for the rest of the week, but some water would be great.''

"Fizzy?''

"Just plain, thanks."

He opened a bottle before handing it to her and selecting a Coke for himself. "If you're ready, I'll take you upstairs so you can get unpacked and settled in for the night."

"Yes, I guess we should do that. Get unpacked, I mean. The day seems to have disappeared. I can hardly believe it's five o'clock already."

She'd got the hunted rabbit look again, which Jordan tried to find amusing and couldn't. Damn, was the mere mention of bedrooms or sleeping arrangements always going to send her running for cover? He was sure she felt the same physical attraction he did, and he wasn't sure why she was so reluctant to acknowledge it. Why wouldn't she allow herself to share something with him that would give pleasure to them both? If he'd hoped that telling her the truth about his affair with Mary Christine would work a miraculous transformation in her attitude, then clearly he was going to be disappointed.

Jordan was tired and irritated enough to lead Emily into the master bedroom, as if he anticipated she would sleep there with him, although he expected no such thing. The room was dominated by a fieldstone fireplace—and a king-size bed. He anticipated watching her reaction to the latter with a certain malicious pleasure.

Not for the first time, Emily managed to surprise him. Far from getting flustered at the sight of the bed with its dramatic blue-and-yellow spread, she didn't seem to notice it. She paid even less attention to the fireplace with its fancy display of lichen-encrusted stones. Instead, she gave a smothered gasp and made a beeline for the armoire standing in the far corner of the bedroom.

His armoire. Jordan's stomach tensed. It was crazy, but he discovered he really cared about her reaction to his work.

She stood in front of it, her gaze rapt. Then she ran her

hands almost reverently over the carved panels of the doors, which depicted two wolf cubs playing in a snow-covered forest clearing.

"You're so lucky to have this," she said, her fingers frankly caressing as she traced the outline of the larger wolf cub's bushy tail. "It's from the Woodcutters Workshop, isn't it?"

"Yes." He actually had to swallow a couple of times before he could say anything else. "How did you know?"

"The craftsmanship is unmistakable once you've seen a couple of their pieces."

"Even so, I'm surprised you could recognize it instantaneously, from way across the room like that."

"I'm an interior designer, remember. It's my job to know about the industry's leading designers. Besides, I think the Woodcutters Workshop is the most exciting producer of custom furniture in the country."

Emily was still examining the carved panels, indifferent to the other contents of the room and even the dramatic view of the mountains from the windows that flanked either side of the fireplace. "I saw an exhibition of their furniture at a trade show in North Carolina about four years ago," she said. "Everything that comes out of their factory is well made and elegantly designed, but the hand-carved signature pieces by J. C. Hunter are more than wonderful. In my opinion, they're works of art."

"I'm…glad you like them."

"I recommend them to clients all the time, but the waiting list is so long, it doesn't always work out. Right after that exhibition, I tried to buy a dining room china cabinet for a client of mine, but every J. C. Hunter piece is custom-produced, and the lead time at that point was at least two years. My client was enthusiastic enough that she agreed to wait. Then she bitched and moaned for most of the two years because she hadn't really believed it would take that long. It was a nightmare keeping her focused on the end result, instead of the wait.''

''Was she satisfied in the end?''

Emily smiled. ''She was ecstatic, thank goodness. Especially when all her friends lavished compliments on her taste. She chose an oak cabinet with a formal design of flowers and ivy leaves, very different in style from this one you have, but still lovely. Personally I like your selection even better. I love the free-flowing feel of the carving on this piece.''

As if she couldn't bear to look away, Emily turned back to the armoire again, bending down to examine the depiction of a robin, perched on the end of a fallen tree trunk. ''God, he does magnificent work,'' she murmured, her fingers tracing the trademark J. C. Hunter signature. ''This piece is even more beautiful than the others I've seen. How long did you have to wait for this to be produced?''

''About three months.''

''Three months! That's all?'' Emily straightened in surprise. ''Hey, what's your inside track, Jordan? Care to share it with me? If I could get J. C. Hunter pieces in a three-month time frame, my success as an interior designer would be guaranteed.''

In the ten years since he'd founded the Woodcutters Workshop, Jordan had never felt the slightest need to explain the truth about how he made his living to his parents or to his older brother. But watching Emily's pleasure in something he had created, he found that keeping silent was impossible. Curiously, telling her the truth was hard to do.

''I know J. C. Hunter personally,'' he said at last.

''You do?'' She looked at him with new respect. ''I'm seriously impressed. I heard he was really young to be such a fine craftsman. Is that true?''

Jordan couldn't believe it, but he felt his cheeks grow hot. Lord almighty, he was blushing! This was crazy. He cleared his throat. "Well, I'm thirty-four. I guess that's pretty young to have run your own business for ten years. But remember, I dropped out of college when I was barely eighteen. So I was apprenticed to a cabinetmaker for six years before I branched out on my own."

She frowned, her gaze narrowing. "What has your age and your career got to do with J. C. Hunter?"

'Well quite a lot." Jordan cleared his throat again. He damn near shuffled his feet. "Actually, I am J. C. Hunter."

Emily's brown eyes widened, the gold flecks unusually prominent. "You're joking, right?"

He shook his head. "No."

"You're J. C. Hunter?" She swung around to look again at the armoire, and then back at him. "You made this?" She couldn't have appeared more astonished if he'd claimed to be the president of the United States, or Elvis, returned from the grave.

Hoping he didn't sound as lamebrained as he felt, Jordan expanded on his explanation. "The initials J.C. stand for Jordan Chambers. And Hunter was my grandmother's name. We were always very close, and she put up some of the capital I needed to get the business started, so I chose the name to honor her. She died two years ago, unfortunately, but she was a wonderful woman. I wish you could have met her."

Emily sat down hard on the bed, looking up at him as if she'd never seen him before. "You're really and truly J. C. Hunter?"

"Yes, I am."

She stared into space for several silent seconds, then she sprang up from the bed and rounded on him. But instead of looking impressed as he'd half hoped, she looked furious. "Does anyone in your family know that you're J. C. Hunter?"

"My grandmother—"

"But she's dead," Emily said ruthlessly. "What about the ones who are alive? Your parents, for example. Do they have any idea what you've achieved, and how successful you are? Do they recognize what amazing talent you have?"

Jordan tried to sound cynically amused, but suspected he sounded bitter instead. "My parents wouldn't recognize my talent if it turned into a dog and bit them on the ass."

"How do you know what their reaction would be?" Emily demanded. "Have you ever tried showing them what you've achieved, as opposed to making sure they believe the worst about you?"

He shrugged. "Of course not. They're much too happy imagining what a disastrous failure I've made of my life. I don't want to spoil their fun."

Far from being pacified, Emily's anger intensified. "What kind of a stupid answer is that? You must be some weird sort of masochist, Jordan. Why else would you allow your parents to ridicule you, and your brother to dismiss your work as if it's of no consequence? Why don't you want them to know you've achieved something extraordinary?"

"My parents have a very narrow view of how their sons should earn a living. Chambers men are supposed to wear starched shirts to work. They sure as heck don't go through a batch of towels a day mopping up sweat. Besides, my parents consider artists and con artists as words for virtually the same activity. If you think they would be happy to know that I'm successfully designing furniture, you're mistaken. When I was a teenager, I won several statewide contests for wood carvings that I'd done. My father was so embarrassed, he cringed when I brought home the winners' plaques. In his world, men who like to paint or sculpt must be gay. Which, of course, is about the worst fate he could imagine for a son of his."

Her eyes flashed fire. "In other words, you haven't told your parents what you do because you're punishing them. You're mad at them because they haven't ever made the effort to see you for the person you really are."

He lifted his shoulder in another dismissive shrug, although he was surprised at how accurate her assessment was. "I've invited both my parents to visit my factory, more than once. If either of them had ever taken me up on my offer, they'd have seen that I wasn't scraping a living by building a cheap line of mass-produced kitchen cabinets. The fact that neither one of them has ever bothered to come and see where I work speaks for itself, don't you think?"

"Yes," she admitted. "It does. You tested them, and they failed the test. They've hurt you."

"Maybe." Jordan could hear the harshness in his own voice. "I'll admit there's an element of 'screw you' in all this. My parents seem determined to believe I'm a failure, so I'm happy to leave them to their misconceptions."

"You have to tell them the truth, Jordan. You need to show them what you've achieved—"

"Why?"

"For your sake, not for theirs." Emily still sounded fierce. "You should take your success and rub their noses in it. Force them to acknowledge it."

Jordan gave a small smile. "Why, Emily, you almost sound as if you care."

"I do care," she said. "You have an amazing talent, Jordan. You've not only established a profitable business, you create furniture that will be treasured in people's homes for generations. That's something to be really proud of."

Jordan had won many design awards for his furniture and made enough money that he'd long ago convinced himself that his family's disdain was a matter of indiffer-

ence to him. Emily's lavish praise of his work was balm
to a wound he hadn't quite realized was there. Still, he was
uncomfortable discussing subjects that were usually off-
limits, and his relationship with his family was a subject
he took care never to examine. He was accustomed to easy
physical intimacy with women, but emotional intimacy
was something altogether different, and he had no clear
idea how he and Emily had ended up so swiftly in such a
private place.

Not sure how to handle a situation that was new for him
in every way, he spoke with studied casualness. "I was a
pain in the butt when I was a kid. Michael, on the other
hand, has always been the perfect Chambers offspring.
Now he's crowning his other achievements by campaigning to be governor of Texas. Under the circumstances, I
don't think my parents are likely to be impressed by the
news that I've acquired a decent reputation for cabinet-
making within the furniture industry."

"Well, they should be. Recognizing your achievements
doesn't undercut Michael's success. Besides, if they're
counting on Michael to burnish the Chambers reputation,
they're going to be disappointed. Governor Kincaid will
be reelected in a landslide, and then Michael will simply
be another ex-candidate searching for employment."

Jordan was surprised by her unequivocal verdict on an
election that was still months in the future. "That's not
what the polls predict. They're suggesting that Kincaid is
vulnerable."

"Do you think polls have any real meaning this far in
advance of the election? Voters aren't paying much attention right now, and Michael looks really good on camera,
but Kincaid has all the advantages of the incumbent. Plus,
he got elected in the first place because he promised to be
tough on organized crime, and he's been very effective in

securing convictions against mob figures. Voters like politicians who keep their promises.''

Jordan grinned. ''Yeah, I noticed Kincaid has been milking the conviction of J. B. Crowe for all it's worth. He can't give an interview without mentioning that the guy is finally getting the punishment he deserves, all thanks to Kincaid's administration.''

Emily nodded. ''And Kincaid has grabbed some great PR opportunities recently with his daughter and his new grandbaby. Alexandra. You see, I even remember the granddaughter's name because she's so cute. Michael can't compete with a cooing little baby granddaughter for voter affections. No man could.''

Jordan raised his eyebrow. ''You sound very sure of yourself. Yet Michael has plenty of moneymen lined up, and money doesn't usually flow to a potential loser.''

''Michael's strength is in pleasing the moneymen, but he's only just started to take his campaign direct to the voters. And Texan voters are smart enough to see that he isn't offering them anything very exciting.''

''Maybe he doesn't have to be exciting to win. Kincaid has had his problems as well as his successes, after all. Michael could win by default, simply because he's not Kincaid.''

Emily shook her head. ''Even though the economy's strong, voters still care about educational reform, and child care for working mothers, and health care for poor families. But Michael's not the right man to capitalize on Kincaid's weakness in those areas.''

''I disagree. Michael's plenty smart enough to exploit any vulnerability his opponent shows.''

''Smart has nothing to do with it. You can't be effective when you're operating from a script, instead of speaking from your heart. Michael needs to care about the issues in his gut, not just because Jeff Greiff has written him a position paper. The truth is, Michael doesn't care about anything in the sort of visceral way that would connect him to the voters. He's too damned patrician to get all sweaty and worked up over policy issues. The whole time we were engaged, I never heard Michael speak with heartfelt conviction on a single public policy issue. Capital punishment? 'Well, Emily, there are sound arguments on both sides.' Gun control? 'It's a Second Amendment issue, Emily. Nothing for me to take a stand on.'" She gave a frustrated sigh. "Heck, I used to get hotter under the collar than he did!"

Jordan sent her an amused glance. "You sound as if you want my brother to get some good old-fashioned fire in his belly. And start breathing it out on anyone who gets within range."

"I sure do," Emily said. "But Michael is going to campaign strictly according to the plan laid out by the political pros. He wants to be governor because he wants to be governor. That's not a reason to run for office, and Texan voters for sure aren't going to elect him just because he feels the Chambers family is owed the governorship by virtue of hereditary entitlement."

Jordan sat down on the bed. "A cynic might suggest that the fact my brother dumped you hours before the wedding has affected your view of how likely he is to win the election."

"Then the cynic would be wrong. I've changed my opinion about a lot of things since Friday morning, but I never thought Michael had a realistic chance of winning the race for governor."

"Funny. I always assumed you wanted to be the First Lady of Texas."

"No." Emily spoke with total conviction. "I'm very interested in some of the issues that politicians have to deal with, but being a politician's wife is definitely not my idea of fun.''

"In that case, exactly why did you agree to marry my brother?''

Color crept into Emily's cheeks. "You can't believe that I might have been in love with him?''

"No. Sorry, Em. I watched the two of you together for three months. I'm damn sure you weren't in love with my brother. Not with the sort of fire and passion you were just talking about, anyway.''

"Perhaps not,'' she conceded. "But at the time we got engaged, we seemed compatible. As far as I'm concerned, that counts a lot in making a marriage successful.''

"There must be a hundred bachelors in San Antonio that you would find compatible as live-in companions. Maybe a thousand. Why pick Michael?''

She sighed. "The truth's pretty humiliating, but if you must know, I've realized over the past few days that I accepted Michael's proposal chiefly because my friends all considered him to be the state's most eligible bachelor.''

"I wouldn't have figured you as a woman who would marry just to show that she can win the prize,'' Jordan said quietly. "You're smart, beautiful, sexy and you have a job you're good at and obviously like. Why would you want to marry Michael—or any other man for that matter—unless you loved him deeply?''

Emily hesitated, and Jordan fully expected her to say something evasive, or even to put an end to a conversation that was cutting closer to the bone than either of them had been prepared for. But once again, she surprised him by answering with evident honesty.

"My attitude toward marriage has always been more practical than most other people's, I guess. I never wanted to fall deeply in love. I still don't. I like to feel in control of myself, and being in love means by definition that you're out of control. Passion causes people to do things that they'll live to regret. I want no part of it.''

He wondered if she realized just how much she was revealing about herself with those few brief—and sad—sentences. ''Being in love and feeling passionate sexual desire can also bring people a lot of happiness.''

''For five minutes,'' Emily said tersely. ''And then, all too often, innocent people are left behind to face the consequences.''

He took her hands into his, reacting instinctively to the pain in her voice. ''I get the feeling you're talking about your own life experiences, Em, rather than discussing general principles.''

''Maybe I am.'' She looked down, but didn't make any attempt to withdraw her hands from his grasp.

''Talk to me, Em. Tell me what happened. Did some man you loved let you down? Treat you badly?''

''No,'' she replied quickly. So quickly that he guessed this time, at least, she wasn't telling the truth.

''Then what?'' he pressed.

In the process of avoiding his gaze, she finally noticed his fireplace, and walked over to it, running her hand absently over the rough stones. ''This is lovely,'' she said. ''I like the flashes of pyrite in some of the stones. It makes an interesting contrast with the lichen.''

''I'm glad you like it, and I'm not going to be that easy to distract, Em. We were talking about you. How about explaining what you have against the idea of love and passion?''

''It's not something that's quick or easy to explain.''

''You know, if you use real simple words and I concentrate hard, I bet I can understand. I'll give it my best shot, anyway.''

She sent him an apologetic glance. ''Okay, I'll try to explain.'' She walked over to the window, stared out for a moment at the view of the meadow, then turned, wrapping her arms around her waist as if for comfort. "I expect you already know I'm adopted."

"Yes. Michael mentioned that to me, months ago."

"Well, according to the adoption agency that placed me with the Suttons, my birth mother was a college student at the University of Texas. That means she was clever enough, and educated enough, to hold down a decent job. It also means that when she discovered she was pregnant with me, she could have found a way to support me if she'd wanted to."

"You can't know that for sure, Em. I've heard lots of stories about the way adoption agencies lied about the backgrounds of the birth mothers. She could have been in truly desperate straits."

"That's true, and I've realized for a while now that my mother may not have been the cute college cheerleader the agency tried to pretend." Emily pushed impatiently at a lock of hair that had fallen into her eyes. "Maybe she was dying of leukemia or something. I know she wasn't married because the agency only accepted single moms. But whatever the truth about her circumstances, it all boils down to the fact that for the sake of a few minutes of physical gratification, my birth mother created a human being that she didn't want, and didn't care about enough to keep."

"I know it must be hard to live with the knowledge that your mother couldn't keep you, but I think you're being surprisingly judgmental on the basis of very few facts."

Emily didn't want to consider the possibility that her attitude was both too harsh and too simplistic. "However you look at it, I was a mistake, an annoying by-product of my mother's sexual desire for some self-absorbed college student. As for my father, he obviously took no interest in me at all. He had an itch. He scratched it. End of story."

Emily drew in an unsteady breath. "Is it surprising if I don't think sexual desire is worth the possible consequences?"

Jordan wondered if Emily had any idea how hurt and desolate she sounded. "You can't really know the circumstances your mother faced. The only thing you know for sure is that she cared enough about you not to have an abortion."

"Which could be for a dozen reasons," Emily said wearily. "Maybe she didn't even realize she was pregnant until it was too late to get rid of me."

"Could be." Jordan knew Emily wouldn't be consoled if he tried to offer her facile or false comfort. "But if I were you, I'd give your mother the benefit of the doubt. You don't really know whether she gave you up because she didn't want to keep you, or for some other reason entirely. Sometimes the bare facts can hide an awful lot of important information, Em. It could have been a heartbreaking sacrifice for your birth mother to hand you over to the adoption agency."

"I know." She tried to smile. "I really do know all that, Jordan, at least at some level. And I'm not usually this neurotic, I promise. You seem to have caught me in one of my more self-pitying moods. Anyway, right or wrong, the facts of my birth have affected how I view marriage and sex and probably a bunch of other stuff, too. I'm not neurotic about sex—"

She broke off and managed a small grin. "Okay, so I'm just a little bit neurotic about sex. Casual sex, anyway. But I believed with the right man, once I felt really secure, we could have a pretty good marriage. Even the sexual part of it."

"And you thought Michael was the right man," Jordan said.

She nodded. "Yes, I did, and the fact that I wasn't

deeply, passionately in love with him didn't seem any reason not to accept his proposal. I wanted a marriage based on shared interests and shared goals. We have the same circle of friends. Whatever else you can say about Michael's campaign for governor, he's working hard at it. I admired that dedication to his goal. My parents liked him. I knew they'd be thrilled if I accepted his proposal—''

"I hope to God you didn't agree to marry Michael to please your parents."

She sent him a wry smile. "No, not really. At the time he proposed, I thought marrying Michael was exactly what I wanted out of life. Then he got so wrapped up in raising funds for his campaign, and I was so busy organizing our wedding that we scarcely ever saw each other unless there were scads of other people around. Who had time to worry about trivial stuff like whether we actually liked each other? Much less loved each other."

"Michael must have found the time to think about the relationship," Jordan said.

"Yes, you're right, otherwise I would be married to him and we wouldn't be having this conversation." Emily gave a laugh that was rich in self-mockery. "How ironic to think that Michael was actually more in touch with his true feelings than I was."

"I wouldn't say ironic," Jordan said. "I would say it was damn lucky. For all of us."

CHAPTER TEN

THE SUN PUSHING ITS WAY through the slats of the wooden blinds woke Emily early on Saturday morning, just as it had for each of the preceding six days of her honeymoon. Stretching lazily, she lay for a few minutes beneath the covers, drowsy and content, debating the merits of getting up or going back to sleep. Finally, the smell of freshly brewed coffee wafting upstairs from the kitchen tempted her out of bed and into the shower.

She stood, letting the hot water pound her shoulders, working out the kinks. Yesterday, she and Jordan had gone white-water rafting, a new experience for her, and the muscles in the top of her arms were protesting the unfamiliar exercise in no uncertain terms. Still, considering the hours they'd spent navigating rapids that Emily swore were only slightly less ferocious than Niagara Falls, she wouldn't have been surprised to wake up this morning with her body paralyzed from head to toe. Anyway, she had no complaints. Yesterday had been such fun that stiff shoulder muscles seemed a small price to pay for the spectacular adventure of shooting rapids through a narrow river canyon, while the sun blazed overhead and swirling freshwater spray cooled her hot skin.

Pulling on shorts and a matching cotton top scattered with poppies—an outfit originally intended to wow folks on the beaches of Tahiti—Emily tugged a brush through her hair and went downstairs, eager for the day ahead. Shivering a little as the cold tile of the kitchen floor struck her bare feet, she poured herself a mug of coffee and carried it out onto the deck where Jordan was sitting, a book resting on his knees. The air was cool, but the sun had already heated the deck and the cedar planks felt warm beneath her toes.

Jordan looked up as she crossed to her favorite chair, sending her a lazy smile. "Morning, Em. You look rested. Sleep well?"

"Wonderfully, thanks. How about you?"

He yawned. "Mmm...pretty well. But I guess I need another cup of coffee before I feel really awake."

He stood up and headed inside. There was something innately purposeful about Jordan, Emily reflected, even when he was doing nothing more important than ambling toward the kitchen in search of coffee. She didn't realize she was staring at him until he turned to give her another smile.

Her body responded with a flash of inner heat that stunned her. She sat down quickly and took a gulp of coffee hot enough to scald her tongue. Even so, it required a good few seconds before she could talk herself back into a rational frame of mind.

Okay, so she was physically attracted to Jordan. But the fact that she was drawn to him said nothing at all about the wisdom of acting on that attraction. Despite the wonderful few days they'd spent together, the fundamentals of their relationship hadn't changed. Their marriage was still a sham, destined to end as soon as Michael's campaign for governor was well under way. More to the point, she still needed security in her relationships more than any other quality, and Jordan was the last man on earth to offer her that.

These perfect lazy days alone with him had allowed her to get acquainted with the man she'd married, and she liked the real Jordan Chambers a whole lot better than the caricature of him that she'd carried around during her engagement to Michael. But she couldn't allow his low-key, offbeat charm to disguise the fact that they weren't well suited as a couple.

She was the ultimate conservative, cautious to a fault. Jordan, on the other hand, saw what he wanted from life, took it and then moved on. To hell with the risks. To hell with the possibility of failure. To hell with regrets for the road not taken. That what he wanted from life was something much more admirable than Emily had once imagined didn't alter the fact that he was about as far removed as any man could be from the solid, reliable, risk-averse husband she had always planned to marry.

Enjoy the moment. That had been Emily's motto for the past week. An unusual one for her, given her obsession with caution and long-range planning. Still, her makeshift motto had worked out pretty well, so far. Once she and Jordan were back in San Antonio, the problems of real life would crowd in, demanding resolution. But for now, she had one more day of freedom, one more day during which she could allow herself to live in the moment, enjoying whatever the day brought, without worrying about the future.

Equilibrium restored, Emily put her mug down on a small side table, then sat cross-legged on the lounger, with her toes tucked under her. Jordan came back out onto the deck, but he didn't speak and neither did she. His silence gave her a few more welcome minutes to pull herself together. Closing her eyes, she breathed in crisp mountain air, letting the sun soak into her skin. She heard the whirr of a hummingbird's wings and opened her eyes just in time to see the passing flash of iridescent green plumage.

"I can't believe we're going back to San Antonio tomorrow," she murmured, beguiled by the bird into forgetting to guard her tongue. The prospect of leaving the cocoon of Jordan's mountain home brought a feeling of regret that would have seemed impossible a week earlier.

"The week's gone fast," Jordan agreed.

"Mmm." She sighed. "I could stay here for another hundred years or so, no problem."

"Or at least until the first major blizzard hits." His voice was warm with laughter.

She pushed her hair out of her eyes and sat up in order to direct a mock glare at him. "You underestimate me, Jordan. As long as you're the designated driver for hauling in supplies, I would cope superbly with a blizzard or two. Besides, now that I have white-water rafting down pat, I'm all set to learn the skiing thing. Raring to go, in fact."

"I wouldn't exactly say that you've conquered the finer techniques of white-water navigation, Em. The idea is to stay out of the water and inside the raft."

"I didn't drown, did I?"

"No, but that's only because I was there to rescue you."

"What an arrogant beast you are," Emily said mildly. "I'd throw a cushion at you or something, if I had a drop of energy to spare."

"Lucky for you that you don't. I'm planning to take you to The Brasserie in Elk Run for our farewell dinner tonight. It's a very special place, and if you're a smart woman, you'll keep on my good side until you've tasted their chocolate torte. It's called Divinity for a reason."

She quashed a little tremor of regret at the words *farewell dinner*. "It's that terrific, huh?"

"It's definitely that terrific, a legend in the county. If it weren't for the fact that the owners want one of my cabinets for their main dining room, I'd never have gotten a reservation at such short notice. You need to be very, very nice to me today."

She gave a mock sigh. "For chocolate torte, I guess a girl can make sacrifices."

"A smart decision, Em." Jordan came and stood behind her, pressing his thumbs against the aching muscles in the vicinity of her collarbone. "Let me do that. Yesterday's rafting looks as if it got to you." His fingers rotated outward in a probing sweep, massaging away the pain.

She hadn't realized that she'd been rubbing her left shoulder until Jordan took over the job. The touch of his hands on her bare skin was simultaneously electrifying and soothing, and for a few moments she surrendered to the sensations he was creating, not allowing herself to question her reaction.

Then years of self-discipline kicked in. She might be sexually inexperienced, but she wasn't a fool. Since the day they'd arrived here—ever since they'd exchanged those troublesome kisses—she'd been aware that her physical attraction to Jordan was building inexorably. There was a constant sexual charge to their dealings that had been entirely absent from her relationship with Michael, and Emily didn't like that charge one bit. Sexual desire tempted women into making foolish decisions that weren't in their long-term best interests. The sensations Jordan was arousing in her right now could rapidly become the sort of dangerous prelude that she'd spent the past six years avoiding.

Emily ordered herself to stand up, collect their coffee mugs and make some cheerful, offhand remark about their plans for the day. Somehow, though, she couldn't quite bring herself to walk away from the shivery pleasure of Jordan's touch. She compromised by holding herself rigidly upright, resisting the temptation to lean back against him while his hands worked their magic. To relax, she knew, would be tempting fate.

If Jordan had spoken, if he'd said anything at all, the spell would have been broken and she would have walked away. But he didn't speak, and the silence pressed in on her, magnifying the thrill—and the surprising comfort—brought by his touch. Tilting her face up to the sun, she closed her eyes and pretended that she didn't notice the moment when he finally coaxed her rigid spine to relax.

Inevitably, her back connected with Jordan's chest. The steady rhythm of his massage faltered for an instant, then continued as before.

Still neither of them spoke. Gradually Jordan's fingers ranged more widely, the stroking motion becoming blatantly caressing. Despite Emily's best efforts at self-deception, when his hands moved downward to cup her breasts, she could no longer keep up the pretense that what he was doing had any connection to massaging overtaxed muscles. Jordan was attempting, with significant skill and patience, to seduce her.

More alarming than his attempt was the fact that he was succeeding. Dramatically succeeding. What she felt right at this moment was skin-tingling, stomach-clenching, pulse-pounding sexual desire. Liberally seasoned with panic and a heady sense of anticipation.

The moment Emily acknowledged how far she'd already walked down the forbidden path, she froze. She wasn't allowed to feel desire. If the circumstances of her birth weren't warning enough of the havoc wreaked by uncontrolled passion, she'd had the lesson rammed home when she was in college. Shawn Dooley, her one and only lover, had taught her a lesson she'd sworn never to forget.

Emily stumbled to her feet, backing away from Jordan until she bumped into the railing that surrounded the deck. "I have—I have to go upstairs," she muttered, although her blood was still humming and her feet seemed to have forgotten how to move.

"Not yet." Jordan's voice held a dangerously rough edge, a note she'd never heard before. Her panic increased, but so did the delicious, tempting sense of anticipation.

He crossed to stand in front of her. "We aren't finished yet."

Before Emily could protest, Jordan tipped her head back and kissed her long and slow and deep. Her body, already seriously aroused, simply melted against his. She seemed to dissolve into the kiss, into the erotic warmth and intimacy of it. She could feel tenderness buried beneath his all-too-evident expertise, and that tenderness captivated her in a way nothing else could have. In Jordan's arms, with his mouth on hers, she found herself dreaming dreams that would never have survived her coolheaded scrutiny otherwise.

Her fantasies became more and more vivid, and much too tempting. Emily realized that she had to break off their kiss now, or she wouldn't have the strength of will to prevent what would follow. A mere ten days ago, Jordan had been nothing more than her fiancé's brother, a man she held in contempt. A week ago, he'd become her husband, a man to whom she owed a debt of gratitude but nothing else. Over the past few days, as they began to know each other, he'd become something close to a friend.

She'd welcomed that final change, even though she'd found it unsettling. But the sort of kisses they were exchanging right now had nothing remotely to do with friendship. They had to do exclusively with passion and lust and torrid sex. They had to do with eager hands reaching out, and overheated bodies writhing in a darkened room until they finally joined in climactic union.

Emily shuddered, tearing herself out of Jordan's embrace. She wasn't repelled—no, she wanted that hot, sweaty, earthy coming-together. She wanted it badly. For the first time in years, she longed to let down her guard and open herself to a man. She wanted to lie naked in Jordan's arms while he made love to her, slowly inciting her to climax. She wanted to be taken with passion, and in return she wanted to rouse Jordan to a level of passion he had never before experienced. She wanted to exercise power over him: the power to make him crave possession of her body.

And that was precisely the problem. Jordan made her feel everything that was forbidden. This week with him had shown her that far from being sexually indifferent, she was all too capable of feeling intense, consuming lust. Ever since her inglorious affair with Shawn, she'd been afraid that she'd inherited the genes that would make her vulnerable to sexual need, and here was the proof that she'd dreaded. A few days in Jordan's company, a few casual caresses, a couple of impassioned kisses, and she teetered right on the brink of begging him to take her to bed.

Jordan moved toward her again, and Emily scrambled to put her defenses in order. She held out her hands, gesturing him away, her mind made up. "No, we have to stop.... I don't want to do this, Jordan. It would be a bad mistake."

"From where I'm standing, it sure doesn't feel like a mistake. For either of us."

She gained a fleeting impression that she'd hurt his feelings, and although that didn't seem possible, Emily decided that there was no way to handle this situation other than with a healthy dose of honesty. She owed Jordan at least that much. "It's not that I don't enjoy kissing you—"

"Because you do."

"Yes," she admitted. "When you kiss me, I get very aroused, very fast. But that's irrelevant."

Jordan sent her a look that was frankly incredulous. "On the contrary, I would have said it was all that mattered."

"Not to me," Emily said. She tried to find words that would make him understand. "Our marriage is a mistake, and getting too intimate will only compound the mistake.

I know your motives were kind when you offered to marry me, but I should never have accepted—"

His gaze narrowed. "Has the past week been that horrible?"

"It's been wonderful." She was afraid that breathless comment sounded far too heartfelt, and so she rushed on. "But that doesn't alter the fact that my reasons for getting married were totally ridiculous. I think I must have been in shock after Michael broke off our engagement, if I can use that as an excuse for behaving so stupidly."

"You're too hard on yourself," Jordan said, leaning against the deck railing. "Under the circumstances, it's not surprising if you felt overwhelmed. And emotionally battered, too."

"Maybe. But in retrospect, I've no idea why I was so obsessed with the need to avoid offending 350 wedding guests. It was absurd to get so worked up about something so relatively trivial in the grand scheme of things. I mean, who cares if the wedding guests turned up and there was no wedding? If I'd been thinking with even half a brain, I would have told my parents the truth, then taken off with Carolyn St. Clair for a quick vacation and left Michael to explain to everyone why he didn't want to marry me anymore."

"If you wanted to destroy his campaign for governor, that's what you could have done. But you're much too honorable to leave Michael in the lurch like that, however badly he'd behaved."

Emily shook her head. "I wish I deserved the compliment, Jordan, but you're giving me way too much credit. When Michael told me he wanted out of our engagement, I thought a lot about my parents, and how upset they'd be, but your brother's campaign for governor didn't figure in my calculations at all." After a moment's pause, she added, "However, now that I know you better, I'm sure it figured in yours."

"What do you mean?" Jordan asked.

"I've been trying to work out why you offered to marry me," Emily explained. "I realized a couple of days ago that you most likely proposed as a way to help save your brother's election campaign."

"You're wrong. Michael's desire to be governor of Texas played even less of a role for me than it did for you."

She smiled wryly, shaking her head. "Nice try, Jordan. A week ago I might have believed you. Now I know better."

"Trust me. I'm not the noble person you're trying to invent. Not at all."

"Okay, if you insist, I'll agree you're a sleazeball who married me for... Fill in the blank, Jordan." She sent him a challenging look. "Now that I know you better, I don't believe you give a damn about the money at stake in the Laurel Acres project, so why did you marry me if not to help out your brother?"

"I do care about Laurel Acres," he said. "My family and yours both have a lot of money tied up in the success of that project. It's really important to both of them that this deal should succeed."

"And you cared enough about that money—that deal—to ask me to marry you?"

He hesitated. "No," he said finally.

"Then if not because of Michael or the Laurel Acres project, why did you propose to me, Jordan?"

He directed a look toward her that Emily couldn't interpret. "It seemed like the smart thing to do at the time," he said.

Emily was neither surprised nor offended by his evasive answer. Jordan didn't want to admit that he'd stepped into the breach in order to save his brother, but she knew her husband well enough by now to realize that he routinely demonstrated a great deal more loyalty toward his family than they showed to him. The fact that he consistently downplayed his efforts to help out was one of his more endearing characteristics.

"You can protest all you want, Jordan. I still suspect you proposed to me because you were trying to pick up the pieces after Michael smashed them."

He gave her a wry smile. "Ten days ago you weren't willing to believe I had any redeeming value at all. Now you have me ready for sainthood. Maybe in another few days you'll be ready to think about me as a regular human being."

"Okay, it's a deal. Let's admit that we're both human, and prone to making mistakes even when we mean well. Which is probably why we have a major screwup on our hands right now."

"I don't see the screwup."

"Our marriage is the screwup," she said softly. "The point is that I'm determined not to compound our mutual mistakes. We're married now, and since the deed is done, we might as well stick it out for the next few months. But let's not muddle the situation even more by introducing sex into a mixture that's already volatile. When Michael's campaign is safely off the ground, I want us to be able to walk away from each other good friends. I really want that—"

"I've never found that friendship and sex are mutually exclusive," Jordan said tersely. "On the contrary."

His words touched an exposed nerve in Emily. She had always cherished the dream that one day she might find a man who would be not only her lover, but also her best friend. Her engagement to Michael had been a tacit admission that in the entire twenty-seven years of her life, nobody had come close to filling that role, not even Shawn Dooley, her one and only lover.

Shawn had been the graduate student, sports jock, Big Man on Campus who'd initiated Emily into the wonders of sex, then taken her on a swift ride through love and romance, getting her pregnant along the way. The final stop had been the point of abandonment her birth mother had once faced. Unlike her birth mother, though, fate had stepped in, and twenty-one-year-old Emily had miscarried her unplanned baby when she was five weeks pregnant.

Those few weeks of unplanned pregnancy had been quite long enough for Shawn to make it plain that, as far as he was concerned, abortion was the only acceptable answer to the situation Emily found herself in. A situation for which he refused to accept any responsibility whatsoever....

"YOU TOLD ME you were on the pill," he said angrily, when she informed him that the home pregnancy test was positive.

"I was, Shawn. You know that the last thing I wanted was to get pregnant. I took the pill correctly, I promise. I never forgot, or took it too late in the day—"

"Then you can't be pregnant," he said flatly.

"Pills aren't a hundred percent effective as a method of birth control," Emily said miserably. *"Nothing is. About two women in a thousand will get pregnant, even taking the pills exactly as prescribed."*

She wanted to cry, but she had too much pride to break down in front of this cold-faced and angry stranger. A stranger who had taken her virginity, shared her bed for the past four months, sweet-talked about the future. And had, apparently, never cared for her at all.

Shawn glowered at her. "So how come we get to be the unlucky couple who prove the statistics?"

"I don't know. Somebody has to be the one who gets pregnant, I guess. Honestly, I would never have chosen for this to happen, Shawn—"

"Then end it. Shit, Emily, if you need money for the abortion, I'll help you out. Anything else, and you're on your own. You know my situation, and I never pretended I was ready to settle down. My dad walked out on us when I was twelve. When he left, my youngest brother was still in diapers. My mother doesn't have a dime to spare, and there are three more boys to put through school. I need to get my career established and pay off my tuition loans. There is zero room in my plans for a kid right now."

"I realize that—"

"There won't be room for years, maybe never. I'll be honest with you, Emily. After raising three younger brothers, the idea of having kids does absolutely nothing for me."

"I understand your situation. Truly, I do. I'm not asking you to marry me. I just need you to give me a little emotional support."

Shawn clicked his tongue impatiently. *"You don't need emotional support, whatever the hell that means. What you need right now is smart advice. And here it is. Have an abortion. Put this pregnancy behind you and get on with the rest of your life."*

"I can't, Shawn." Emily choked back a sob. *"I'm not going to have an abortion or put the baby up for adoption."* Shawn's total lack of understanding was making her angry. *"I'm going to keep her. Or him. It's my baby and I'm not going to give my baby away. I just can't."*

He shrugged. *"Okay, have it your way. It's your pregnancy, Emily. Your call. But it's not a smart decision, in my opinion. And I'm telling you now, up front, I want no part of it, and I'm not going to give you one penny of support."*

His words effectively ended their relationship and destroyed any romantic dreams Emily had been cherishing about Shawn playing an active role in raising their child. She'd still been working up the courage to tell Raelene and Sam the truth when she'd started to miscarry the baby.

Strangely, even though she'd dreaded everything about her pregnancy and been terrified of the prospect of single motherhood, Emily was devastated by the loss. She knew that she wasn't ready emotionally, financially or any other way to care for a child. But reason didn't have much to do with what she felt as she watched her baby bleed out of her womb.

Grief had kept her shut in her room, not eating, not sleeping, not even crying, and the Emily Sutton who emerged from the dorm just in time to take her final exams was a very different woman from the Emily Sutton of five weeks earlier....

EMILY FELT the brush of Jordan's finger against her cheek and realized she was crying. Crying, she discovered, for old hurts that had never healed properly, because they'd been buried deep for more than six years, festering instead of healing.

"What is it?" Jordan asked. "You left me. You were about a million miles away."

"Not quite that far." Emily banished Shawn and her miscarriage to the past. Maybe she needed to take some of those feelings out and examine them again, but this wasn't the time or the place.

Emotions once again under firm control, she spoke briskly. "Jordan, we've spent a terrific week together, you and I. I've had a great time, and I've really enjoyed your company. We only have one more day together and then we have to go back to San Antonio and face our friends, our work. This last day here is special. Let's not complicate things between us. Please?''

Jordan looked down at her, his gaze dark, his expression inscrutable. "It's a deal," he said. "We won't complicate things between us. As a matter of fact, I've always believed in keeping things simple.''

For some reason, Emily didn't find his answer one bit reassuring.

CHAPTER ELEVEN

DURING THE YEARS he worked undercover for the Dallas police force, Dylan Garrett had been too busy staying alive to waste much time wondering if he enjoyed his work. The height of his ambition had been to avoid getting killed, while putting criminals behind bars where they could do no further damage to law-abiding citizens.

Since establishing Finders Keepers with his twin sister, Lily, his aims had become more diffuse, and in some ways more difficult to achieve. He still wanted to make a difference in people's lives, but he wanted to enjoy himself in the process. When he and Lily discussed their goals in starting the agency, he had even mentioned his hope that he might actually find time for a personal life.

That hope quickly proved an illusion. Ever since he'd taken on the case of Julie Matthews Cooper, the missing wife of his friend Sebastian Cooper, Dylan felt as if he'd been spinning his wheels, running at top speed simply to crash into one frustrating dead end after another.

It had reached the point that he couldn't even think about Julie without getting a knot in his gut the size of a huge fist. Although having his gut tied in knots wasn't too much of a change where Julie was concerned, Dylan thought wryly. She'd been driving him quietly crazy since he met her during his junior year in college, and her power to mess with his emotions had increased exponentially ever since.

It had been bad enough two years ago when she married

Sebastian Cooper, his longtime friend. It was even worse now that she had mysteriously disappeared. Dylan couldn't—wouldn't—consider the possibility that Julie, the golden girl of his fantasies, might be dead.

The San Antonio police were convinced that she was the victim of some unspecified accident and, in Dylan's opinion, they weren't putting enough resources behind the investigation of her whereabouts. He had just come from a meeting with Bill Myers of the San Antonio homicide division, a cop who'd qualified as detective at the same time as Dylan himself. Bill was a good guy, a hard worker, but he lacked the spark of imagination that was necessary for cracking the really tough cases. Bill worked by the rules and followed the instruction manual to the letter, so Dylan hadn't been surprised this morning when Bill insisted the latest reassessment of the evidence pointed to the firm conclusion that Julie Cooper was dead.

Listening to the detective's verdict, Dylan had bitten his tongue, shoved his hands into his pockets, counted to a hundred, and just managed to avoid telling Bill that the cops were being played for suckers. Far from being firm, the evidence for Julie's death was vague, conflicting and inconclusive. In Dylan's opinion, it was precisely the sort of evidence somebody might plant, hoping that the authorities would be dumb enough to fall for it.

The police seemed to have obliged by tumbling headlong into the traps set for them, but Dylan wasn't so easily fooled. And it wasn't just because he was still so much in love with Julie Cooper that his heart damn near stopped beating every time he considered the possibility that her body might be rotting at the bottom of the San Antonio River. No. His reasons for doubt were a smidgen more professional than that. In his considered opinion, the evidence of her death was simply too circumstantial to be convincing.

Given that he clung to the belief that Julie Cooper was alive, the question Dylan found most urgent was who wanted to convince people that she was dead? Was she being held against her will, for some as yet unspecified purpose? Or had she disappeared voluntarily? And if she'd chosen to disappear, what the hell reason could she have had for causing her husband and friends such terrible worry?

The harder Dylan wrestled with that problem, the further away he seemed to get from finding any acceptable answers.

In the meantime, the only solid fact he had to work with was one he didn't like at all: namely, that since the day Julie went missing, not one worthwhile clue had surfaced as to where she might be. Dead or alive.

And if that wasn't enough to keep him awake at night, as an added bonus, Sebastian was almost driving him completely insane with daily demands for an update on the status of the investigation. At one point Dylan had thought Sebastian might be giving up hope, accepting that Julie would never come back. But his behavior lately had dispelled those doubts. Sebastian cared deeply about his wife, and would never rest until she was found. Which left Dylan in the ironic position of busting his gut to find the woman he loved so that he could have the dubious satisfaction of seeing her welcomed back into another man's arms.

Trying hard not to dwell on any of these multiple ironies, Dylan strode along San Antonio's famous River Walk, anxious not to be late for his meeting with Emily Sutton. Two boatloads of tourists chugged past him in opposite directions, but he was so accustomed to the colorful sight that he barely noticed them, and the guides' running commentaries impinged as nothing more than background noise.

Rounding a sidewalk tub of cascading petunias, he dragged his thoughts away from Julie's disappearance and made a quick mental inventory of the status of his search for Emily's birth mother—another case that was currently frustrating him. What should have been a routine investigation was proving to be a great deal more difficult than he'd anticipated. He'd arranged this meeting with Emily partly because he'd promised her an update as soon as she returned from her honeymoon, but also because he needed to find out if she had any clue as to who—apart from herself—might be interested in finding out the details of her birth. Because somebody had been poking around in the entrails of her past, Dylan was sure of it.

With five minutes to spare, Dylan arrived at Perk at the Park, his favorite coffee shop on the River Walk. He took a seat under the welcome shade of a giant green-striped umbrella and read through today's handwritten menu.

When he returned to San Antonio to open his own investigative agency, he'd started coming to Perk at the Park because the place was owned by Kelly Adams, an old friend, and he wanted to support her business venture. He continued to come because she sold the best coffee, sandwiches and home-baked cookies in San Antonio.

He was just about to request a glass of ice water while he waited for Emily to arrive when he saw her crossing one of the bridges that spanned the river. He stood up and waved to attract her attention, and she sent him an answering wave, along with a quick smile. She looked fabulous, Dylan thought. The copper highlights in her thick, wavy chestnut hair gleamed in the sunlight, and her skin glowed with the sort of perfect light-bronze tan that usually occurred only in magazine advertisements for suntan lotion.

Her honeymoon had agreed with her, Dylan reflected, watching as she came closer. At their first meeting, Emily had struck him as an exceptionally pretty woman, but she'd projected not an ounce—not an atom—of sexual allure, living up to her reputation as the elegant Ice Princess of San Antonio society. The elegance was still there, but now, even at a distance, she radiated an aura of subtle sensuality.

Jordan Chambers must be almost as amazing a lover as his reputation suggested, Dylan thought with a touch of silent amusement.

"Hi, Dylan. I hope I haven't kept you waiting too long?" Emily entered the welcome shade of the umbrellas, pushing her sunglasses up onto her head as she shook his hand. Despite his love for Julie, Dylan felt himself respond briefly to the tug of Emily's new sexual charisma.

"Well, if it isn't Mrs. Chambers," he said, shaking her hand and smiling as he used her married name.

She stared at him blankly for a moment, then gave a quiet laugh. "Every time someone calls me Mrs. Chambers, I have to resist the urge to peek over my shoulder to see if my mother-in-law is standing behind me."

He grinned. "An old married woman like you should be used to it by now."

"I think it might take more than a week or so to get used to being married," Emily said with feeling.

"So I've heard." Dylan pulled out a chair for her. "My godparents celebrated their fortieth wedding anniversary in May, and they tell me with that hurdle behind them, they're hoping to get their newlywed bumps smoothed out sometime real soon."

Emily laughed and Dylan handed her the menu.

"Have you had lunch already?" he asked. "I know it's late, but I haven't had time to eat anything since I grabbed a stale granola bar at six this morning."

"I already had lunch with my parents, thanks. But you go ahead and eat, Dylan, and I'll keep you company with an iced coffee. I saw a man at the table next to us order one for himself, and it looked great.''

"Kelly makes the best coffee in town," Dylan said. "And customizes it to taste. Do you like yours extra strong? With extra milk? Extra ice? Want to indulge in a scoop of mocha ice cream?''

"I'll pass on the ice cream, but some extra foamed milk would be wonderful.''

"Coming up," Dylan said. "Excuse me for a couple of minutes while I give Kelly our order, will you? This place is strictly self-service.''

Dylan ordered himself a roast beef sandwich and a glass of fresh-squeezed lemonade, carrying his meal back to the table along with Emily's iced coffee.

"Okay, let's get straight to business," he said, offering her the sugar and then unfolding his napkin. "I'm very glad you could find time to meet with me today. I have some news for you—''

"You've found my mother?" Emily turned pale beneath her tan, her coffee spoon suspended in midair.

"No, not that," he said quickly. "I'm sorry to have raised false hopes." Putting down her spoon, Emily pressed her hand against her rib cage and drew in a deep breath. "It's okay. I jumped to conclusions. It was nothing you said.''

Dylan watched, relieved to see the color slowly return to her cheeks.

"I never realized how important this search was to me until just now," Emily said. "I guess I really do care a lot about finding my mother. Funny, even though I hired you specifically to make the search, I never knew how badly I wanted to see her. To talk to her just once, you know? Even if she never wants to see me again after our first meeting….''

Dylan sent her a sympathetic glance. "We'll get there,

Emily. It takes time and perseverance, that's all. And right now, it looks as if it's going to take a little more time and perseverance than I anticipated. Let me tell you what I've done so far.''

"Yes, please.''

"In detective work, it's always smart to start with what you know for sure and work outward from there. We know two things about the circumstances of your birth with more or less certainty. Namely that your birth date is March 16, 1974, and that you were adopted through Lutheran Family Services of San Antonio—''

"Which is now defunct, of course, so it's not a very useful piece of information.''

"More useful than you might think,'' Dylan said. "It wasn't hard to find a record of all the people who were working at the agency in the first half of 1974. Once I had a complete list of the employees, tracking them down was as simple as sitting in front of my computer and clicking the mouse a few times.''

She gave a tiny grin. "Don't make it sound too easy, Dylan. You're ruining your mystique.''

"Hey, I'm going to build it right back up again. Finding out the current location of the employees was easy. After that it got difficult. Real difficult, real fast.''

"How so?''

"Well, if you include three part-time clerks, two nurse-midwives and a receptionist who also answered the phone, there were twelve people working at Lutheran Family Services around the time you were adopted. That translates into twelve potential leads. Some employees were likely to know more than others, obviously, but all of them might be useful potential sources of information. I found current addresses for ten former employees, which isn't bad at all—''

"Not bad? It sounds amazingly good to me," Emily said.

"I was hopeful we were going to crack the case quite quickly when I found all those addresses," Dylan admitted. "Of course, in any investigation of this sort, the list of potential leads quickly narrows down, and this case was no exception. Two of the ten employees whose addresses I found are dead, and two have moved out of state. Another former employee is in Dallas, and one has moved to Lubbock, but that left four staff members still living here in San Antonio. And two of those four were actual case workers, not clerks, so I was optimistic that I'd be able to generate some information that would at least take me to the next stage of the investigation."

"But from your tone of voice, I'm assuming that didn't happen?" Emily asked. She spoke coolly, and if Dylan hadn't spent his adult life trying to read what people were concealing, he doubted if he would have been aware of the longing ruthlessly subdued behind that calm facade. He wondered why Emily fought so hard to keep her feelings repressed, then spared a moment of sympathy for Jordan Chambers. He hoped the poor guy was well trained in the fine art of reading unspoken emotions.

"Sadly, you're right," Dylan said. "I contacted all four of the former employees who still live here in San Antonio and all four of them refused point-blank to meet with me once they knew that I was trying to reunite a baby born on March 16, 1974 with her birth mother. The outcome amounted to four potential leads resulting in zero useful information."

She frowned. "Isn't that what you would have expected, though? Adoption records are supposed to be kept confidential, after all."

"You're right, but based on my past experience with this sort of case, I would have assumed at least two of the four women would agree to meet with me, even if they refused to give me any information once we did get together.''

"Were you just unlucky, do you think? Might one of them reconsider if you approached them again?"

"I don't believe so. After our phone calls, despite their reluctance to talk, I paid personal visits to each of them and once again they all refused to speak to me. So having struck out with the locals, I contacted one of the employees who'd moved out of town.''

"Did you have better luck with her?" Emily asked.

"Yes, and no. Lizbeth Hoffmann is a nurse-midwife who worked at the adoption agency for fifteen years, from 1970 until it closed in the mid-eighties, exactly the time period we needed. She'd transferred to Lubbock to be near her grandchildren once she retired, and since that would have meant a plane journey if I wanted to interview her in person, I had to be content with contacting her by phone. Still, she was quite friendly at first. She told me she no longer approved of the system of closed adoptions and regretted having been involved in so many secret placements.''

"That sounds very promising. Just the sort of person you must have been hoping to find.''

"Yes, but unfortunately, the good news stops there." Dylan scowled at the memory of his frustrating phone conversation with the former midwife. "Encouraged that I'd found an ally, I asked Mrs. Hoffmann if she'd retained any records from her time with Lutheran Family Services that she could refer to in order to refresh her memory about specific cases.''

"And what did she say?"

"She admitted that she might have a few personal records that she'd kept, but she wasn't promising anything. She was perfectly friendly in her warning, she just gave the impression that she didn't want me to get my hopes up. Then she asked me for the birth date of the baby I was interested in reuniting with its mother. Your birth date, in other words—''

"So you gave it to her…"

"I did." Dylan sighed. "And Mrs. Hoffmann's reaction was instantaneous. The minute—the second—I told her that the baby I was interested in was a little girl born on March 16, 1974, she clammed up on me. Closed down tighter than Fort Knox."

Emily frowned. "But why? Why would mentioning my birthday trigger such an intense reaction?"

"I've no idea. Mrs. Hoffmann suddenly claimed that she was never involved with the births, which all took place in the local hospital. She insisted she had nothing to do with the subsequent adoption placements, so she had no useful information to pass on. Then she told me never to call back, and hung up the phone. Slammed down the phone, more like it."

Emily stirred the melted ice in her glass, looking troubled. "That's a really odd reaction. First Mrs. Hoffmann wants to help, then she tells you never to call again as soon as she hears my birth date?"

"That's about the gist of it. Yes."

Emily frowned. "If Mrs. Hoffmann worked at the agency for fifteen years, she must have been involved in the prenatal care of dozens of single moms—"

"I'd guess as many as four or five hundred."

Emily's frown intensified. "That makes her reaction even more weird. Out of all those babies, are you suggesting that there was something so extraordinary about my birth that she recognized which child you were talking about the minute you told her the date I was born?"

"It gets even stranger," Dylan said. "When I thought back on my interviews with the employees who are still living in San Antonio, I realized that their point-blank refusal to speak to me always came after I mentioned your birthday.''

''Good grief, what could possibly be so special about my birth? Was I the only survivor of quintuplets, or something?''

Dylan gave a wry grimace. ''Funny you should mention that, because I began to wonder the same thing. In the end, though, I concluded that these women all recognized your date of birth because someone else had recently asked them about the same adoption. Found out something useful, perhaps, and then suggested they'd be smart to keep quiet about what they knew.''

Emily's head jerked up, shock darkening her eyes. ''What leads you to that conclusion?'' she asked.

''Among other things, the conversation I had a couple of days later with Donna Freni,'' Dylan said.

''And she is…?''

''Donna is a former agency employee who moved to the Dallas area. She joined Lutheran Family Services right out of college, and she's now in her fifties, and working as a family counselor for a big HMO in Plano. By chance, I had to make a business trip to Dallas in connection with another case, and I decided to make a detour so that I could call on Mrs. Freni in person, rather than pleading for information over the phone.''

Dylan pushed aside his half-eaten sandwich, his appetite killed at the memory of yet another dead end. ''After my experience with Mrs. Hoffmann, I pumped Donna Freni for all the information I could before I even mentioned your date of birth, but she wasn't willing to cooperate. From a few hints she let slip, I'm pretty sure she has actual records of all the adoptions she participated in among her personal papers. The trouble is, she refused to share anything she knows with me.''

"But why? Why would Mrs. Freni take the records unless she intended to share them at some point. And how could she be intimidated into silence? Dylan, what's going on?"

"How could she be intimidated? Easily. As you yourself mentioned, adoption records are supposed to be kept confidential. People aren't usually prosecuted for breaking the law, but they could be."

"You think someone threatened these women with prosecution if they revealed anything they knew about my birth?"

Dylan nodded. "Yes, I do. I've questioned a lot of witnesses over the years, and I recognize when people are too scared to talk. These women were scared."

"But who are they scared of?" Emily reacted so strongly that she almost knocked over the dregs of her iced coffee. "Dylan, that makes no sense. Who in the world would care enough about my birth to run around Texas threatening potential witnesses to keep them silent?"

"If your biological father was a very important man, or if your birth mother was the daughter of a very prominent and wealthy family, there might be all sorts of incentives for making sure people in the know are warned to keep quiet."

Emily didn't say anything for a few minutes. Finally she raised her eyes, her expression wistful as she met Dylan's gaze. "Well, you warned me what might happen when I started to delve into my family origins. But despite everything you said, I guess I always hoped my birth mother would be just as anxious to find me as I am to find her. It's a bit of a shock to discover that instead of longing to meet me, she's so reluctant to acknowledge my existence that she's intimidating people just to make sure I never darken her door."

"You're jumping to conclusions again," Dylan said.

"It's way too early to assume that your mother doesn't want to meet you. You asked me who could possibly be interested in the details of your birth, and I gave you one reasonable answer. But at this point in the investigation, we have no way of knowing that it's your birth mother who's been coercing these witnesses into silence. That's no more than a wild guess."

"But if not my mother, or someone in her family, then who?"

"Well, that's a major reason why I wanted to see you today, Emily. Can you think of someone in your current circle of acquaintances who might be interested in finding out the details of your birth? Think hard before you answer."

Emily stared into the distance, but her gaze was focused inward. After a few moments' silent contemplation, she shook her head. "Apart from myself, I have no clue as to who might have an interest in finding my birth mother. Or preventing me finding her, as the case might be. My adoptive parents, maybe? But that's impossible. I know Sam and Raelene would never attempt to trace my birth mother without telling me what they planned."

"Are you sure?"

"Of course. They love me, they have my best interests at heart—"

"And you love them, and have their best interests at heart. But you still initiated an investigation without saying a word to them."

"I only wanted to save them from hurt feelings," Emily murmured, evidently taken aback by his comment.

"Maybe they had the same thought," Dylan suggested.

Emily paused only for a few seconds before shaking her head. "No, Sam and Raelene have nothing to do with this. It just wouldn't be in their natures to go behind my back on something so personal. Besides, I'm a hundred percent positive they would never intimidate all those women from the adoption agency into keeping silent. They're so kind-hearted they couldn't threaten a mouse into staying out of the pantry. And apart from my adoptive parents, who else among my friends would care about finding my birth mother?''

"Nobody among your friends, probably. But what about your enemies?''

"My enemies?'' Emily looked bewildered at the word. "Dylan, I don't have any enemies.''

"Everyone has enemies,'' he said curtly.

"Well, okay. Yes, I have enemies, of course. Julie Mae in high school was mad when I made the cheerleading squad and she didn't. I have a cousin, Sam's niece, who dislikes me every bit as much as I dislike her. Then there are always a few guys who believe that buying me dinner gives them a divine right to sleep with me, and are seriously annoyed when I tell them no—''

"None of those sound likely candidates. How about business rivals?''

"Way back when I was just starting out as an interior designer, Mark Reddy accused me of underbidding in order to snatch a couple of jobs from his long-standing clients, but that's about it. These days, my biggest client is my dad. I do the interior design work for all his model homes, including the layout of the kitchens and bathrooms. I earn a decent living, but what I do isn't exactly cutting edge. I'm just not important enough to have crossed anyone's radar screen as a professional threat.''

Dylan stirred the slivers of ice at the bottom of his glass, all that was left of his lemonade. "There's one sense in which you're a very important person.''

She smiled. "Tell me. I'm all ears.''

"Your relationship with Michael Chambers. You were engaged to a man who might be the next governor of

Texas, and that made you very interesting to a lot of people. You personally may not have any enemies, but what about Michael? Rival political campaigns are notorious for dirty tricks.''

The look she directed at him was disbelieving. ''Okay, I feel like Miss Naive U.S.A. here, but are you suggesting that Governor Kincaid had me investigated to see if he could find some dirt to use against Michael?''

''It's surely within the bounds of possibility,'' Dylan said.

Emily pulled her sunglasses down, her fingers drumming on the tabletop. ''I'm willing to accept politicians do crazy things, but Governor Kincaid is a decent man. I can't believe he would authorize funds for such a silly wild-goose chase.''

''Why silly?''

''Because tracking down my birth mother would be a complete waste of time and energy for him. I've lived with the Suttons ever since I was a week old. Whoever my birth mother is—even if she's spent the past twenty-seven years in jail for murder or some other truly horrible crime—well, so what? How could Kincaid exploit my birth mother's crimes to sling mud at me, much less at Michael?''

''Sometimes people throw wildly, just in the hope that some of the dirt will stick,'' Dylan suggested.

''But nothing about my mother's past could be made to stick to Michael. Surely Kincaid would run the extreme risk that the mudslinging would boomerang and leave him with filth all over his hands and face.''

''Even so, never underestimate the depths to which political campaigns can sink,'' Dylan said. ''There's always some crazy intern willing to break the rules and launch an attack against the opposition.''

Emily looked at him consideringly. ''You really think Kincaid might be behind this, don't you?''

"Not Kincaid," Dylan said. "I have too much respect for his intelligence, let alone his integrity, to believe he would choose to win by slandering his opponent. But I wouldn't vouch for all his election campaign team."

"If you approach Kincaid's campaign manager, you know he's just going to deny being involved."

"Which is why I'm not going to bother approaching him," Dylan said. "For right now, I'm just going to concentrate on making an end run around whoever is responsible."

"How can you continue your investigation if none of the former agency employees are prepared to talk to you?"

"There's always someone, somewhere, who's willing to talk. A secret is only safe when all the people who know the truth are dead, and that sure isn't the situation here. For a start, there are still those two former employees of Family Services who moved out of state. I'll try to make contact with them this week, and report back to you. Maybe whoever silenced all the other employees didn't get to those two. Then if that fails, I can start tracking down hospital records. That's longer and a lot more complicated than going to the adoption agency, but it can be done."

Emily sent him a grateful smile. "Thank you, Dylan. I really appreciate all the hard work you've done for me on this."

"Thank me when I've got something more useful to report to you than a bunch of puzzles and dead ends." Dylan glanced at his watch, then rose to his feet. "I'm sorry to cut this short, but I'm already running late for my next appointment back out at the ranch."

"I understand," Emily said, heading toward the steps that led up to the street level of downtown San Antonio. "I'm running late myself."

"I'll look forward to seeing you tomorrow night, at the reception your parents-in-law are throwing for the Texas

Fund for Children,'' Dylan said. "My sister's fiancé, Cole Bishop, has just taken over as executive director of the fund, so Lily insisted I had to buy a ticket and attend. I know you and Carolyn are both active volunteers. That's where you first met, isn't it?''

As soon as he mentioned the party, Dylan could have sworn he saw a flash of consternation in Emily's eyes, but she recovered herself within seconds, and smiled at him with all the cool assurance of a woman who'd been attending charity functions and handling difficult social situations since her presentation at the cotillion on her seventeenth birthday.

"Yes, that's where Caro and I first got to know each other. And I already met Cole at the last board meeting, right before my wedding. He made a presentation to the board and he seems to have some really excellent ideas for revamping the administration of the fund. Which, to be honest, had gotten more than a tad messy over the past few years.'' She smiled shyly. "He's also amazingly good-looking.''

Dylan laughed. "My sister would agree with you on that, I'm sure.''

"And since you're planning to attend the party, I hope there'll be a chance for me to introduce Jordan to you. I think you would enjoy each other's company.''

Composed, gracious, seemingly unaffected by the heat that blasted at them, Emily said a courteous goodbye as soon as they hit street level. She thanked Dylan again for his help in finding her birth mother and walked briskly toward the parking garage where she'd left her car.

He watched her departure with wry admiration, recognizing a fellow spirit who disliked to wear her heart on her sleeve. Emily put on a good show, he reflected, but the prospect of attending tomorrow night's ball in support of the Texas Fund for Children had obviously given her serious pause.

You didn't have to be a genius to work out why. Attending such a prestigious event less than two weeks after she married the "wrong" brother would no doubt be a daunting prospect even for a woman with all of Emily's legendary poise. Dylan decided he was looking forward to meeting Jordan Chambers. The man who could persuade San Antonio's own Ice Princess to toss everything aside for love had to be quite a guy.

CHAPTER TWELVE

JORDAN PUSHED OPEN the swinging glass door that led to his brother's campaign headquarters, a suite of offices on the ground floor of a handsome fifty-year-old building on Commerce Street. He was greeted by a pretty receptionist who looked barely old enough to vote, with a halo of fluffy blond curls and a sweet smile.

Jordan glanced at her name badge and returned her smile. "Hi, Kimberly. I'm Jordan Chambers. I'm here to see my brother."

"Oh yes, Mr. Chambers. How nice to meet you! I saw pictures of your wedding on the news last week. It was lovely. Your wife is just beautiful."

Kimberly blushed and broke off abruptly, as if remembering that the Chambers-Sutton wedding might not be the very wisest subject to bring up for discussion in this particular setting, given that her salary was being paid by the fiancé who'd been dumped.

Somewhat breathless, she switched to business and tried again. "Mr. Chambers...Michael...gave strict orders that he wasn't to be disturbed. Is he expecting you, Mr....er...Chambers?"

"I'm sure he knew I'd be stopping by sometime today," Jordan said with perfect truth. Michael might be brick stupid on occasion, but he must have known this confrontation couldn't be put off much longer. "Just point me in the direction of my brother's office, and I'll take full responsibility for the interruption."

Kimberly's expression remained uncertain, so he flashed her one of his patented, melt-your-panties smiles, then felt guilty when she instantly responded. Still, Jordan excused himself, it was pretty damned hard to remember to behave like a sober married man when your honeymoon had been an eight-day exercise in physical torture, and your wife-in-name-only kept insisting that she wanted the divorce finalized as soon as possible.

Emily's continued insistence on celibacy, in addition to her equally annoying insistence on a quickie divorce, was enough to put Jordan in a distinctly grouchy mood as he knocked on the door Kimberly had indicated. *Grouchy,* in fact, was a mild word to describe his state of mind. Ready to bite the head off anybody who offered him even marginal provocation would have been a more accurate description.

Flinging open the door without waiting for a response to his knock, Jordan walked into a sparsely furnished office where Michael and his campaign manager, Jeff Greiff, were deep in conversation. Various flow charts and colored graphs were spread out on the coffee table in front of them.

"I gave instructions not to be interrupted." Michael looked up, not attempting to hide his annoyance at the intrusion. His annoyance faded to surprise when he saw his brother. "Oh, Jordan, it's you. How are you?"

"Fine."

"You wouldn't know it by looking at you," Michael said with snide satisfaction. "The honeymoon doesn't seem to have agreed with you. Where did you go?"

"I'm fine. The honeymoon was fine. You and I need to talk." Be damned if he was going to reveal the existence of his home in the Colorado mountains, Jordan thought.

Michael frowned. "Later, maybe. Sorry, little brother. As you can see, I'm knee-deep in crap. This isn't a good time."

"We're just discussing the latest polling data," Jeff put in, trying to explain his employer's curtness. "It's important for Michael to get a good grasp of these numbers as soon as possible. A lot of difficult decisions are hanging in the balance right now, and we need to reconcile the needs of the voters with the needs of the moneymen."

Jordan turned very slightly, just enough to bring the campaign manager into his line of sight. "Ever considered the possibility of making decisions based on what you think is right, as opposed to what the polling data say?" he asked with deceptive mildness.

"We can't do that!" Jeff sounded horrified by the mere suggestion. "Good heavens, that would be far too risky."

"How so?" Jordan kept his question amicable.

Michael looked impatiently toward his brother, his features sharpening into scorn. "God, Jordan, what's with you this afternoon? I mean, how naive can you get?"

"I don't know. You tell me."

"Okay, let me spell out the political reality for you. Bottom line, I have to get elected before I can worry about what's right and wrong. It's no good having a million great ideas for reform and new legislation if I can't get elected. To get elected, I need money. Lots of money. To get money, I have to be sure my stated policy positions don't offend the guys with the money."

"How about finding a few issues you care about and then persuading the voting public to agree with you?"

"Bypass the moneymen, you mean? And how do you propose that I persuade voters to adopt my point of view if I can't buy TV ads?"

"Get out and meet the voters in person," Jordan suggested. "Explain exactly what you want to do for them, and for the state."

Michael gave an impatient snort. "Yeah, that's a really good way to go. Back in 1950, it might even have gotten you elected. Nowadays, explain any of your proposed policies too closely, and your opponent will eat you alive with attack ads.''

Jordan looked at his brother for a long, silent moment. ''What are you planning to do if you lose this election, Michael?''

''He's not going to lose,'' Jeff said quickly. ''Michael is beginning to catch the attention of the voters. More than thirty percent of them recognize his name already, and it's more than a year to the election. If you can believe it, your wedding to Emily Sutton actually improved his numbers among suburban moms by 2.75 percentage points.''

''I'm real glad to have been of service,'' Jordan said. ''Anytime I can help out with a discarded fiancée, just let me know.''

Michael's gaze narrowed, as he finally registered the fact that his brother might not be feeling one hundred percent cordial about the events leading up to his wedding. ''Look, little brother, I'm up to my ass in alligators right now. Does this conversation have a point? Are you here for some specific reason?''

''Yes. I need to speak to you.''

''Then go ahead. Speak.''

''I need to speak to you privately.''

Michael glanced toward his campaign manager, then gave an airy wave of his hand. ''Don't worry about Jeff. He knows all my secrets.''

''Maybe, but he doesn't know any of mine, and I'd like to keep it that way.'' His patience exhausted, Jordan bundled up the various spreadsheets and graphs of polling data and shoved them into Jeff Greiff's arms. Then he walked over to the office door and held it open.

''I believe you should find something in that little pile there to keep you busy while I talk to my brother,'' he said pleasantly. "Goodbye, Jeff. I'll be sure to have Kimberly give you a buzz when Michael is free again."

Jordan's manner was so commanding that Jeff obeyed without protest. With a startled glance toward Michael, he scurried through the door and Jordan quietly closed it behind him.

"Was that little drama really necessary?" Michael directed a scowl at his brother, then walked to the window. He yawned and made a show of watching the traffic zoom past. "Your honeymoon definitely doesn't seem to have agreed with you," he said. "What's your problem? Was Emily as boring in bed with you as she always was with me?"

Jordan let the red mist clear from his eyes before he answered. "As far as my wife is concerned, you get one free ride, Michael, and you just had it. If you ever speak disrespectfully about Emily again, be prepared to face the consequences."

"For God's sake, Jordan, let's not fight about Emily Sutton. She's trash, and definitely not worth it."

Jordan didn't even realize he'd swung a punch until his fist connected with his brother's jaw. Michael staggered back, banging into the wall, cradling his chin in his hands. "Are you crazy?" he mumbled. "Damn, I think you've broken my jaw!"

"I doubt it. Your jaw is as thick as the rest of the bones in your head. Besides, I gave you fair warning."

Michael stumbled to a small fridge in the corner of the room and pulled out a bag of ice, holding it to his face. "Look, it may come as a surprise to you to hear this, but I don't exactly harbor tender feelings toward your new wife."

"Why not?" Jordan asked. "She's doing a pretty damn good job of protecting your ass from those alligators you were just talking about."

"Protecting me?" Michael's handsome features aligned themselves into an expression of incredulity. "How do you reach that amazing conclusion? And before you answer, let's just say I'm having a little difficulty accepting that on Friday morning Emily Sutton was engaged to me, and by Saturday evening, she was married to you."

"Cut the crap," Jordan said tersely. "Have you forgotten who you're talking to? I know that you dumped Emily on Friday morning, not the other way around."

Michael continued to look aggrieved. "Okay, so what? Maybe I did dump her. But I had my reasons, and I certainly didn't expect her to run straight to you for consolation! Just how long had the two of you been carrying on behind my back, anyway?"

Belatedly, Michael seemed to decide his final question might fall into the category of comments his brother considered disrespectful, because he hastily backed away, his arm raised to protect his jaw.

"Don't judge Emily by your own rotten standards," Jordan said coldly. "You're the one who was unfaithful, not her. And before you start protesting your innocence, I know all about your trysts with Hector Romero's wife."

Michael spluttered a protest, then fell silent when Jordan looked at him with something akin to pity. "It makes no odds to me, Michael, but if I were hoping to become governor of Texas, I'd try a little harder to keep my fly zippered. Especially around other men's wives."

Michael gave a hard crack of laughter, then winced and pushed the ice back against his jaw. "That's rich, coming from you."

"Yeah, well, I'm not trying to get elected to public office." With Emily it had mattered, but with his brother, Jordan didn't attempt to deny the rumors that falsely linked his name to a succession of bored married woman. "Besides, I wasn't engaged to anyone until Friday of last week.

And then again, Hector Romero isn't one of my biggest campaign donors."

Michael turned away. "Is that why you came here? To lecture me about my sex life?"

"No. As far as I'm concerned, you can screw your way to electoral oblivion if that's what you want. It seems to me that if you don't lose because of sexual misconduct, you're going to lose because you're allowing Jeff Greiff to micromanage your campaign into the dust."

"You're dead wrong," Michael blustered. "Jeff Greiff has a winning record, and you don't understand the first thing about running a high-tech, professional campa—"

"Right, so you've told me, many times. But I'm not here to debate your strategy for winning the election. I'm here because I want to know the real reason why you broke off your engagement to Emily. Three months ago you told me she was the perfect wife for a man running for political office. It was one of the smarter things you've ever said, because she obviously is a gift to any aspiring politician. So why the sudden change of heart?"

Michael shrugged, evading his brother's gaze. "We weren't compatible—"

Jordan quelled a rush of impatience. "Try again, Michael. And be warned, I'm going to stay here until I get the truth out of you. Remember, you're the one who has a tight schedule today, not me." He tried not to think of the backlog of work piled up at the factory waiting for him after his eight-day absence, the phone messages, sales calls, people wanting to consult with him. Not to mention the actual hands-on work of carving.

Michael remained stubbornly silent for a full minute, then he shrugged. "All right, what the hell. I'll tell you the truth. Why not? There's nothing you can do about it now you've married her."

He crossed the room and sat down behind his desk, and

Jordan controlled the urge to haul his brother out of the chair and shake him until his teeth rattled.

"Start at the beginning," he instructed his brother, trying not to let any trace of his intense interest show. "Speak in short, clear sentences, and keep going to the end."

"I guess you know that Emily's adopted," Michael began.

"Yes. So you informed me several months ago." How in hell could that be relevant to a broken engagement, Jordan wondered.

Michael picked up a brass paperweight and slowly turned it in his hands. "Well, shortly after we got engaged, Emily and I were having dinner with Mom and Dad—maybe it was even the meal at the club when you were there. When I introduced the two of you for the first time."

"I remember the occasion." The meeting was etched in Jordan's mind with blinding clarity. He'd finally fallen head-over-heels in love at first sight—and the woman he'd fallen for had just promised to marry his brother. Yeah, he remembered the meeting all right. He'd gone straight from the dinner to the bar where he'd picked up Mary Christine Bernauer.

"If you remember the dinner, you may remember that Emily mentioned something about wanting to have at least two children, maybe even three."

"I do remember, actually. You said that was fine by you."

"Yes, I've always felt that a man isn't complete without children, you know. And, I'll be honest, I thought that if Emily got pregnant next spring, and we announced it just in the last month of the campaign...well, it couldn't hurt with the women voters, could it?"

"Probably not. Had you shared this particular campaign tactic with Emily?"

"Not really, not in any detail. She wanted to have kids,

so did I. There was no point in discussing the specifics.''
Michael frowned. ''I'm really going to have to think about
finding some other woman to marry. Children always look
good on a politician's résumé. As long as there aren't too
many, so that environmentalists start to wonder if you're
overutilizing the planet's resources and—''

Jordan leaned across the desk. ''Michael, get to the point
of this story within the next thirty seconds, or I kill you.
Your choice.''

Michael recoiled. ''Geez, what bug's biting you today?
What the hell have you got going on in your life that
you're always in such a damn hurry?''

''Michael...'' Jordan murmured threateningly.

''Well, okay. You want the truth, here it is. You know
that Mother was never as enthusiastic about the match with
Emily as Dad. Dad won Mother over by pointing out that
Sam Sutton was giving us way more favorable terms on
the Laurel Acres deal because of the marriage. Mother
recognized that we needed the money, but getting Emily
as part of the deal was a hard pill for her to swallow.''

''Could you explain why precisely?''

''Because Emily's adopted, of course.'' Michael appeared genuinely surprised that his brother had failed to
grasp something so self-evident. ''Anyway, Mother took
me aside after that dinner and suggested that although I
had to go through with the marriage for the sake of the
election and the Laurel Acres deal, starting a family with
Emily was a high-risk proposition, and I should avoid it.
Since we didn't know anything about Emily's true genetic
background at all, she recommended that I put off starting
a family so that I could arrange a divorce as soon as the
election was over. By that time, the Laurel Acres project
would most likely be completed, so the marriage would
have served both its purposes.''

Jordan was beginning to feel very, very angry. ''You

and Mother have both been acquainted with the Suttons for several years, so you know that Emily had been raised by a wonderful couple, with a superb set of values. You know that Emily is smart, because she graduated summa cum laude from college with a degree in Fine Arts. You know that she's compassionate because she works her tail off for the Texas Fund for Children, and the Literacy Council, not to mention several other less fashionable charities. You also know that she's professionally competent, since she's been recognized as one of the best interior designers in San Antonio. In other words, you and Mother both knew that she was smart and charming and beautiful, and you still didn't think she was qualified to be the mother of your children?''

"My God, you're in love with her," Michael said, looking at his brother in amazement. "You've actually fallen in love with her. I can't believe it. Jordan Chambers, San Antonio's most notorious stud, has fallen for little Emily Sutton, the all-American prude.''

Jordan walked around the desk and hauled Michael to his feet, ignoring his brother's attempts to break free. "My feelings for Emily, whatever they may be, have absolutely nothing to do with this conversation. You're supposed to be explaining why you broke off your engagement to Emily. What you've just said explains why Emily is incredibly lucky to have escaped marrying you. It doesn't explain why you dumped her less than forty-eight hours before the wedding. Tell me why you put the Laurel Acres project and your election at risk or, so help me, you're going to need your jaw rewired before you deliver your next campaign speech.''

"Let go of my neck, for God's sake." Michael finally twisted out of Jordan's hold. "Okay, here's the bottom line. You asked for it, and I'm giving it to you, so don't blame me if you don't like what you hear.''

"Just tell me why you dumped Emily."

"After mother's heart-to-heart, I got to thinking that marrying Emily might be a dangerous move on my part. I mean, who knew what kind of baggage she might be bringing with her? I'm not just talking genes here. What if the circumstances of her birth were really bad? I mean, running for public office you make a lot of enemies. What if one of them started digging around and came up with something about Emily that could hurt me?"

"So you started to investigate Emily's background," Jordan said.

"Yes." Michael nodded. "I turned an investigative team loose with instructions to find Emily's birth mother."

Jordan unclenched his teeth so that he could speak. "Which they did, presumably, or we wouldn't be having this conversation."

"Yes, they did. They reported back to me on Friday morning, and right away I knew that whatever problems it caused, I would have to cancel the wedding."

Jordan's stomach lurched so violently, he thought he might be sick. What had the researchers discovered? That Emily would never be able to have children? He could handle that. What if she was destined to die at forty from some terrible disease?

By an act of will, he concealed his panic and spoke coolly. "What did your team of researchers discover, Michael?"

His brother's voice hovered between horror and a sort of gloating pleasure that he could reveal something so terrible. "They discovered that Emily Sutton's birth mother was an illegal immigrant. A poverty-stricken, broken-down, two-bit whore. And God alone knows who her father is. Her mother sure couldn't have the faintest idea—"

As Jordan's hands rose, Michael broke off, jumping back so fast he knocked over his chair. "You can't fight with me for telling the truth!'' he yelled, huddling in the corner by the desk where Jordan's fists couldn't reach him. ''Face facts, Jordan. Your wife's mother earned her living selling her body on the streets of San Antonio! Obviously I couldn't marry Emily. Think of the scandal if some journalist got hold of the same story I did! It's okay for you to marry her, since you're just a carpenter, and you're never going to have any status in public life, anyway. But it's different for me. I have to carry on the Chambers tradition. For God's sake, can you imagine what Kincaid's people would have made of Emily's background if they'd ever found out the truth about her birth mother?''

''I can imagine exactly what Kincaid's people would have made of it,'' Jordan said coldly. ''Nothing. Because that's what it's worth, Michael. Precisely nothing. Emily's mother may have been a prostitute, but she apparently cared enough about the baby she conceived to carry her to term and arrange for her to be adopted by wonderful parents. You're campaigning on a pro-life platform and I would say Emily is the poster child for your point of view on the abortion issue.''

''Just because Emily has turned out okay so far, you have no idea when nature is going to kick in and she'll revert to type.''

Jordan looked at his brother with a sense of genuine sadness. ''How in hell did your values get to be so screwed up, Michael? Are you really so insecure that you need to bolster your self-esteem by having a wife with genes preapproved by our mother?''

''Oh, please,'' Michael said disdainfully. ''Trust you to pretend a person's heritage doesn't matter. Just wait until Emily's pregnant with your child, and you're wondering how the hell the kid's going to turn out with half its genes an unknown quantity. Then maybe you'll wise up as to why I wouldn't marry her.''

"I doubt it," Jordan said quietly. "And if I were going to worry about genes and hereditary, right now I'm thinking it's the Chambers genes that would have the hairs on the back of my neck standing up."

"You would say something ridiculous like that," Michael said acidly. "You never fitted into our family, Jordan. You've always stuck out like the proverbial sore thumb."

"Could be," Jordan said. "Although my grandmother sure seemed to think that I had a role to play in saving the Chambers family fortune."

Michael's mouth turned down in a bitter line. "I'll never in a million lifetimes understand why Grandmother Hunter left all her money to you. And as for Laurel Acres...it's totally outrageous that she tied Dad's hands, saying he could only use the land for a development project approved by you."

Jordan smiled, although there wasn't much mirth in it. "There's no mystery as to why Grandmother Hunter left her estate to me. She wrote her reasons right in the first paragraph of her will."

"Yes. She said you were the only member of the family who didn't give a damn whether you got her money or not. What kind of a reason is that? The old bat was as crazy as you are."

"Fortunately a doctor and two lawyers disagree with you. In the meantime, I've approved the Laurel Acres deal with the Suttons, and only the Suttons, so you'd better hope it's a success, since your income depends on it."

"Until I'm governor of Texas."

Jordan drew in a deep breath. "Yeah, until then. And since your campaign manager is probably chomping at the bit to get back in here and draw some more pretty colored charts, I'll get out of here as soon as you've answered two more questions for me. First, what's the name of Emily's birth mother, and second, where can I find her?''

"Her name is Maria Vasquez, and you can find her in the cemetery.''

Jordan's head jerked up. "In the cemetery?''

"Yes, I guess she's buried somewhere in town. Maria Vasquez is dead,'' Michael said. "She died last month of lung cancer.''

CHAPTER THIRTEEN

JORDAN'S APARTMENT IN San Antonio was a converted loft on the top floor of a six-story building close to the Mexican Market. The brick walls had been painted white, and the two thousand square feet of space had been partitioned into living, eating and sleeping areas only by ficus trees, book-shelves and strategically placed pieces of large furniture. The two bathrooms were enclosed, but otherwise there were no interior walls to interrupt the flow of tiled floor and massive windows.

As a professional interior designer, Emily appreciated the practicality of the layout for a bachelor who lived alone and often worked at home on design concepts. As a wife in name only, she found the floor plan seriously deficient. It was hard to pretend you weren't living with someone when there was nowhere to escape except the closets and the bathrooms to avoid seeing him.

On returning from their honeymoon early yesterday afternoon, Jordan had insisted that Emily should take over the corner of the loft that had been set up as the master bedroom, but his courteous gesture afforded her almost no privacy, since the double-sided bookcases that served as a boundary between sleeping and living areas were less than four feet high and failed to blur her view of the leather sofa where Jordan had spent the night.

The guilt she felt at imposing this uncomfortable sleeping arrangement on her husband had done absolutely nothing to improve the quality of her rest. Which would, in any case, have been seriously impaired, given that every breath Jordan drew seemed to reverberate inside her body until she wanted to cry out with the frustration of being alone in the vast emptiness of his king-size bed.

Now it was Monday evening, bedtime was mere hours away, and they would soon have to go through the whole birdbrained procedure again. As they would tomorrow, and every night for however long their marriage lasted. In Colorado there had been two separate bedrooms for them to sleep in. Here in San Antonio, the inconvenience of their marriage of convenience was revealed in all its stark absurdity.

The trouble with the institution of marriage was that it demanded intimacy, Emily thought, as she painstakingly basted the chicken breasts and red peppers she was baking for dinner. A marriage in name only might have worked for aristocrats in the nineteenth century, when massive houses and hordes of servants imposed distance and formality. But as a method of coping with everyday living in the twenty-first century, it left a lot to be desired.

The sound of the old industrial elevator clanging to a halt produced a fluttering sensation in the pit of Emily's stomach. A sensation that she recognized immediately as excitement. She shut the oven door and gave up trying to pretend, even to herself, that she hadn't spent the past hour waiting on tenterhooks for Jordan's arrival.

He came into the loft, his too long hair rumpled, and the stubble of the day's beard already beginning to darken the line of his jaw. Emily's stomach performed its usual back flip, warning her that this was going to be another long, hard night of trying not to notice that Jordan was the most attractive man she'd met in this particular lifetime.

He tossed his portfolio of drawings onto the dining room table, and strode across the living room area to the kitchen.

"Something smells wonderful," he said, halting a couple of feet away from her. "Hi, Em. How was your day?"

Since they returned to San Antonio, Jordan had been scrupulous about maintaining a physical distance between the two of them, and Emily knew she ought to be grateful for his consideration. She wasn't, of course. Why would she expect the smallest trace of rationality in her reactions to Jordan?

"My day was very busy," she said, resisting the urge to reach out and touch him. Or lean over and kiss him. She turned away, occupying her hands by stirring the rice, which didn't need stirring. "I survived the usual quota of minicrises in the office, but otherwise things weren't too bad, given that I'd been gone for almost two weeks."

Jordan detoured past the oven before going to the fridge and pulling out a bottle of beer. He flipped off the cap with his thumb, then unfastened the buttons at the neck of his shirt before taking a long, thirsty swallow. "How about the lunch date with your parents?"

"Surprisingly, it went very well. Mom and Dad were so happy to see me they hardly asked any difficult questions at all." Emily fixed her gaze at a point somewhere to the left of Jordan's ear, since her eyes had apparently developed a defect that caused them to focus with laserlike intensity on the tanned and muscled expanse of her husband's chest.

Jordan took another swig of beer. "That's good news. I was afraid they might have been harassed by reporters looking for human interest stories to fill a few empty column inches."

"The only people who seem to have harassed them are my relatives. Apparently, my various aunts, uncles and cousins are all burning up with curiosity as to how I came to switch grooms hours before the wedding ceremony, and they've been bombarding my parents with questions. Mom and Dad think it's rude of them to be so inquisitive. They're fielding all inquires with variations on the theme of how you and I fell passionately in love at first sight, and are destined to live happily ever after for the next hundred years or so.''

He smiled at her, eyes warm. ''You must be relieved. I know you were dreading being cross-examined.''

''I sure was. I hate lying to them, you know?'' She pulled a face. ''Unfortunately, Mom and Dad have now done such a great job of convincing themselves we're in love, I worry about how upset they're going to be when we get divorced.''

''Don't buy trouble, Em. We have months before we need to decide what we tell your parents to explain our divorce.''

Emily mentally added the word *divorce* to her lengthening list of words like *honeymoon, bed, love, sleeping arrangement, sex* and *celibacy* that caused instant acceleration of her pulse rate and a tightening of the permanent knot in her stomach.

''I know you're right,'' she said, trying to make light of the problems ahead. ''Unfortunately, I have a twenty-seven-year history of obsessing about the future. You need to understand that you're looking at a woman who's so compulsive that she starts out each business day making three copies of her schedule. And then revises the master copy at lunchtime.''

''Three copies?'' Jordan tipped his head in a question, then hastily shook it instead. ''No, it's better if you don't try to explain.''

She laughed. ''Yes, it probably is. Anyway, how was your day? I expect you were even busier than I was. At least everyone at my office was prepared for me to be out of reach for a couple of weeks. You weren't able to give your people any warning.''

"Yeah, it was your basic madhouse for most of the day. I fielded a lot of calls from customers wanting to be personally reassured that their furniture is going to be delivered in time for the holidays." Jordan ran his hand through his hair, frowning. "The general manager has done a great job keeping the standard production lines moving smoothly, but I'm seriously behind schedule on my signature pieces. I'm sorry, Em, but I'll have to work the next couple of weekends to catch up. Will that screw up any important plans of yours?"

So much for Jordan, the layabout, who never did any work, Emily thought. Did his family know anything about him at all? "No, of course it won't mess up my plans," she said quickly. "You aren't accountable to me for your time."

She meant only to reassure him that she wasn't about to turn into a nagging wife, constantly demanding his attention, but she was afraid her words came out sounding curt, and she tried to soften her response. "Having just said that, I have a big favor to ask. Are you free tomorrow evening by any chance? I realize this is really short notice to spring something on you."

He grinned. "You're asking so nicely that I bet I'd be real smart to say I'm completely tied up at work, can't get away, have to be in Timbuktu."

Her mouth quirked wryly. "I have a suspicion a quick trip to Timbuktu would be a lot more appealing to you than what I have in mind."

"Spit it out, Em. Tell me the worst."

"Tomorrow is the night your parents are opening up their house to the public and throwing a gala reception on behalf of the Texas Fund for Children. Cole Bishop has just been hired as the new executive director, so the board decided to throw a party, partly to introduce him to important donors, and partly to raise money. To be honest, what with one thing and another, I'd clean forgotten about it, but I really need to put in an appearance.''

''Because you're a member of the board?''

She nodded. ''And because Cole Bishop has a lot of new ideas he wants to introduce, and I support almost all of them. Given that the board is stuffed full of members who believe that anything new must be bad, Cole is going to need all the support he can get. The catch is that Michael will be there, along with a lot of your parents' friends, and I'm getting an acute case of cold feet. Would you mind very much coming with me? It's black tie, and I know how much you hate getting dressed up and making small talk for hours at a stretch, but it would make the whole evening so much easier for me.''

''Of course I'll come with you,'' Jordan said quietly. ''I don't mind getting dressed up for a good cause. Besides, if I get too bored, I'll just find you and make you dance with me until I'm in a good mood again.''

Emily let out a breath, returning his smile. ''Thank you, Jordan. I really appreciate this.'' She hadn't realized how much she'd been dreading his refusal until he accepted with such easy willingness.

He walked across the kitchen, breaking the invisible barrier that had kept them separated ever since they left Colorado. Crooking his finger under her chin, he tilted her face gently upward. ''How could you think I would refuse, Em? Obviously all the gossipy tongues in San Antonio would start wagging if you turned up at such an important event minus your new husband. Especially since said husband isn't the groom everyone was expecting you to marry. Putting on a scratchy starched shirt for three or four hours doesn't seem like too high a price to pay to help you avoid that.''

She was caught up in the way he looked, in the way the overhead light made his thick hair gleam and the way the shadow of beard darkened his skin, which was actually quite fair, despite his dark coloring. His skin would feel rough beneath her fingertips, she thought. If she just reached up her hand, she would be able to touch his cheek, stroke the line of his jaw....

Emily tried to speak, then had to swallow before the words would come out. "I really appreciate your willingness to help, Jordan."

"Don't mention it," he said. "It's not a big deal. Who knows? We might even enjoy ourselves." He dropped a fleeting kiss on her mouth and walked away before she could protest. Or return the kiss.

Thank God he hadn't given her time to return the kiss, Emily thought. So far this night was going worse than she'd anticipated. The knowledge that she had approximately three hundred more nights just like this one to get through didn't help lighten her mood one bit. At this rate, she would be a certifiable lunatic before the end of the month, let alone before the end of their marriage.

At what point, she wondered, did physical desire become such a driving physical need that a person just decided to give in, to hell with the consequences?

Better not pursue that line of thought. "Dinner's ready whenever you are," she said brightly. "I laid the table here in the kitchen because I thought the one in the living room looked as if you use it for your design work."

"I do." Jordan grinned. "I didn't have much use for a dining room table until I got real smart and found myself a wife." He yawned. "Geez, it's been a long day."

His yawn made Emily feel guilty all over again because she knew he hadn't slept properly on the sofa, and yet she didn't dare invite him to share her bed. She could predict, with exquisite clarity, exactly what would happen if the two of them ever ended up lying next to each other in a bed. And what would happen between them was something she had dedicated the last six years of her life to avoiding.

Fortunately, bedtime was still a few hours away. Right now, they had dinner to enjoy, and that was likely to provide a pleasant hour for both of them. In Colorado, mealtimes had gone smoothly, whether they ate out at a restaurant or stayed home and cooked for themselves. She and Jordan always seemed to have a dozen different topics to talk about, and their rare moments of silence felt companionable rather than tense gaps that needed to be filled with chatter. In fact, Emily realized as she took the chicken from the oven, she'd been waiting all afternoon to share this time with Jordan.

Ever since her meeting with Dylan at Perk at the Park, she'd been mulling over the idea of telling him about her search for her birth mother. She wanted his opinion on possible reasons for the frustrating wall of silence that Dylan had encountered when he began to investigate. For obvious reasons, she was reluctant to talk to Raelene and Sam, and she didn't want to burden Carolyn St. Clair with a story that came loaded with unsorted emotional baggage. Not to mention the fact that Caro might find it uncomfortable to discuss her employer's work methods with a client.

Jordan, on the other hand, was likely to have a fresh perspective that would enable her to understand why she'd found today's interview with Dylan Garrett so unsettling. Somehow, she was optimistic that Jordan would have the power to put to rest her strange, restless sense of foreboding.

Emily served their dinner, determined to allow Jordan time to eat in peace before she burdened him with the details of her meeting with Dylan. She was still pushing her fork around a half-empty plate when Jordan reached out and covered her hand with his.

"Okay, Em, tell me what's wrong. You've been mauling that poor piece of chicken quite long enough."

With a rueful sigh, she put down her fork. "And here I thought I was doing such a good job of providing entertaining dinner conversation."

Tenderness came and went in his eyes before being replaced with impatience. "Em, you don't have to entertain me. You're not a hired companion, you're my wife—"

"Not really," she said quickly. *Wife* was another one of those words that hovered close to the top of her anxiety list.

"You're my wife," he repeated firmly. "At least temporarily. If something's bothering you, tell me. Don't wait for some mythical right moment to slip the topic into the conversation."

"I'd wait forever if I did that," she said ruefully. "This isn't the sort of subject you can slip into a conversation. It's about my mother."

His eyes narrowed in immediate concern. "What's wrong? She looked so well at the wedding. I hope she didn't give you bad news about her health?"

"I didn't mean Raelene." Emily pushed her plate away, realizing she wasn't about to eat any more dinner. "I meant my birth mother."

Jordan put down his fork with what seemed to Emily exaggerated care. "Your birth mother?"

"Yes." Emily's mouth was desert dry, and she took a sip of ice water. "Nobody knows about this except Carolyn St. Clair, but a few weeks ago I decided I wanted to start a serious search for my biological mother. For some reason, I had the feeling time might be running out for us, and I wanted to see if we could find each other after all these years."

Jordan didn't answer immediately, and when he did

speak, his voice was deeper and rougher than usual. "Have you ever tried to find your birth mother before, Em?"

"No," she said. "For the first twenty-six years of my life, I honestly didn't think much about her. Of course I remembered her on my birthdays, and wondered if she was thinking about me, too. But my adoptive parents are wonderful, and it seemed disloyal to consider making a serious search for her, even after I went away to college."

Jordan laid his hand next to hers on the table. "I can understand why you felt like that, Em, although Raelene and Sam might have been more understanding than you would expect. They're a remarkable couple."

She looked down at their hands, which were almost touching. "They are, but I think this might be difficult even for them. Especially my mom. In college I joined a support group for students who were adopted—"

"I thought you said you never thought much about your adoption?"

"I didn't. But most kids want a group identity at that age, I guess, and I decided being adopted was going to be mine. The focus of the group was on searching for your birth parents, and we had quite a few experts come to talk to us. Detectives, psychologists, social workers, even a lawyer. The one thing every one of those experts agreed on was that searching for your birth parents was almost guaranteed to put stress on your relationship with your adoptive parents. I was curious to see if the experts were right. So when I came home for summer vacation at the end of my freshman year, I just hinted to Raelene that I might be interested in seeing if I could find my biological mother. She tried to hide her reaction, but I could see she was devastated."

"So you abandoned the idea," Jordan said.

"Yes. At that point, finding my birth mother wasn't nearly important enough to me to risk hurting Raelene and

Sam. When I returned to college, I dropped out of the support group and took up volleyball instead. End of story till this year."

Jordan's hand moved slightly, the tips of his fingers covering hers. "You're a kind daughter, Em."

"Not really. You could just as easily say that I'm selfish. The Suttons poured out so much love, why would I be tempted to rock the boat?"

"You're not giving yourself nearly enough credit."

She sent him a sudden smile. "I think I told you the same thing about yourself just a few days ago."

He returned her smile. "Hey, looks like we're both better people than we ever imagined. Anyway, what made you change your mind and decide to start looking for your birth mother?"

"I began to dream about her." Emily shifted uncomfortably on her chair, shrugging off a sudden chill. "Suddenly, out of nowhere, about two months ago, these dreams started. I've never admitted this to anyone, Jordan, but for a couple of weeks, the dreams were so vivid they began to carry over into the day. I couldn't seem to escape from them. I got this weird notion stuck in my head that my mom was trying to contact me. Telling me I needed to find her." She gave a laugh that was intended to be mildly self-mocking and instead sounded scared. "How's that for spooky?"

"Spooky," he agreed, but lightly as if it wasn't any big deal. "What did your birth mother say exactly, when she told you to start looking for her?"

"I'm not sure. Not the exact message. That sounds strange, but the image of her that came in my dreams was nothing like the all-American college coed the adoption agency had described her as being. My dream mother was dark and petite and looked Hispanic. In fact, she spoke in my dreams in Spanish...."

Emily's voice trailed away when she noticed that Jordan's expression sharpened into a new intensity the moment she mentioned that her mother spoke Spanish. "What is it?" she asked. "What have I said?"

"Nothing important. Do you speak Spanish, Em?"

She shrugged. "I've lived in San Antonio all my life, so of course I speak a little, but I'm not fluent. I had dreams of going to Italy to study fabric design, so I took Italian in college."

"But you obviously understood enough of what your mother was saying to decide that she wanted you to start searching for her."

Emily nodded. "You know what dreams are like. They have their own crazy internal logic. I always understood exactly what my mother was saying while I was asleep, even though part of my brain seemed to realize that I ought to be having difficulty grasping her Spanish. I even 'recognized' some of her words as being regional expressions from the Yucatan peninsula. How's that for weird? Then as soon as I woke up, I wouldn't be able to remember what her Spanish words meant, not exactly. I was just left with this compulsive need to start looking for her."

Jordan's hand was completely covering hers now, but Emily chose not to move her own hand away. The warmth of his touch was comforting, dispelling the chill that always gripped her when she remembered those distressingly vivid dreams.

The silence that greeted her confession gradually became oppressive, and she gave an uncomfortable laugh. "Okay, you don't have to sit there trying to find something polite to say. Go ahead and tell me how crazy it was to start searching for my birth mother because she was calling to me in my dreams."

"It doesn't seem crazy to me at all," Jordan said. "That wasn't why I was silent."

"What rational explanation could there be for my dreams? Much less the fact that I found them compelling enough to act on?"

"I can think of several good, rational explanations. Here's one. Despite your protests to the contrary, you've been wanting to find your birth mother for a long time. You suppressed that desire for the sake of the Suttons, but it was a real sacrifice on your part. It's quite logical that if you censored all thoughts of your birth mother during the day, then your subconscious would take over and force you to confront your secret wishes while you slept."

Emily smiled ruefully. "Well, thank you for that. I guess my subconscious sending me subliminal messages sounds less nutty than my mother's spirit wafting through the ether to invade my dreams with a plea for me to find her."

"I have to get another beer," Jordan said abruptly, pushing back his chair. "Can I get anything for you?"

"No, thanks. I'm fine."

When he came back to the table, his expression seemed to Emily to be on the grim side for a man who'd just assured her that he didn't think she was even slightly crazy.

"So tell me what you did once you'd decided to start searching," he said, taking a long swig of beer. "Did you try to go it alone, or did you hire professional help?"

"I hired professionals," Emily said, explaining about Carolyn's job at Finders Keepers, and how she'd hired Dylan Garrett the day before the wedding on her friend's recommendation.

"Dylan promised to get back to me as soon as he had anything to report, and he was as good as his word," she said. "He called me this morning at the office and asked if I could meet him at Perk at the Park, down on the River Walk, because he had some information he needed to review with me. I agreed to meet with him right after I finished lunch with my parents.''

''Did he have anything important to tell you?'' Jordan asked, and Emily wondered if she was imagining the note of sympathy she could hear in his voice. What was there in the story she'd recounted to evoke his sympathy?

''I'm not sure I'd call it important,'' she said. ''His report to me was more puzzling than anything else, and it's been bothering me ever since I heard it.'' She explained how Dylan had contacted many of the people who'd once worked at Lutheran Family Services, and how all of the former employees had clammed up, refusing to speak to Dylan the moment they knew he was trying to track the mother of a baby born on March 16, 1974.

''It seemed very strange that all these adoption professionals would remember my birth date the second Dylan mentioned it. It's almost thirty years since I was born, so why would they remember me? After all, they must have dealt with hundreds of adoptions in the course of their careers.''

''Did Dylan have an answer for you?'' Jordan asked.

''Yes, he did. But first I suggested maybe I was one of triplets, or quads, all farmed out to different families. I guess that would be memorable, even to adoption professionals. But based on the pattern of how his interviews developed, Dylan came to the conclusion that people were refusing to talk because they'd been bribed to keep silent. Bribed recently enough to remember instantly which birthday they weren't supposed to talk about. Or, even more likely, he suspected they'd been intimidated into keeping quiet.''

''Intimidated? As in threatened if they dared to speak out about what they knew?''

''Yes,'' Emily said. ''Apparently it would be easy to apply pressure to keep potential informants quiet, since it's technically against the law to disclose the details of sealed adoption records.''

Jordan took another long, slow swallow of beer. Emily could no longer ignore the fact that for some reason he was taking longer and longer to respond to what she was saying.

''And that's all Dylan Garrett had to tell you?'' he asked finally. ''That the agency employees he'd interviewed didn't want to cooperate.''

''Yes, that's all.''

''Then if his sources wouldn't cooperate, I guess Dylan didn't actually manage to find out anything concrete about your birth mother,'' Jordan persisted.

''No, nothing.'' Emily struggled to explain why the afternoon's meeting with Dylan had troubled her so much. ''It really bothers me that somebody might be intimidating those former employees into keeping quiet. Why? Who would care? What's the purpose? On top of the puzzle of *why*, it angers me that I'm being thwarted in my efforts to find my mother. When I started this search, I realized I might never find her, so I'm mentally prepared for failure. But I'll be damned if I'm going to sit back quietly and give up the search because some outsider, for reasons unknown, has decided to intimidate people into refusing to talk.''

CHAPTER FOURTEEN

HE WAS GOING to have to tell her the truth, Jordan realized. He'd been debating all afternoon exactly how much he should tell Emily about his conversation with Michael. Driving home, he'd reached the conclusion that he would tell her nothing. The coward's way out, maybe, but he hadn't seen any purpose in thrusting information on Emily when she'd shown no signs of wanting it.

But that decision had been based on the belief that Emily had never attempted to find her birth mother. Now he knew she had been secretly yearning to find her birth mother for years. Under the circumstances, silence was no longer an option.

It was clear that he couldn't conceal the facts. What wasn't clear was how in hell he would find the words to tell Emily that the mother she'd finally started to search for was dead. In a coincidence he would very much like to have ignored, it seemed quite possible that Maria Vasquez had died soon after Emily started to be plagued by dreams of her birth mother. Now there was a psychic phenomenon that he was definitely not ready to explore.

And that wasn't the worst of it. Hard as it would be to tell Emily that her birth mother had died, Jordan knew it would be even more difficult to explain how he happened to be in possession of this piece of information. Telling Emily what he'd found out this afternoon, while revealing only the barest minimum about Michael's role, was going to require some mighty fancy verbal flimflam.

He sure as hell didn't want to reveal the part Michael had played in all this. He was ashamed that his brother had behaved so badly, but he was even more concerned about how devastated Emily would be to discover the real reason her fiancée had dumped her. There was no kind or tactful way to explain that Michael had called off the engagement because he found Emily's dead mother too offensive to be admitted to a perch on the branches of the Chambers family tree.

Jordan realized that his fingers were drumming on the edge of the table, and that Emily was looking at him with visible concern. No more beating around the bush, he decided. It was time to speak up.

"I went to see Michael this afternoon," he said.

"Michael?" Emily looked at him, more puzzled than anything else.

"Yes, we had some family business to take care of." What the hell could he say next? *I asked my brother what his real reason was for dumping you, and he said it was because your birth mother was a whore, and you have tainted genes, unworthy for the production of a Chambers heir.*

Jordan gave up on preparing mental speeches and let his instincts take over. He pulled his chair next to Emily's, putting his arm around her shoulders and taking her hand into his.

"I have some sad news to give you," he said quietly. "When I was talking with Michael today, he mentioned that he'd happened to come across some information about your birth mother."

"About my mother?"

No wonder she sounded incredulous. Jordan gripped her hands tighter. "Yes. It's an odd coincidence, but your dreams were right on about her being Hispanic, Em. Apparently she was a Mexican immigrant, and her name was Maria Vasquez.''

''Maria Vasquez.'' Emily murmured the name, her voice soft. Her mouth slowly broke into a small, radiant smile and joy sparked in her eyes.

''My mother's name is Maria Vasquez.'' She changed his *was* to an *is* and laughed with pure delight, consciously or unconsciously ignoring his warning that he had sad news.

Her smile widened. ''Oh, my God, I know my mother's name! Where does she live? Can I go to meet her?'' She was already half out of her chair.

Gently, he tugged her back down. ''I'm afraid not, Em.'' Jordan steeled himself to tell her the rest. ''She's dead. I'm really sorry, sweetheart, but Maria died a little while ago.''

The joy disappeared from Emily's eyes, to be replaced by a bleakness that made Jordan ache. ''My mother's dead?'' she whispered.

''Yes, she is. I'm so sorry, Em.''

She said absolutely nothing. Then a single tear splashed onto the back of their clasped hands, but she didn't seem to notice it.

''I wish I didn't have to give you such sad news,'' he said.

''I'm not really surprised,'' she replied, her voice remote. ''At some level, it's what I've been dreading. All along I've had this sense of urgency. Like I had to find her really soon, or it would be too late.'' She took a shaky breath. ''Now it is too late.''

He couldn't deny the simple truth of it, and Jordan had rarely in his life felt more powerless. Cursing silently, he watched as another tear fell onto their hands, and then another. There was no storm of tears, just a quiet, restrained grief that tore at his gut until he couldn't stand it any longer.

To hell with keeping his distance and showing restraint. He pulled Emily to her feet and cradled her in his arms, stroking her hair, and rocking her gently back and forth, whispering words of comfort.

Suddenly she was sobbing, her face turned into his chest, the sobs racking her body and soaking his shirt. He let her cry, and—since this was his own uptight Emily—the storm didn't last for long. In a very few minutes she had herself back under control. He reached behind him and found a box of tissues, handing it to her without speaking.

"Thanks." She wiped her eyes and blew her nose. "You must think it's silly to be so upset when I've never even met her, but I guess I'm crying for all the lost opportunities in our lives. For the chance to know each other that we'll never have."

Jordan touched her cheek with the back of his hand. Her skin felt hot, as if all the emotion she wouldn't let herself reveal burned inside. "I can tell you one thing about her beyond a shadow of a doubt. She'd have been very proud of you, Em."

The sadness in her eyes faded just a little. "Do you think so?"

"I know so," he said with complete truth.

She looked at him wistfully. "If only I'd started looking for her a little earlier. If only we could have met just once—"

"Don't," he said, taking her hands and tugging her close again. "Don't do this to yourself, Em. The what-ifs in life can drive you crazy if you don't watch out."

"You're right. There's no point." She broke away from him to reach for the glass of water standing on the table. Ever his practical Em, she drank deeply, set down the empty glass and started on the painful process of turning

her grief into constructive action. "I guess I should call
Dylan Garrett tomorrow and tell him to call off his search
Do you know where Maria is buried, Jordan? I'd like to
visit her grave. It's nothing morbid or anything. But I need
to go, just once."

"I don't know where Maria is buried," Jordan said.
"But I can pass on whatever information I have to Dylan
Garrett and I'm sure he'll be able to find out your mother's
burial site within a couple of hours. There aren't that many
cemeteries in San Antonio, after all."

"I'd appreciate that. I'd like to pay her my respects. I
wonder what she died of? She must have been quite
young."

Michael had said something about lung cancer. Jordan
decided not to pass on that fact. Better if any more details
about Maria's death were left to Dylan Garrett to explain.
As for Maria's life…if he could square it with his conscience, he would call Dylan tomorrow and ask him, man
to man, to go easy on revealing the details of exactly how
Maria Vasquez had made her living.

Jordan watched as Emily carried her plate over to the
sink and scraped the remains of her meal into the garbage
disposal. She suddenly looked up, her forehead wrinkled
into a frown.

Oh, hell, he thought. She's starting to wonder how Michael stumbled onto information about Maria Vasquez. After all, she'd been paying a top-notch investigator to conduct the same search, and he'd come up empty. Her
mystification was almost inevitable.

"I'm confused," Emily said, her plate sitting forgotten
on the counter. "I know you told me Michael gave you
this information about my mother, but how did he find out
about her? Was it some amazing coincidence?"

Could he risk claiming coincidence? Probably not, Jordan decided. Emily would want to know exactly what

chain of events had led to such a curious twist of fate, and he couldn't think of any story that would withstand scrutiny. He needed to head her off with a plausible mix of omissions and half truths before she asked him a question he wasn't willing to answer. Emily didn't need to know that her birth mother had earned her living on the streets.

"You probably know that Michael's campaign has access to teams of investigators who are experienced in digging up information on just about anyone and anything. He asked them to try to find your birth mother."

"Why?" Emily's gaze was justifiably bewildered. "Why in the world would Michael do such an odd thing?"

Jordan had a flash of inspiration. "He wanted to find your birth mother as a surprise wedding gift for you." He tried hard to make the lie sound convincing. "But when he learned that your mother was dead, he decided it was best not to say anything to anyone. He didn't know you were searching for Maria yourself, of course."

Phew! That all sounded pretty reasonable, Jordan figured.

"How unexpectedly thoughtful of Michael." Emily added detergent to the dispenser in the dishwasher while Jordan mentally wiped sweat from his brow and wondered what subject he could introduce to create a diversion.

"Would you like me to brew us a pot of coffee?" he asked.

"Sure, that would be nice." Having put her own dinner plate into the dishwasher, Emily wandered over to the table for his. She stopped halfway back to the sink and stared into the distance. With the relentless persistence of an incoming tide, she produced her next question.

"Do you know when my mother died, Jordan?"

He shook his head. "No, I'm sorry. I didn't ask Michael for the exact date."

She stared down at his plate, as if not quite sure how it

had arrived in her hands. "I guess I still don't quite understand how the subject of my birth mother came up in a conversation you were having with your brother."

Jordan paid great attention to the simple act of scooping coffee grounds into the filter basket. "I don't exactly remember myself."

She sent him a look that was more regretful than angry. "What are you hiding from me, Jordan?"

"Nothing—"

"Don't lie," she snapped. "I may have deceived myself about a lot of things while I was engaged to Michael, but in other ways I had a very clear understanding of his character. For one thing, he's entirely conventional and utterly predictable. And before you rush to his defense, I consider those to be very desirable characteristics. I've always been conventional myself, and I admire predictability—"

She might understand Michael's character, Jordan reflected, but she sure didn't understand her own. "I don't see where this conversation is going, Em."

"Michael was going to buy me a diamond necklace as his wedding gift to me," she said quietly. "To make doubly sure that he bought exactly what I was expecting, he took me with him to the jewelers when he went to select it."

"Finding Maria was his *surprise* gift. That means you weren't to know about it—"

She shook her head. "Don't even try to convince me, Jordan. Your brother would have been no more likely to search for my birth mother as a wedding gift than he would have been to take up bungee jumping."

"But he did search for your mother, so for once you have to accept that you've misjudged him." Jordan took two mugs from the cupboard. "Here, let's take our coffee into the living room, shall we?"

"Sure." Emily closed the dishwasher and set it going.

He had the feeling that if he'd suggested standing on their heads to drink their coffee, she'd have agreed just as easily.

"Of course!" she exclaimed, her gaze in focus again. "Oh, my God, of course! That explains everything."

"What explains everything?" Jordan was horribly afraid that he knew what she was going to say next.

"Why Michael was looking for my birth mother. He was afraid there might be something scandalous in her background that would cause problems for his campaign. That's why he had his team of investigators searching for her. He wanted to be sure she wasn't going to pop out of the woodwork in midcampaign and embarrass him. Or worse, that Kincaid's campaign would spring her on him when he least expected it."

Jordan accepted the inevitable. Emily was, unfortunately, way too smart to be deceived. Lying wasn't going to achieve any useful purpose at this point. In fact, it was an insult to her strength of character to keep trying to distort the truth. "You're right," he said finally. "Michael was afraid your mother might present potential problems to his campaign. That's exactly why he initiated the investigation. I'm sorry, Em. I shouldn't have lied to you."

"I understand. You were trying to protect your brother, which is a habit of yours. It's odd, you know. Michael always appears so self-confident, and yet he must be pathetically insecure deep down inside." Her forehead wrinkled in thought, and she seemed to be talking as much to herself as to him. "Although I don't really understand why he would expect voters to pay any attention to my birth mother. I'm an adult, responsible for my own actions, and it's the Suttons who raised me. What relevance could Maria's life have?"

Jordan hesitated only for a moment. "Do you want me to answer that honestly?"

"Most definitely yes. I'm sick of being lied to by you and your brother."

Jordan decided to be brutally honest, to compensate somewhat for his earlier half truths. "Then I would say that in an ideal world, Maria's activities would have zero impact on Michael's campaign for governor. But in the real world, in a tight race, I can imagine scenarios where rumors about your birth mother could have enough of an impact to affect the outcome. If she were tied to organized crime, just to give an example."

"Is that what Michael's investigation uncovered?" Emily asked. "That Maria had ties to organized crime?"

"No, of course not—"

"But his investigation did uncover something terrible," she said slowly. "Of course it did. How could I have been so blind? That's why Dylan didn't get anywhere with his investigation. Michael, or more likely one of his cronies, threatened the agency employees with prosecution if they told anyone else what they'd told already told him."

Emily was getting visibly enraged. "And that also explains why Michael—Mr. Conventional personified—dumped me only hours before our wedding. His investigative team dug out the dirt on my birth mother right before he came into the study and said we had to call off the wedding."

"Even if that's true, do you care?" Jordan asked. "Given what you know now, would you want to be married to Michael?"

"Of course I wouldn't!" she yelled. "But that doesn't excuse Michael's slimy behavior." She rounded on him, eyes flashing. "Did you know about all this when you offered to marry me?"

"No. I found out this afternoon."

"When you went to Michael and demanded to know why he'd dumped me. I see it all now." She paced up and down the kitchen a couple of times, her entire body radiating anger. "Okay, exactly what did Michael find out about my mother, Jordan? And before you invent any more charming lies, remember that I'm her daughter. The least you and your brother owe me is a few honest answers."

He'd bungled this whole situation to the point where he had no option but to tell her the truth, Jordan decided. And since there was no way to make the truth pretty, he gave it to her straight.

"Maria Vasquez was an undocumented immigrant from Mexico," he said. "According to the evidence Michael's team unearthed, she earned her living as a prostitute."

"I see." Emily's voice was heartbreakingly steady. "And my father?"

From somewhere, Jordan dragged up the courage to meet her gaze. He kept his voice carefully neutral. "It seems unlikely that Maria knew who your father was."

"I see," she said again. Her face slowly drained of color, but her chin angled defiantly.

"I really need some privacy right now, Jordan. Please don't follow me."

She turned away and walked toward the bathroom, but Jordan swiftly interposed himself between her and the door.

"I asked you for some privacy," she said, her voice icily calm.

"I know."

"Then move away. There's nowhere in this damned apartment to be alone except in the bathroom."

"Grieve for your mother," he said. "Be angry with me and my brother if you want. But don't confuse the two emotions, Em."

Her eyes glittered. "What the hell is that piece of psychobabble supposed to mean?"

"Don't take out your anger on your mother because

Michael investigated something that wasn't his business, and then didn't tell you what he'd found out. And while you're straightening out confused emotions, you might remind yourself that you're not to blame because Maria died before you could find her.''

She spoke through gritted teeth. ''I realize that—''

''I hope you do. And I hope you also realize that knowing Maria worked as a prostitute doesn't tell you everything there is to know about her. That's the way my brother thinks. Don't fall into his simplistic pattern of thinking, Em.''

''Right, I won't.'' Emily's voice wobbled. ''I'm sure my mother was a whore with a heart of gold. I'll bet she had the purest damned heart in the state of Texas.''

He had never seen Emily like this, raw with the bitterness of her emotions. ''It could be that your mother had a very loving heart,'' Jordan told her quietly. ''After all, she chose to be pregnant with you for nine months, when having an abortion must have been an easier option for her.''

Emily squeezed her eyes tightly shut, and when she opened them again, some of the frightening desolation had gone. ''You're right. I was angry with Maria for not being the perfect mother because that was less painful than feeling anything more complicated.''

''I have a shoulder handy if you need one to cry on.''

''Thanks, but I don't feel like crying right now.'' She moved closer, putting her hand flat against his chest. ''I owe you, Jordan. That's the second time in the past two weeks that you've saved me from making a really bad mistake.''

He wondered if she could feel the hammer of his heartbeat beneath her fingertips. To him, each thump felt powerful enough to rouse the dead. Better move out of the danger zone before he did something unforgivable, he decided. Emily was vulnerable right now, and only a prime quality bastard would take advantage of her fragility. He stepped back, his spine pressing hard against the bathroom door, and tipped his hand to his forehead in a mock salute. "You're welcome. Jordan's Roadside Rescue is always at your service."

The feeble attempt at humor did nothing, not one damn thing, to dampen the desire that had him in its thrall. The muscles in his stomach were tying themselves in hot, slippery knots, and his arms ached with the effort of not reaching out to hold her. How was it, he wondered despairingly, that with Emily, he could jump from sympathy to lust in one mindless leap?

Emily didn't have the sense to walk away from him. She remained standing in front of him, hands hanging loosely at her sides, the rich coppery brown of her hair accenting the continued pallor of her face. At some deep gut level, Jordan knew he wouldn't meet with much resistance if he tried to make love to her right now. An offer of sympathy, a few slick moves, and she was vulnerable enough to succumb.

Of course, an honorable man would never take advantage of her emotional fragility, but then, as his mother would say, when had anyone ever accused Jordan Chambers of being honorable? His back was to the wall, literally and figuratively, and he had no more fight left in him. How could he resist taking her to his bed, when he'd fallen in love months ago? When he'd spent the past ten days falling deeper and deeper in love? He knew, damn it, that he could bring Emily enough physical pleasure to ease the ache of her loss. Under the circumstances, was it really wrong to seduce her?

The argument continued to rage inside him for several long, silent moments, but Jordan knew the real battle was already lost. Emily's vulnerability wasn't going to protect her. On the contrary, it called out to his primitive mascu-

line urge to defend by domination. And if he needed further justification, the awareness that he'd seen in her eyes
provided it, allowing him to believe that at some profound,
elemental level she wanted him as much as he wanted her.

Shaking off the last twinges of guilt, Jordan stepped
forward to take her into his arms and, as he'd instinctively
known, she didn't resist. He bent his head slowly toward
her, giving her time to turn away, but she didn't. He
touched his mouth to hers.

For an instant, he felt her resist. Then she drew in a
shuddering breath and clung to him, her mouth moving
hungrily beneath his. Her kiss was already full of desire,
waiting to be answered and then taken to the next level.
He held her as he'd dreamed of holding her, possessively
hard, erotically close. Through the fog clouding his brain,
Jordan marveled at the miracle that made him harder the
more he wanted her, while Emily became softer and ever
more yielding.

He didn't speak. Didn't dare to introduce any words that
might shatter the hot, brittle shell that kept them bonded
together. Emily was silent, too, but when he unfastened
the buttons of her blouse and found her breasts, she gave
a soft moan. A sound of pleasure so intense that he felt it
to the core of his being.

He took off her clothes with practiced ease, shedding
items as he moved them closer to the bed. She smelled of
woman, overlaid with a soft verbena fragrance that was
simultaneously discreet and erotic. Essence of Emily, he
thought, encapsulated in a perfume. The taste of her was
on his tongue, the feel of her on his skin, the rasp of her
unsteady breath in his ears. Aroused as he was almost beyond reason, a tiny part of his brain nevertheless stood on
one side and counted down the seconds until he could be
inside her. Like a master musician, lost in the glory of the
symphony while at the same time utilizing technical ex-

pertise to create the perfect sounds, Jordan realized that he was employing every seductive trick he knew to lure Emily into the bedroom without breaking the spell of their mutual desire.

And then she was there. Lying in his arms, in his bed, her hair splayed out on his pillow, her body naked to his gaze. He even had his condom ready. A few more minutes, another couple of accomplished moves, and he could make her his.

Except that she was crying. Typical quiet, restrained Emily tears. But for some reason, despite the tears, she wasn't resisting him. Her body was still soft and slick, her movements languid with desire. Jordan had enough experience to be damned sure she wasn't faking it. It would be so very easy to pretend he hadn't seen the tears.

Temptation painted the edges of his vision scarlet, so he closed his eyes. His heart pounded loud and fast in his chest. Too loud. Too fast. He rolled onto his back, opening his eyes to stare at the ceiling, trying to reclaim the shreds of his integrity. Shame washed over him, a cold Arctic wave, cooling red-hot desire.

When he was fairly sure that he would be able to speak in something that could pass for a normal voice, he sat up in the bed and looked down at Emily.

He touched his fingertip to one of the tears, half-dried on her cheek. "Why didn't you tell me to stop?" he asked.

Her eyes darkened, but she didn't look away. "Because I didn't want you to stop."

"You were crying."

"Yes."

His eyebrow quirked. "Want to expand on that answer just a little?"

"I cry when I feel deep emotions. Happy emotions as well as sad."

His blood began to hum again and hope had his heart

pounding with all its previous force. "You didn't want me to stop?"

"No. I didn't want you to stop."

Jordan leaned back against the headboard, folding his arms across his chest. "If you ask me really nicely, I guess I could be persuaded to start all over again."

Emily reached up and put her arms around his neck, pulling him down, kissing him in a way that had the symphony roaring in his head again.

"Is that asking you nicely enough?" she murmured.

"I'm not sure." He let out a long, unsteady breath. "Repeat the request and I'll let you know."

She kissed him again. "You're shaking," she said when they finally drew apart.

"Am I?" He gave a rueful laugh. "It's been a rough night."

She kissed him a third time. "Getting better?"

"By the second."

Emily started at his chest, then walked her fingers down his body with slow deliberation and clear intent. Jordan concentrated on not totally losing his mind. He forgot all the skill he'd acquired in previous sexual encounters. His vaunted expertise, normally guaranteed to provide his partner with the thrill of a lifetime, vanished. He wanted to make this experience perfect for Emily but he couldn't think, couldn't plan, couldn't orchestrate. Hot with passion, beside himself with need, he followed blind instinct. He stroked her until she trembled, kissed her until the taste of her was absorbed into every atom of his being, and when he knew he could hold out for only a few minutes longer, he slid between her thighs.

He hadn't been prepared for Emily's soft cry when he entered her, nor for her shudder of pleasure as he began to move. Most of all, he hadn't been prepared for the surge of profound emotion that overcame him as he watched delight and stunned incredulity chase across her face as she hurtled toward climax.

He followed her down, soaring into the depths.

CHAPTER FIFTEEN

THERE WAS ABSOLUTELY nothing like sex for clouding a man's brain and ruining his powers of concentration, Jordan reflected. Unless it was love. He had staggered through most of the day in a state of lustful infatuation that left him only a scant step more functional than a drunk coming off a two-day binge. Now, with his parents' party looming ahead, he was attempting to act like a suave, sophisticated man-about-town when all he really wanted to do was take Emily home and rip her clothes off. Why in hell was he trussed up in a monkey suit, attending the Texas Fund for Children gala benefit, when they could be lying in bed, blissfully naked and making love?

He drew the car to a halt, finally able to take his eyes off the road and look at his wife. Perhaps it was worth sacrificing a few hours of nakedness, just to see Emily dressed up for the party. She was one of those fortunate women who always looked attractive, but tonight she wasn't just attractive, she was beautiful. Stunningly, breathtakingly beautiful. He knew she'd called Dylan Garrett early this morning and asked him to locate Maria Vasquez's grave site. Whatever other demons she'd been forced to wrestle with during the past twenty-four hours, she'd clearly come to terms with her mother's death, at least temporarily. Tonight she had decided to take on the world—and San Antonio's gossips—with all flags flying.

He opened the passenger door on his SUV and Emily stepped out of the car, exposing a long length of leg, encased in glittery dark stockings. He'd decided back in the apartment that her dress, a plain black sheath, must be glued to her body, since it had no other visible means of support. It was also slit at the left seam from hem to upper thigh. Upper, *upper* thigh, Jordan realized belatedly, as Emily maneuvered herself out of the car.

He handed his keys to the bug-eyed parking valet, not sure whether to punch the guy on the nose for his slack-mouthed admiration of Emily's legs, or shake his hand and compliment him on his excellent taste.

Jordan offered Emily his arm. Fortunately, she accepted, or there would have been a major altercation right there on his parents' marble steps. Having seen the parking valet's reaction to her outfit, Jordan planned to remain a permanent fixture at her side for the rest of the evening. And if his behavior bore more resemblance to a chest-thumping caveman than the sophisticated man of the world he was supposed to be...well, so be it. A wife with legs like Emily's tended to bring out the primitive traits in a man's character.

As luck would have it, Michael was the first person they met after they'd shown their tickets to the uniformed attendant guarding the door and passed into the drawing room. Michael nodded to his brother, about to move on without speaking, then did a visible double take when he saw Emily.

"My God, Emily! What have you done to yourself?" Michael demanded, his voice hovering between appalled and lascivious.

"I married your brother," Emily said, and swept past, leaving Michael to stare after her with an expression remarkably similar to the one displayed earlier by the parking valet.

Jordan followed his wife. He rather liked the way she'd said, *I married your brother*. He was still mulling over the possible implications of that remark when they were stopped once more.

"Emily, how nice to see you again." Jordan didn't recognize the ruggedly good-looking man who was shaking his wife's hand.

The man spoke again. "I heard from Dylan that you got married a couple of weeks ago. Congratulations."

"Thank you, Cole." Emily turned. "Jordan, I'd like you to meet Cole Bishop, the grandson of Eve Bishop, who's virtually the founding mother of the Texas Fund for Children. Cole has recently taken over as executive director of the fund. Cole, this is my husband."

"Good to meet you, Jordan." Cole Bishop held out his hand.

Jordan shook the man's hand, which was strong and callused. This was a guy who'd obviously worked hard with his hands in the not too distant past.

"Emily told me you have some interesting new ideas for improving the efficiency of the fund's operations," Jordan said, dragging his gaze from his wife's altogether delectable fanny so that he could do his part to keep the conversational ball rolling.

"I have a couple of ideas I'm anxious to work on," Cole agreed. "We may be a charitable organization, heavily dependent on volunteers, but that doesn't mean we have to be inefficient. On the contrary—"

He broke off, and his sunburned features softened briefly into tenderness as a tall, slender woman slipped her hand into his.

"Sorry to interrupt," the woman said, her gaze bright as she looked up at Cole. "Carolyn St. Clair pointed out that you were talking to Emily, and she suggested I should come over to meet her." She smiled, her green eyes sparkling. "Hi, Emily. I'm Lily Garrett, Dylan's twin sister. The other founding partner of Finders Keepers."

"And my fiancée," Cole said.

Lily smiled up at him. "That, too, I guess."

Cole's gaze rested for a moment on his fiancée, the love between them almost palpable. Then he inclined his head toward Jordan. "This is Emily's husband, Jordan Chambers."

"I'm so pleased to meet you," Lily said. "I've been hoping we'd be introduced ever since I heard a rumor that you were J. C. Hunter, the famous cabinetmaker. Is the rumor true, by any chance?"

"Yes, it is," Emily said, before Jordan could decide how to reply. "And I know wives aren't supposed to brag about their husband's achievements, but I think the furniture he makes is magnificent."

"You won't get any argument from me," Lily said. "I'm a great fan of yours, Jordan."

"Thank you," he said stiffly, thinking this was exactly why he'd always kept his work as J. C. Hunter secret. He hated the idea of having to answer endless questions about his craft, trying to explain the inexplicable, where he got his inspiration, when he'd first known that he wanted to be a wood-carver, how many hours it took him to complete each design. And yet there was something undeniably appealing in having an attractive woman like Lily looking at him as if he were some sort of creative genius. Not to mention the pleasant shock of hearing Emily publicly state that his furniture was magnificent.

"Cole's grandmother has promised to buy me one of your signature chests as a wedding gift," Lily said. "She'll be really impressed when she hears that I've met you in person. Although I'm not going to let her near you when we select the design for the wood carving. Knowing Eve, she'd want a picture of the Alamo on the side, and the Texas state flag on the lid."

Jordan laughed and made a suitable reply. The room was

becoming more crowded by the minute. Cole was called away to talk to a prospective donor, and Lily accompanied him, leaving Jordan and Emily unexpectedly face-to-face with his mother.

"Hello, Jordan." Amelia Chambers didn't smile or hold out her hand. "I'm surprised to see you here."

"Emily persuaded me to attend." Jordan shoved his hands in his pockets, not knowing what else to do with them. If he hugged his mother, she would only squirm.

Amelia Chambers gave the barest nod of acknowledgment to her daughter-in-law. "Hello, Emily. My goodness, you look as if you caught too much sun on your honeymoon. It's not fashionable to be tanned anymore, you know. And what an unsuitable frock you're wearing!"

Emily's chin tilted. "And why, exactly, is it so unsuitable?"

"Well, my dear, I should have thought that would be obvious, even to you. I'm sorry to say it makes you look as if you earn your living in the world's oldest profession."

Emily looked absolutely stricken and Jordan was washed by a wave of fury so explosive he was surprised that the top of his head didn't blow off. He looked at his mother with biting contempt. "Tell me, Mother, I've often wondered. Are you rude intentionally, or is it just that you were never taught basic good manners and don't know any better?"

Amelia's eyes narrowed in shock, and the base of her throat flushed a mottled red. "I suppose I should expect that sort of crude insult from you, Jordan. As you very well know, the Beaumont family has a pedigree that stretches back to a daughter of Louis XV of France—"

"A bastard daughter," Jordan couldn't resist pointing out.

His mother ignored him. "My father made sure that I

received extensive training in the duties of a woman in my social position, and I can assure you that I have a flawless understanding of the rules of etiquette.''

"Knowing which fork to use when you eat asparagus and how to address a visiting archbishop isn't the same thing as having a grasp of basic good manners,'' Jordan said.

"I'm not surprised you would feel that way, Jordan. You've always been a most unsatisfactory representative of the Chambers family.''

"Jordan isn't a 'representative of the Chambers family','' Emily said. "He's your son.''

"I am aware of that fact.'' Amelia's gaze flicked over Emily. "You two undoubtedly deserve each other,'' she said coldly. "All I can say is thank heavens Michael didn't marry you.''

"Amen to that,'' Emily said. "What do you know, Mrs. Chambers? We've finally found a subject on which we're in total agreement. Thank heavens Michael didn't marry me.''

Emily walked away, afraid of what she might say or do next. Jordan quickly caught up with her and put his arm around her waist, leading her to the relative peace and quiet of the library. How had Jordan survived growing up in a house where he had to face his mother's hostility every day, she wondered. Right at this moment, having a birth mother who had earned her living as a prostitute seemed like a very much better bargain from fate.

She crossed to the window, breathing hard, and Jordan followed her. "It helps if you just keep telling yourself that my mother is a very unhappy woman,'' he said quietly. "She was supposed to marry a French count and live in a château, but he ran off with his hairdresser instead. His male hairdresser. She's never been the same since.''

Emily laughed, the cloud of anger lifting. "You're making that up."

"No, I swear it's true. My grandmother told me the story."

"Your grandmother Hunter?"

"Yes. My mother's mother."

"Why is her name Hunter?" Emily asked. "Your mother's maiden name was Beaumont, wasn't it?"

"Yes, but Grandma Hunter married three times. Her marriage to Grandpa Beaumont lasted just long enough for her to give birth to my mother. Then she asked Grandpa Beaumont for a divorce on the grounds of terminal boredom. When he wouldn't agree, she had an affair that was so blatant he felt compelled to divorce her for adultery. Which, as you can imagine, created a huge scandal back in the forties. Then she married twice more in rapid succession. The third time, in the early sixties, she married Ben Hunter and finally got it right. Still, it can't have been easy for my mother growing up, even before the count ditched her for his hairdresser."

"You're going to have a hard time persuading me to feel sympathy for Amelia," Emily said.

"Then let's forget her and go drown our sorrows in dessert. Whatever else you can say about my mother, you have to admit she knows how to throw a party. She always uses Le Grand Gourmet to cater this sort of an event, and they bake a chocolate torte that's almost as good as the one they make at The Brasserie in Elk Run."

Emily touched her hand to his. "You go and test-drive the chocolate cake. I need to talk with a few board members, try to win them over to supporting Cole Bishop's administrative changes. You know what it's like with these volunteer boards. Sometimes persuading them to innovate is about as easy as persuading a chicken to lay a goose egg."

"I'll give you an hour," he said softly. "By then, I'm pretty sure my patience will have run out."

She pulled an apologetic face. "I know this must be really boring for you—"

"Not especially." He lowered his voice. "I'm just tired of waiting to discover what you have on under that dress."

"Nothing much." She blushed and looked away. "I can't believe I said that."

"You're not exactly revealing state secrets," Jordan said dryly. "My best guess is that you're wearing the dress, your panty hose and a splash of perfume. There isn't room for anything else."

She smoothed the fabric over her hips, the gesture betrayingly anxious. "I've had this in my closet for two years, and tonight is the first time I've ever had the courage to wear it." She looked at him, full of doubt. "Was your mother right, Jordan? Do I look like...does this dress make me look like a...prostitute?"

"Not even a very high-class one." He took her hands, pulling her close. "It makes you look exactly what you are, Em. A very beautiful and desirable woman."

She swallowed over the sudden lump in her throat. "Thank you, Jordan."

"Make love to me like you did last night and you're more than welcome."

Carolyn St. Clair chose that precise moment to put in an appearance. She pretended to be blithely unaware of Jordan's final remark, although the grin she couldn't quite smother suggested that she'd heard every word.

"Dylan has been trying to find you for the last half hour, Emily. He has some information that he's anxious to pass on to you. He's in the big room on the right as you come in...."

"The drawing room," Emily suggested.

"Yes, that must be the one."

"I was just about to leave in search of chocolate torte that's rumored to be of world-class quality," Jordan said. "Come and taste some with me, Carolyn." He kissed Emily swiftly on the cheek. "Go talk to Dylan. I'll catch up with you in a few minutes."

DYLAN WAS STANDING by the doors that led out onto the drawing room terrace, speaking to a man Emily had never seen before. She hesitated to interrupt, but as soon as Dylan saw her, he waved and beckoned for her to come and join them.

"This is Sebastian Cooper," he said. "We're old friends from way back. Sebastian, this is Emily Chambers. Her husband is Jordan Chambers."

"Hi, Emily." Sebastian shook her hand, his ebony eyes charismatic in their intensity. "It's good to meet you. I know Michael, of course, and I'm enthusiastic about his campaign for governor, but I've never had the pleasure of meeting your husband."

Emily smiled, responding instinctively to Sebastian's charisma. "He's in the dining room, tempting Carolyn St. Clair to eat too much chocolate torte."

"Maybe you'd like to join them?" Dylan suggested.

"Is that a hint?" Sebastian asked laughingly.

"Emily and I do have something to discuss," Dylan agreed.

Sebastian gave a mock bow. "I'm devastated to be banished from your dazzling presence, Emily. If your conversation with Dylan gets too boring, send a message and I'll rush to the rescue."

She laughed. "I'll certainly do that." Her smile faded as soon as Sebastian turned his back. She'd forgotten him by the time he left the room. She looked up at Dylan. "Carolyn said you had some information for me. Is it—is it about Maria Vasquez?"

"Yes, it is." Dylan's gaze was compassionate. "Look, why don't we step outside onto the terrace? It's so hot tonight, I figure we have a chance that we might actually be able to talk out there for a couple of minutes without being interrupted."

"Fine, yes, of course." Emily followed him out onto the terrace, her thoughts already in such turmoil that she barely noticed the oppressive humidity of the summer night.

"I went to work on tracking down the burial place for Maria Vasquez as soon as I got your phone call this morning," Dylan said. "You'd given me permission to get in touch with Michael, so he was the first person I called. He was reluctant to cooperate at first, but I eventually persuaded him that it was in his best interests to share with me all the information he had in regard to your mother."

"I'm surprised that you managed to persuade him."

Dylan's smile was cynical. "I suggested he wouldn't want my search for Maria Vasquez's grave to find its way into the newspapers, and he agreed that he most certainly wouldn't. After that, it was fairly easy to persuade him to part with all the information he had. He told me that Maria died of lung cancer while in St. Anthony's Hospital. His investigative team gave June 1, 2001 as the date of death."

"June 1?" The color leeched from Emily's face. "That had to be just when I started dreaming about her," she said. She gazed across the street, looking at the house opposite without seeing a single feature of its elegant facade. It was a moment before she could continue speaking. "Did you manage to find out where she's buried?"

"No. In fact, the situation isn't exactly what we thought it was." Dylan drew in a deep breath. "Emily, a fund-raising party isn't the very best place for us to be having this particular conversation, but there's a real urgency to the situation and I thought, on the whole—"

He broke off. "I'm sorry. I'm not being very professional or coherent about this. Let me try again. Once I had the basic information from Michael, it was routine to check with the hospital on what had happened to the body of Maria Vasquez after she died. It soon became apparent that the hospital had a problem with its paperwork, because nobody seemed able to answer that simple question. I was transferred from one clerk to another, until finally I got transferred to a nurse, Judy Simmons."

He paused for a moment, but Emily didn't ask any questions. She couldn't. Her tongue felt as if it had swollen to fill her entire mouth. "Judy Simmons doesn't work in records," Dylan said. "She works in oncology. With patients who have cancer. In the end, it turned out I'd been put through to her because there's a patient in the terminal stages of lung cancer on her floor. The patient's name is Maria Vasquez."

Emily tried to speak and failed. She cleared her throat and tried again, her tongue still clumsy when she attempted to make it shape words. "It's a common name, Maria. Even Vasquez isn't that unusual."

"True. It wasn't beyond the bounds of possibility that one Maria Vasquez died of lung cancer on June 1, and another Maria Vasquez was in the hospital suffering from the same disease today. But I decided I wasn't getting anywhere trying to straighten out the confusion by phone. I was also frustrated by the fact that I didn't seem to have made any real contribution to this case so far, and although I like to charge high fees, I like to produce some service that's worth the high prices. So I canceled my appointments for the rest of the afternoon, got into the car and drove to St. Anthony's before Judy Simmons reached the end of her shift. I explained to her that Maria Vasquez had been identified as the mother of one of my clients, and that we'd been informed that she died of lung cancer on

June 1.'' Dylan shrugged. "We're fortunate that medical records are strictly confidential while people are alive, but death certificates are a matter of public record, so Judy was willing to cooperate in finding where Maria's body had been taken.''

Emily realized she was holding her breath, and hastily let it out. Dylan took a sip from the glass he'd carried out onto the terrace before continuing with his story. "When Judy Simmons checked the records that are supposed to show which funeral parlor had been given custody of the body, she discovered that an error had been made in entering Maria's case file into the hospital's computer system. The actual hard copy of Maria's records was accurate and showed that the hospital had halted the lung infection that brought her into the hospital. They also showed that Maria had been discharged to the care of her regular doctor on the first of June. Unfortunately, a temporary data entry clerk had transcribed the incorrect number code into the computer, so that anyone referring only to the computer to find out the fate of Maria Vasquez would be told that she was dead.''

The streetlights edging the sidewalk blurred and danced in front of Emily's eyes. She gripped the decorative wrought-iron balustrade and clung to it with grim determination, anchoring her hold on reality. She finally managed to make her voice work one more time.

"This is more than a little overwhelming, Dylan. Are you telling me that my birth mother is alive and in St. Anthony's hospital right now?''

"Yes," he said. "But it's not entirely good news. Your mother's dying, Emily. She has another lung infection, and the cancer has spread. Her body's major systems are starting to fail.''

"How long does she have left?" Emily asked.

"We're not even talking weeks here, we're talking days.

I've visited with Maria and she's asking to see you. By the time I got back from the hospital, you and Jordan had already left to come here, so I followed you. The truth is that Maria is currently conscious and lucid, but nobody's sure how long that will last. It's way past visiting hours, of course, but under the circumstances, the hospital is willing to bend the rules. If you'd like to meet your mother tonight, Emily, she's waiting to see you.''

"I'll get Jordan," she said. "We can be out of here in two minutes."

CHAPTER SIXTEEN

THE NURSES' STATION on the oncology floor was a pool of brightness in contrast to the dim, nighttime lighting of the hospital corridors. Emily and Jordan followed one of the nurses to Maria Vasquez's room, the tap of Emily's high-heeled evening sandals sounding loud and intrusive as they passed rows of closed doors.

The nurse paused outside a door near the end of the corridor. "This is Maria's room. I'll have to ask you to wait outside for a few minutes. I need to check with her one more time to confirm that she still wants to see you."

"I understand," Emily said. Her voice sounded almost normal, which was amazing since the rest of her body was in turmoil and she had the disorienting impression that she was viewing everything through the wrong end of a powerful telescope.

The nurse opened the door and slipped inside, closing it behind her.

Jordan put his arms around her. Feeling the sleeve of his dinner jacket brush against her bare skin, Emily realized the dress she was wearing had almost no back and that she'd forgotten to bring her pashmina evening shawl from the car. No wonder she was shivering in the chilly temperatures of the air-conditioned hospital.

Kissing her lightly on the forehead, Jordan pulled her against him, wrapping his arms around her so that her head was resting against his chest. Warmth gradually replaced the bone-deep chill as she listened to the comforting sound of his heart beating beneath her cheek.

"Maria will see you," Jordan said, stroking her hair. "This is just a formality."

"I know. It shouldn't be so hard to be patient. I've waited twenty-seven years, so a few minutes more shouldn't matter."

The sound of coughing came from inside Maria's room. Not ordinary coughing, but harsh, rattling coughs, followed by shuddering gasps, as if she fought to drag in every breath.

Emily didn't realize she'd started to shake until Jordan's arms tightened around her. "Do you want me to come into Maria's room with you, or wait outside?" he asked, distracting her from the frightening sounds coming from the other side of the door.

Through the tumble of her emotions, Emily identified a flicker of surprise. It had never crossed her mind to exclude Jordan from this first meeting with her biological mother. She'd simply assumed he would be there.

"I want you to come in with me," she said. Dimly, she recognized that there was something significant about wanting to have Jordan with her, but she was too mentally numb to work out what.

The horrible coughing finally stopped and the nurse emerged into the corridor, leaving the door ajar behind her. "You can go in," she said, her voice a low murmur. "Maria is anxious to see you. Don't let all the equipment alarm you. It's really not much more than an IV and an oxygen supply to help with her breathing, and some electronic monitors that are mostly for our benefit in keeping track of her status. Today has actually been a good day for her. We've made some headway with the infection."

"Does that mean there's new hope?" Emily asked quickly.

The nurse shook her head. "I'm sorry," she said. "It just means we've delayed the inevitable for a little while. Anyway, why don't you go on in?" She gave an unexpected smile, and patted Emily on the arm. "Maria will be pleased you're all dressed up. She just loves fashion and pretty things."

Jordan held the door open for her and Emily walked past him. The only light came from a fixture on the wall, dimmed so that the room was scarcely brighter than the corridor outside. Even that low light couldn't conceal the ravages that disease had wrought on the petite, wasted woman lying against the cranked-up hospital bed.

Emily took a long, shaky breath, and then another. Her feet felt weighted to the floor, like one of those plastic dolls that never moved however hard you punched them. After twenty-seven years of waiting to meet her mother, she could find no words. Her voice had disappeared, drowned under the flood of emotions pouring through her body.

Maria found her voice first. It was harsh and breathless from her ruined lungs, but softened by a note of awe. "I have been waiting so long, and now you are here. The nice detective who visited this afternoon told me your name is Emily."

"Yes. My parents named me Emily Rose in honor of my two grandmothers."

Maria's gaze was riveted on her daughter's face. "You are so beautiful. I always knew you would be." A tiny smile tugged at her dry, cracked lips. "Your papa, he was one handsome fellow. I can see you have taken his eyes. They are warm, like golden Mexican honey, not plain old brown, like mine."

Shock wiped all thought of tactfulness from Emily's brain. "You know who my father is?"

Maria frowned. "Of course I know who was your papa."

Emily pressed her hands to her stomach. "I didn't realize. They told me— I thought—"

"You thought your father was some man—some john I never spoke to except to ask him for money." There was no bitterness in Maria's voice, only a wealth of sadness.

"No...yes...it doesn't matter—"

"It matters," Maria said hoarsely. "Later, I will tell you about your papa and you will tell me your whole life. But first I will tell you all that is most bad that I have done. Did you know I went to jail for prostitution? I see from your face that you did not. That was twelve years ago. The judge who sentenced me, he said I was a hopeless case."

"I didn't know. I'm so sorry."

"Don't look so sad, Emily Rose. You know, in the end, jail was a good thing for me." Again the quick flash of a smile. "That judge pissed me off, you know? I decided I would show him just who he was calling hopeless. I spent three months in jail. When I came out, I was lucky because my old pimp, he was in jail on drug charges, so there was nobody to order me around. I found a job waiting tables, and then a friend got me a job in the shoe factory. Now I am shift leader, and this Christmas, it will be ten years that I have worked a steady job. Decent pay, retirement benefits, health care, the works."

Maria gave a wry chuckle that turned into a painful cough. "Since they will never pay me those retirement benefits I worked so hard for, I guess the boss will pay for me to die in style, no?"

Emily moved closer to her mother's bedside. Suddenly it seemed entirely natural to bend and kiss her mother's pain-wrinkled forehead. "I just found you, Maria. Please don't talk about dying."

Maria flushed with pleasure at the kiss, then her frail shoulders shrugged beneath the hospital gown. "Not to talk about it will change nothing. The past is what it is, you know? I smoked three packs of cigarettes a day and never quit until last year. I started when I was fifteen, and kept right on going." Again the fugitive smile. "Enjoyed every damn pack I smoked, too. Do you smoke, Emily Rose?"

"No, I never did."

"That's very good. Your papa never smoked, either. He was always nagging me to quit. But then, when we were together, he was crazy about health and fitness. He was quarterback of the football team at the University of Texas, and he was determined to become a famous pro football player. If he wasn't eating wheat germ or some other disgusting food, he was doing push-ups."

"Did you and my father live together?" Emily asked.

"For a little while. Until I told him I was pregnant."

"And then he left you?" Emily said.

"You are angry, but he wasn't a bad person. He was only young and selfish, and one of those faults, time takes care of for everyone."

"He abandoned you and the child he'd helped to create," Emily said fiercely. "How can you make excuses for him?"

"I have had twenty-seven years to learn forgiveness." Maria shook her head. "Not long after you were born, he injured his knee, and his career in football was ended. In those days, I was like you. I was angry with him and glad for his pain. I thanked God because He had punished your father. Now I am dying, I regret that I showed your father no kindness in my thoughts. As for God, I believe He has better things to do than destroy a young man's dreams. Of course Robert's bad knee wasn't a punishment from God."

Emily exchanged glances with Jordan, who so far had remained completely silent. Maria sounded entirely coherent, but Emily couldn't help wondering how much of the story about her football hero father was fact, and how much was wishful fantasy. "Do you know where my father is living nowadays? Could you...would you tell me his name?"

"I can tell you his name, and he lives right here in San Antonio." Maria smiled. "Your papa, he is a famous man, Emily Rose. His name is Robert Pardoe."

"Robert Pardoe?" Emily exclaimed. "The television news anchor?"

Maria nodded her agreement. "He is your father," she said.

"But I've met him." Emily swallowed hard. She turned to Jordan, unable to grasp the fact that she had already met her biological father. "He's a volunteer at the Texas Fund for Children." She suppressed a gasp of laughter that was too close to hysteria for comfort. "We worked together last year on raising funds for a preschool on the west side. I worked side by side with my own biological father and never knew it."

Maria's eyes, large and poignant in the skeletal thinness of her face, brightened. "If you have spent time with him, then you should know that you look a lot like him. You have the same tall body, the same eyes, the same shape of hands...."

Maria's recital of the similarities trailed off into a bout of coughing that left her gasping for breath. "Jordan, you'd better call the nurse," Emily said, trying to help her mother, her heart in her throat.

"No!" Maria's command was whispered, but absolutely firm. "I talked too much, that's all. Now it's your turn.

Tell me first, who is the handsome man you have brought with you?''

"This is Jordan Chambers, my husband.'' Emily linked her arm through Jordan's and drew him up to the bed. "We've been married less than two weeks.''

"It's a very great pleasure to meet you, Maria.'' Jordan took her hand, with its trailing IV tubes, and held it within his own. If he was shocked by the paper-thin skin, and weightless bones, he gave no sign of it.

Maria looked from Jordan to Emily and gave a sly wink. "Great body,'' she croaked. "Handsome, too.''

Emily smiled. "He is, isn't he? I must have good taste in men.''

"Does he look as good out of his tux as he does in it?''

"Better,'' Emily said. "Definitely better.''

Maria sighed, but it was a contented sound. "You will make beautiful babies, you two. Lots of them.''

"Well, at least two, anyway.'' Emily's eyes met Jordan's across the bed, and the look he gave her was hot enough to scorch all the way to her toes.

We'll start working on it tonight, he mouthed.

Emily blushed, and Maria nodded with approval. "You are in love with him,'' Maria said. "That is very good.''

"Yes, it is,'' Emily said, holding Jordan's gaze. "I love my husband very much.'' She thought how strange and somehow fitting it was that the first time she acknowledged her true feelings for Jordan should be in her mother's presence. Maria had been cut off from all the important events in her daughter's life. Except for this one.

"And you love my little girl?'' There was a note of anxiety in Maria's voice when she turned her head toward Jordan, as if no man could be entirely trusted to do right by the woman who loved him.

"I'm crazy about your daughter,'' he said softly. "In

fact, I fell in love with her the very first time I ever saw her, which was months before she realized she was in love with me. I had to work *damn* hard to persuade her to have me, you know.''

''It never hurts a man to do the chasing. He appreciates the prize more if he runs hard to catch it.'' Maria's eyes closed.

''Are you tired?'' Emily asked. ''Do you want us to leave?''

''I'm tired, but I don't want you to leave. I wish to hear everything about your life. Tell your fine husband here to pull up a chair, and you can tell me the story of Emily Rose.''

Emily sat down on one side of the bed, Jordan on the other. He held one of Maria's hands; she took the other. Starting with the puppy the Suttons had bought for her fifth birthday, Emily recounted some of the happiest moments from her life, realizing all over again how incredibly lucky she'd been to have such wonderful parents. Maria never opened her eyes, but whenever Emily stopped talking, she would move one of her hands and utter a quick plea for more stories.

It was over an hour before the nurse came into the room and glanced in surprise at Maria's peacefully sleeping form. She beckoned, silently indicating that Jordan and Emily should leave the room, and this time Maria slept on, making no protest.

The nurse looked tired, but she gave them both a warm smile. ''Well, the pair of you seem to have worked a minor miracle. This is the most restful sleep Maria's had since she was admitted. Her blood pressure's good, her pulse rate has stabilized. We thought the monitors must be malfunctioning.''

''That is good news,'' Emily said.

"We'd like to come back tomorrow," Jordan said.

"Of course. Here's a card with visiting hours, phone numbers, everything you need to know. And I have your phone number if we might need it in an emergency."

The nurse left unspoken what they all understood. That restful sleep was not going to cure Maria's cancer, and the emergency the nurse referred to was Maria's death.

"Thank you for being so kind," Emily said. "And thank you for bending the rules tonight so that I could meet my mother."

"You're welcome. To be honest, this isn't a place with a lot of happy endings. It's great to know that you and Maria managed to find each other before it was too late. She's convinced she has psychic powers, you know. She told me when she was in here back in June that she was sending out messages to you and that you'd get here soon."

She had to be punch-drunk, Emily decided, because it no longer seemed even a little bit difficult to accept that Maria had sent out a psychic call, and she had responded. Hadn't she known in her heart of hearts that her dreams came straight from her mother?

Jordan walked with Emily to the elevator. Once they were inside, she slumped against the side, her legs suddenly too shaky to support her.

Jordan leaned close, framing her face with his hands. "Are you okay? I was afraid the nurse telling you about Maria's summons might put you over the top."

"I'm still standing. Under the circumstances, I think anything more would be aiming high."

"You're amazing, Em. On an emotional trauma scale of one to ten, the past couple of months have to be registering about a hundred for you."

"A thousand is more like it." The elevator doors glided

open to reveal the main floor of the hospital, but Emily didn't move. "I think my body's gone on strike. I've forgotten how to walk."

Without speaking, Jordan lifted her up into his arms and carried her across the lobby, indifferent to the interested gaze of the man polishing the floor and the security guard at the inquiry desk. He didn't put her down again until they were in the parking lot, next to his car.

He always knew just what she needed, Emily reflected. When to push, and when to cosset. When to tease her out of the blues, when to leave her to brood in peace. She wondered if there were any words to tell him how grateful she was that he'd come into her life. And then she realized how easy it was going to be.

"I meant what I said just now, Jordan. I love you. That wasn't just something I said to make my mother happy. I really do love you." Overwhelmed with the truth of it, she lifted a hand to his cheek.

He laid his hand over hers. "I told the truth, too. I've loved you ever since my brother escorted you into the San Antonio Federal Club, looking as if he didn't have the faintest idea what an extraordinary woman he had on his arm."

She smiled, feeling only amused tolerance for Michael's stupidity. "I think your brother appreciated my potential as arm decoration. It was all the other parts of me that he was indifferent to."

"Poor, foolish man."

Emily met his eyes, her gaze steady. "For what it's worth, if it matters to you at all, your brother and I never slept together. Our relationship wasn't intimate in any way."

"It shouldn't matter, but it does. Some leftover primitive male gene, I guess." He lifted her hand and kissed it in a gesture that made her pulses race. "I'm glad that Michael has absolutely no idea what a fantastic, creative lover you are, Em."

She laughed, but her breath caught in her throat. "I think my partner had something to do with my startling expertise last night."

Jordan grinned. "I sure as hell hope so." He took her other hand, linking fingers. "Let's go home, Em. I want to make love to you again and then fall asleep with you lying next to me. You know, the old married couple thing."

"The old married couple thing?" Emily repeated, then smiled as she climbed into the car. "That sounds like a wonderful idea. Take me home, Jordan."

Home. She realized that the word had slipped out so easily because when she was with Jordan, she felt a glow deep inside that sprang from an emotion even more profound than happiness. Last night she had not only learned that she could be a passionate and sensuous woman. She had also experienced a bone-deep contentment that sprang from the knowledge that this man was her soul mate—the creative, unconventional and supremely sexy man she never guessed she craved as her life partner. She'd married for all the wrong reasons, but she'd been rewarded by finding her true self. Jordan had given her the courage to drop the protective disguise she'd worn for most of her adult life, and the sensation of freedom was intoxicating. Emily discovered she was looking forward to making the acquaintance of the vulnerable, passionate woman who had been hiding beneath those suffocating layers of prim conformity.

She was so overwhelmed by the meeting with Maria that she couldn't talk much during the drive home. Her thoughts were full of her birth mother and the precious few days or weeks they might still have together, but the silence inside the car was companionable rather than heavy, and every time they stopped at a traffic light, Jordan reached over to rest his hand on her knee and give her a little pat.

The gesture started off by being gentle and comforting. By the time they reached the building that housed their loft, Emily's nerve-endings were alive, and each touch of Jordan's hand brought shimmering sexual tension in its wake. She marveled at the ease and speed with which he'd brought her out of exhaustion and into a state of desire. The longing to make love to Jordan was like an underground river, rushing unseen beneath everything else that they did together, strengthening the bonds between them because they were both swept along by the same current.

Until she married Jordan, she'd been scared of falling in love, terrified at the loss of control that she associated with sexual passion. She wondered why she had taken so much longer than most people to realize that true love was nothing more—and nothing less—than an intoxicating mixture of friendship and passion, cemented by trust. Looking back, she could hardly believe that only a few weeks earlier her cool, asexual relationship with Michael had seemed the perfect foundation for marriage. Heavens, she'd been seriously screwed up! Until Jordan, love had struck her as something dangerous and complicated. Now it seemed blissfully simple.

Jordan parked the car and they walked into the loft hand in hand and made straight for the bedroom. The hunger for physical intimacy seemed life-affirming after the emotionally draining encounter with Maria. Emily tossed her wrap and evening purse onto the chair. Jordan shed his jacket and tugged at his black tie, then his fingers fumbled with the onyx studs of his dress shirt.

Watching him, Emily was seized by a rush of sexual longing so intense that for a moment she couldn't move. Jordan had hands that were steady and skillful enough to produce carvings of surpassing beauty. It was unbearably erotic to realize that he became clumsy with desire in her presence.

"Let me do that," Emily said huskily, when she could speak.

Jordan forgot to breathe as Emily slipped the studs out of his shirt and let them drop onto the carpet. She threw his shirt away, indifferent to where it fell. She bent, her hair brushing against his bare skin as she ran her mouth over his chest, then stepped back so that she could slip the thin silk straps of her dress from her shoulders. As he'd guessed earlier, she wore nothing beneath the dress except a pair of panty hose. The effect was still stunning, and he let his breath out in a harsh gasp.

Jordan had never seen a woman so beautiful. He wanted to make love to her now even more than last night, when her body had been unknown to him. Along with desire, he felt a surge of tenderness. This was Emily, his wife. His wife. He framed her face with his hands, pulling the pins from her hair and letting them drop onto the floor.

"I love you," he said.

"I love you, too." She looked up at him, her eyes sheened with tears. "Jordan, thank you."

"For what?" He brushed away a single drop of moisture from her cheek.

"For being there tonight. For asking me to marry you. For being you."

Having grown up in a family that didn't understand the first thing about what made him tick, Jordan discovered there was a special joy in hearing the woman he loved offer acceptance of everything he was.

"It's me who should be thanking you." He took Emily's hand and held it against his cheek, moving his lips to press a kiss into her palm. Then he grinned, lightening the mood. "Come to bed and let me show you how grateful I am."

She answered his smile, although her eyes were still a little misty. "I'm so glad I married you, Jordan. You have the best ideas."

EPILOGUE

CAROLYN ST. CLAIR was late. These days, it seemed she was always late as she tried to cope with problems in her personal and professional lives that had begun to intersect in ways that had destroyed her usual efficiency. She hurried the last few yards to Perk at the Park, slipping into the seat across from Emily and struggling to catch her breath.

"Hi Emily." She sipped from the glass of ice water her friend had thoughtfully provided. "Sorry I'm late."

"That's okay." Emily smiled. "I only got here a few minutes ago myself."

"I've been playing catch-up all morning." Carolyn gave a rueful grin. "This past week would have worked out just fine if I never needed to sleep and there had been twenty-five hours in each day."

Emily made a sympathetic sound. "You should have called and cancelled. We could have had lunch another day."

"No. It's Saturday, I refuse to think about work anymore right now. Besides, I wanted to find out how everything went last night. I'm dying to hear the whole story of the meeting with your father. So did Robert Pardoe turn up as promised?"

"Yes, he came." Emily toyed with the menu.

"And? And?"

"It was very strange at first. We'd met several times last year, working on that fund-raising project I told you about, so in one sense you could say we were already acquainted. But it was quite different to meet him knowing he was my biological father."

"What excuses did he have for abandoning Maria when she was pregnant?"

"Quite a good one, actually. He admits that he refused to help Maria when she first told him she was pregnant. Then a week later, his conscience got the better of him and he tried to find her. Not to offer marriage, but at least to provide financial help."

"Why couldn't he find her?"

"Because Maria had deliberately chosen to disappear. She'd lied to him about her situation. Robert didn't know she was an illegal immigrant, and the address she'd given him was a fake, so he could never find her." Emily gave a shrug. "Maybe he didn't exactly beat down the doors of San Antonio looking for her, but I do believe he at least tried."

"Which I guess is more than a lot of college kids would have done," Carolyn said.

"Especially a football star who had half the girls on campus competing for his attention," Emily agreed.

"Robert Pardoe has a reputation for being really interested in the welfare of young kids who get caught up in the juvenile justice system," Carolyn commented. "Maybe that's his way of making up for not helping Maria."

"Yes, he said as much to me. He told me that one of the big regrets of his life has been not knowing if he had a child somewhere in the world. Or worse, he wondered if Maria might have had an abortion because his initial reaction had been to refuse to help her financially. He seemed pretty relieved when I told him that I had great adoptive parents, and that they'd provided a loving home, a terrific education. Everything a father could want for his child."

"Except the chance to know you."

"Odd you should say that. Robert said almost exactly the same thing."

Carolyn watched a couple go past, pushing a toddler in a stroller. "Robert's married, isn't he? I seem to remember reading that in an article about him in the local paper."

"Yes, and he has two teenage sons. My biological half brothers."

Carolyn sat up, startled. "You have two teenage brothers?"

"Yes, amazing, isn't it?" Emily stirred her straw in her iced coffee. "We made a tentative arrangement that I should meet them sometime next month. Apparently Robert Pardoe is from an enormous family. It turns out I have enough new aunts, uncles and cousins to fill a jumbo jet if we ever decide to have a family reunion."

Carolyn shook her head. "Gee, that must be a really strange feeling."

"It sure is." Emily laughed a touch ruefully. "Having grown up as an only child, it's going to take time to get used to the idea that I have twenty-three biological first cousins."

Carolyn grinned. "Thank goodness you didn't know about them before you and Jordan got married. At least you avoided horrible family arguments about how many of them were to be invited to the wedding. Can you imagine Amelia's face if she'd had to plan seating arrangements for Maria, Robert and his wife, and your parents? Not to mention the twenty-three extra cousins!"

"Amelia would have had a heart attack. Or pretended to have one as an excuse to retire to her bed," Emily said, laughing. "But Raelene and Sam would probably have taken it all in stride. They're really the kindest, most generous parents anyone could have. Look at how understanding they were about Maria. They knew I was only going to have a few weeks with her, and they could have filled that time with recriminations. Instead, they went out of their way to be sure that every day we had together was as happy for both of us as it could be. And Sam would have paid all the expenses for her funeral if Jordan hadn't insisted that we wanted to do it ourselves.''

''This has been an incredibly emotional few weeks for you,'' Carolyn said sympathetically. ''I can hardly imagine what you've been going through.''

''It's been stressful,'' Emily admitted. ''But I'm just so grateful that Maria and I managed to have some time to get to know each other. When I start wishing that we could have had longer, I remind myself how lucky I was to find her at all.'' Her voice was briefly husky. ''Between marrying Jordan and having Raelene and Sam as parents, I don't have much cause for self-pity.''

Carolyn smiled a little wistfully when she saw the way her friend's expression softened as she said her husband's name. ''From that sickeningly mushy expression you're wearing, I guess I can conclude that the Sutton-Chambers marriage isn't about to break up anytime soon?''

''No, I've pretty much decided to keep Jordan for the next sixty years or so.''

''That sounded heartfelt.''

Emily's cheeks tinged with pink, and her voice became dreamy. ''It was. I had no idea that falling in love could be so wonderful, Caro. I know people write poetry about it, and sing romantic songs, but as far as I was concerned, that was all in the realm of fantasy. I never imagined it could happen to me.''

But it had, Carolyn thought. Emily and Jordan were so much in love that they glowed when they were together. And if Emily could find her true love a mere twenty-four hours before she was planning to walk down the aisle with the wrong brother, then maybe there was hope for Carolyn to find her own happy ending. One day. Maybe.

Miracles could happen, after all.

TRUEBLOOD, TEXAS *continues*
next month with
A FATHER'S VOW
By Tina Leonard

The day Ben Mulholland walked in to Finders Keepers, Carolyn St. Clair's life changed forever. The man she'd loved and lost six years ago was asking for her help, and she couldn't refuse. His little girl needed a miracle, so Carolyn would move heaven and earth to find one. Maybe in the process she and Ben would rediscover their own magic.

Here's a preview!

CHAPTER ONE

CAROLYN, THIS IS Marissa," Ben said.

He didn't know that Carolyn had devoured the pictures of him and his new bride in the newspaper six years ago when they'd married.

The two women assessed each other and, fortunately, the little girl Marissa held by the hand leapt into Ben's lap so they could break eye contact.

"Carolyn," Ben said, his voice soft and gentle, "This is my daughter, Lucy."

And his daughter's bright smile sent all the misgivings she'd been nursing right out of her head. "Hello, Lucy. You sure are pretty."

"I know." She grinned at Carolyn. "Everyone says I look like Mommy."

Carolyn smiled. "You do."

"But I'm going to look like my daddy when I grow up." She turned in her father's lap, then kissed him on the nose and patted him on the cheek with a soft, pudgy hand. "I'm going to marry my daddy when I grow up."

Well, that makes three of us in the same room who considered marrying Ben Mulholland, Carolyn thought wryly.

"I need thirty more minutes," Ben said over Lucy's shoulder as he looked up at Marissa.

Marissa nodded. Her gaze flicked to Carolyn while she reached to take Lucy's hand. "It was nice meeting you," she said. "Ben has a lot of faith in you. I hope you can help us."

Help us. The plural caught Carolyn off guard. This was, then, a family situation that had brought Ben to her. Nothing she need fear. The past was not going to jump out at her with painful memories. "I'll do my best," she told Marissa sincerely. "Although I have yet to hear the situation, I most certainly hope Finders Keepers can resolve it."

Lucy and Marissa went out, the door closing behind them. Carolyn glanced down at the blank notepad in front of her, the cassette she had not yet loaded into the recorder. "She's beautiful, Ben," she said, meaning Lucy but knowing the word encompassed his ex-wife as well.

"Lucy is my sole joy." He leaned forward and Carolyn's gaze involuntarily jumped to his face. "She means the world to me. I can't even tell you how much I love my daughter." It seemed that the earnestness left his eyes for a moment as he focused inward. Then he said slowly, "She has leukemia, Carolyn."